Overturned

Overturned

'deluge of
law n. 1 a r
try or comm

ANNETTE RAYNOR

For my mother Rita
who made all things possible.
I love you.

Preface

July 1, 2002

**President Bush nominates Harding
to U.S. Supreme Court**

July 20, 2002

**Senate Judiciary Considers Harding
for Highest Court**

The Senate Judiciary Committee may meet as soon as Wednesday, July 31, to consider the nomination of Owen Harding to the U.S. Supreme Court. President Bush has nominated numerous anti-choice judges to the federal judiciary; however, this is his second anti-choice nomination to the Supreme Court. The Senate Judiciary turned down his earlier nomination of Prudence Offin.

The Supreme Court determines whether a state or federal law conflicts with a provision of the U.S. Constitution. *Roe v. Wade*, in fact, was a case where the Supreme Court in 1973 determined that a Texas law that banned abortion conflicted with the Constitution's right to privacy. If the Supreme Court finds that a law conflicts with the Constitution, it declares the law "unconstitutional." From then on, the law is unenforceable.

Congress cannot change a decision by the Supreme Court that declares a law unconstitutional. There are only two ways to change such a decision: (1) Congress and the states must pass a constitutional amendment to change the Constitution, or (2) the Supreme Court may overrule a previous decision or modify it in a significant way. While *Roe v. Wade* has been significantly modified since 1973, it has never been overruled.

Justices decide most cases by a majority vote. The alignment of the court's majorities shifts over the years as justices retire and are replaced. When *Roe v. Wade* was decided in 1973, the vote was seven to two. When the court last considered whether *Roe v. Wade* should be overruled in 1992, the vote was five to four (*Planned Parenthood of Southeastern Pennsylvania v. Casey.*) In a recent decision, *Stenberg v. Carhart* (2000), the court voted five to four to strike down a Nebraska statute that would have severely curtailed abortion rights.

If Owen Harding is nominated to the Supreme Court, the alignment of the court will shift once again, with five justices pro-life and only four pro-choice. This would put *Roe v. Wade* in significant jeopardy of modification or complete overturn for the first time since 1973.

September 15, 2002

Senate Approves Nomination
Owen Harding Elected to U.S. Supreme Court

The U.S. Senate elected Owen Harding, supreme court justice of Texas, to the U.S. Supreme Court today. The Committee on the Judiciary approved President Bush's nomination at the end of July, moving his nomination to the Senate floor for a full vote. Judge Harding has served on the Texas supreme court for five years and is an avid pro-life supporter.

June 21, 2006

Overturned! Abortion Outlawed!

The Supreme Court voted five to four in *Mather v. Tutola*, declaring the fetus an "unborn child," thereby ruling abortion unconstitutional. While the 1973 ruling has been modified over the years, this is the first time *Roe v. Wade* has been overturned.

May 30, 2021

U.S. Justice Chesterfield Dies

United States Supreme Court Justice Thomas Chesterfield died unexpectedly of a heart attack yesterday evening. Justice Chesterfield was seventy-eight years old. Nominated to the Court by President Bush, he took his seat in August 1991.

Chapter 1

"SHE'S dying!"

"She is not dying. She is hemorrhaging. Let's go."

"We can't go! We can't leave her like this! She paid us, and we killed her!"

"Relax. A simple call to 911 from the payphone on the corner and help will be on the way. Now let's go."

"I really think we should take her to the hospital! We can leave her on the curb. She really doesn't look good! I don't think there's time to wait!"

"We can't take her to the hospital. Abortion is illegal in this country, and I am not about to risk a double murder rap. Now help me clean up so we can make the call."

He calmly collected the tools and soiled sheets, shoving them into the black garbage bag. His assistant was too far gone to be of any practical use. This didn't surprise him in the least. There were two types of people in the world: leaders and followers. Followers were ignorant and weak, rarely any help in a time of crisis. He figured he would have to take this situation into his own hands and move as quickly as possible. With any luck, they would be out of there in a minute or two. The girl would be fine once the ambulance arrived. As for what the authorities would do once they realized she had terminated was not his affair—her mistake would be her problem. If she didn't want a child, she shouldn't have become pregnant. On some level he really didn't care whether she lived or died—it seemed appropriate that God should decide her

1

fate. Whatever the outcome, he was satisfied. Five thousand dollars for one hour's work was definitely worth the risk.

He surveyed the room one last time, grabbed his muttering assistant by the collar, and left the abandoned house. They quickly loaded the blue Buick, drove to the corner, placed an anonymous call to 911, and sped off.

She died before they left the house.

Chapter 2

SHE stared out the window overlooking Broadway in the theater district. It was her favorite café, allowing her a quick bite, great cappuccino, and a seat by the window. She used to hate eating alone, but after nearly eight years as an agent, she was finally used to it. Actually, she preferred it—no conversation, just her thoughts or the comfort of "people watching." She would stare out the window, enjoying the antics on the street and giving her overactive mind a break. In New York, you could always count on a good show if you stopped long enough to watch, especially on Broadway, where the neon lights created a carnival atmosphere. Her cell phone vibrated as soon as her sandwich arrived. As she looked at the LCD panel, she knew she would not be eating. After a brief hesitation, she answered the call.

"Gina Vincent here. What's up?"

"Agent Vincent, this is Brooklyn Dispatch. We have a homicide in an abandoned house downtown. We believe it's a failed termination. Can you get out there?"

"Downtown Brooklyn," she said, looking at her watch and calculating. "I'm in Midtown, and it will be at least forty minutes for me to get through the tunnel. Ask them to keep things tight until I can get there—I'll be about an hour."

"I'm sure that will be fine. The local precinct was clear: they can't handle the caseload, so they will be more than patient in waiting for you."

"Tell them I'm on the way."

She hung up, paid her bill, grabbed her sandwich for the ride, and left her coffee on the table. She knew she didn't have to rush. The cops had given up trying to handle the workload. Abortion had been illegal for only six months before the caseload surpassed their ability to investigate, prosecute, and house the incredible number of female convicts. Still, it was nearly fifteen years since 2006 when *Roe v. Wade* had been overturned, so why was the caseload still so high? You would think after all this time they would just have their babies and give them up for adoption. The risk of prison or death due to black market abortions seemed far worse than simply bearing the child. Being unmarried, never pregnant, and nearly thirty years old, she thought maybe she just couldn't relate. Whether she understood it or not just didn't matter; this was her job, and she did it extremely well.

For as long as Gina Vincent could remember, she had wanted to be a federal investigator. She was only ten years old on 9/11, but the images, forever burned in her memory, still called to her. Her heroes were the firefighters, police, and Port Authority personnel who raced, without hesitation, into the buildings to save others with little concern for their own welfare. She recalled the details in her mind as clear as the Tuesday morning it happened.

She had been standing at the bus stop playing tag with her friend Lisa, noting the bright blue sky and the faint but unmistakable smell of fall. They arrived at school at 8:50 a.m., the same time they arrived every day, which put them there after the first plane had hit but before the second plane did. As they took their seats, she thought it bizarre that the teachers were clustered around the counter in the front office. Her own teacher arrived and appeared preoccupied when class started at 9:05. By 9:30, the students knew that something was up because the teachers looked wild. They could feel the tension, or was it panic—hard to tell, but it was something. They whispered to one another in the halls with very concerned faces, shaking, nodding, and then running off to the next faculty member. Finally, after the collapse of the towers, it was too serious for them to hold back any longer. All students were to report to the cafeteria for an impromptu assembly. By this time, parents were inexplicably and suddenly picking up their children. Gina remembered at least six of her classmates were pulled from class before 10:00 a.m. Her own parents arrived at 12:30, after they had had a chance to relieve themselves from work and pull themselves together (at least according to her mother's memory of the day). Any student who had not been picked up by a parent was hand-delivered to a family member. The plan was simple: a teacher would be on each bus ensuring the student arrived home to family or friends. In some cases, the worst was true: both parents had perished, requiring the school to access emergency contacts.

By 1:00 p.m. that Tuesday afternoon, Gina's family was able to locate every family member working in New York City. Phone lines were jammed as each person called an "impromptu network" of family to ensure they knew all were safe, with each call ending in tears of relief. Gina's family entered what she liked to remember as "lockdown." The only calls her mother made were to clients who needed her help or to neighbors who were looking for loved ones.

Gina could still see the despair on her father's face and the tears in her mother's eyes as they struggled with their grief. Her mother didn't get out of her pajamas for nearly a week, while her father stayed home from work muttering about how things just didn't seem to matter. They were stuck in a virtual vacuum—all of the New York tri-state area was. People were either guilt-ridden for surviving or overwhelmed with grief for those who had died. Not a person in New York, New Jersey, or Connecticut was unaffected. Everyone—and I mean everyone—knew someone who had lost someone.

In the following days, the classmates who lost parents, the schoolteacher who lost her husband, the mother who lost her son became all too real. Gina's parents struggled to find their role in the aftermath, attending the services, donating to memorial funds, offering any support or aid they could in an effort to ease the pain of those who were grieving. It was an obligation that those spared would take on without question and would bear for the rest of their lives. If people lived in the geography, they felt it was their duty to remember and "fill in" for those who had paid the highest price for the freedom they had simply come to take for granted.

As Gina grew older, her feelings about the day intensified. For her the anniversary required her attention, her review of the details, her obsession with the stories and videos. How could the FBI not have known? How could they not speak the language? Federal investigators not trained in the beliefs, religion, or language of the criminals? Surely knowing the criminal mind and lifestyle was necessary to bring them to justice. Gina knew she would be a federal investigator—one who would make a difference.

Her chance came when the FBI established the new division in 2016. The Federal Bureau of Life Investigation became necessary after nearly ten years of failure to handle the abortion caseload. She would have preferred the standard FBI assignment, allowing her the opportunity to protect her homeland, but the new division offered the opportunity for advancement. She was sworn in as an investigator for the Federal Bureau of Life Investigation on January 30, 2016, at the age of twenty-five. After five years, she still loved the position but had second thoughts about the assignment. It was difficult to arrest women—mostly young, impoverished girls— for aborting their pregnancies. Why couldn't they understand the consequence of their actions? Finding the abortionist, on the other hand, was an entirely different matter. Each arrest saved multiple lives, and after all, preserving life was what the law had in mind, wasn't it?

Her car stopped at the approach to the Battery Tunnel, and she knew she would be waiting a while. The bridge may have been a better choice, but it was too late now; she would just have to wait. She was sitting in the middle of evening rush hour, and she couldn't do a damn thing about it. Once she was into Brooklyn, it would take only a few more minutes to reach the address dispatch had given her. Gina knew the neighborhood: mostly abandoned brownstones and dilapidated housing. Revitalization had begun during the early part of the new millennium, but it just never seemed to turn over. Crime was rampant in the area—prostitution, illegal gambling, drugs, and of course the business of termination. The lack of low-income housing, never addressed by any administration, allowed property values to continue to skyrocket and then collapse. It took years to process the foreclosures and many of the abandoned properties continued to lay to waste in the current day. The poor had moved into worse living conditions than ever before. Squatters were prevalent in the abandoned factories, and drug houses were everywhere.

Finally, the traffic moved, and the tunnel opened up as if there were no reason for the holdup in the first place. As she looked at the brownstone-lined streets, she thought about how pretty the neighborhood must have been when the homes were first built. She imagined a comfortable neighborhood teeming with a mix of immigrants, children playing stickball, vendors lining Third Avenue, and pushcarts moving down the streets. That would have been over one hundred years earlier, and time had worn the area down. She tried to remember the last time she had been in the neighborhood—it had to be over six months ago, and the place looked worse than ever.

She pulled up in front of an abandoned row-style colonial and studied the block. It looked like every other block downtown, with brownstones or row houses in varying stages of disrepair. She surveyed the patrol units parked in front of her and marveled at the crowd that would always gather at a crime scene. As she stepped out of her car, a sense of dread gripped her heart. Gina was not predisposed to premonitions, so her fear startled her. This call was going to be very different—she just didn't know why.

Chapter 3

AS Gina approached the front door, she noted two squad cars and three police officers at the scene. A burly patrolman—Officer Kenny, by his tag—stopped her at the door.

"Gina Vincent, federal investigator," she announced, flashing her identification.

"Oh, we've been waiting for you. We haven't touched her; looks as if this should be straightforward for you. She's lying in a pool of blood in what appears to be a back-alley termination. We figured we would wait for you before we dusted for prints."

"Thank you, . . . Officer Kenny?" she said, squinting at his name tag.

"Sorry, yes, it's Officer Patrick Kenny. Let me take you inside." His cheeks blushed a bright red at the oversight of not introducing himself.

Gina immediately liked Officer Kenny. He didn't seem aggravated by her arrival and was quite accommodating. The local police did not really care for federal investigators, and neither did they really care for the burden of the "illegal termination" workload. Every cop in the country would probably vote "pro-choice" if given the opportunity. They were losing hardened criminals and watching violent crimes increase due to their inability to investigate and respond sufficiently. Officer Kenny led her through an empty living room into the kitchen. The house looked as though it had been condemned. There were charred patches on the floor where a fire once burned to keep squatters warm. Rusted appliances and cabinets and murky brown trails where water and filth had built up lined two walls. The girl lay on the floor, nude from the waist down.

"How did you find her?"

A young patrolman with pale white skin answered, "Dispatch got a 911, we came out, and there she was." Staring at the floor, he continued, "I am Officer John Scott, and I was the first to find her. She is definitely not from this neighborhood. Nike sneakers, Ralph Lauren polo sport shirt, matching skirt heaped in the corner over there. Good skin and teeth, very clean."

Gina, observing him for the first time, realized he was a rookie. Only the rookies spent the time to really look at a scene, felt the emotion of a crime, and truly tried to make sense of it all. She couldn't remember the last time she met an officer who felt as strongly as Patrolman Scott did.

"Thank you, officer. You seem to have completed a thorough investigation without disturbing the scene. I appreciate your detail. Has the skirt been moved?"

"No, but there is something underneath it, so you may want to start there," he said, pointing to the skirt. Her comments on his work made him feel good even though his heart squeezed in his body each time he looked at the girl.

Gina approached the corner where the skirt lay on the floor, but as she bent down to get a closer look, she saw the girl's face. Really saw her. The girl was beautiful. She hadn't noticed at first while she took down the observations of the young officer, but now that she really saw the girl, she couldn't believe how pretty she was. She had blond hair, green eyes, small features, and was about 5'7" and 125 pounds, with well-defined, muscular legs and an overall athletic build. The sinking feeling in her stomach returned. This girl was not from this neighborhood and was maybe 17 years old. Gina put on her gloves, bagged the skirt, and saw the wallet. It was a wallet-purse designed to hold a cell phone, credit cards, cash, and keys. Inside there was only student identification—New York University, Ashley Rydell.

"We have identification. She is a student at NYU. Her name is Ashley Rydell. Officer Scott, would you contact NYU and call me when you have reached the dean's office?"

"Sure thing, Agent Vincent. It will just take a minute." He went to the living room to make the call in private.

Gina looked at Officer Kenny. "What do you think, Pat?"

"I've personally seen at least a dozen in the last year, and it never gets any easier. Such a waste. This girl is leaving many broken hearts behind. I'm going to canvass any neighbors and finalize our report for you. I'll leave you to the business of notification," he said as he shuffled out of the kitchen. Men never seemed to handle these scenes very well. It was if they knew women reproduced but were never quite sure how.

Officer Scott returned with his phone, announcing the NYU dean's office. She took his handset and nodded an approval. "Gina Vincent, federal investigator. To whom am I speaking?" Jotting down a name in her notes, she continued, "I have some inquiries in reference to one of your students. I will need you to confirm her student information for me. Do you have an Ashley Rydell enrolled?"

Gina's face paled, and her knuckles whitened. "No, I understand. Yes, please plan to meet me within the hour. I will be able to explain the nature of the incident when I get there. Thank you," she said as she blankly stared at the phone in her hand.

"Agent Vincent, are you okay? Can I help you with anything?" Officer Scott faltered as he took his phone.

"Seems as if we are going to have our hands full. Miss Rydell was the daughter of Senator George Rydell of Illinois, the same Senator Rydell who sponsored the pro-life movement. Officer Scott, could you please secure the scene and wait for the coroner? We need to ensure the confidentiality of her identity until I can speak with the senator. It's going to be bad enough for him; the last thing we need is a media circus."

"Sure thing. We'll release the other patrol car, and Officer Kenny and I will finish up. We'll keep it quiet until we hear from you. Should I tag her Jane Doe for the coroner?"

"No, I don't think anyone will put two and two together just from her name. It will be out of our hands long before the medical examiner realizes who she is."

Gina called her office and filled them in on the details. She needed to notify her superiors, and her assistant was doing just that. Now she had to get to NYU to meet with the dean. They still did not know the nature of the crime, and the woman she had spoken with seemed as if she might have a nervous breakdown.

It was nearly 9:00 p.m. when she reached the university. She hoped there would not be mass hysteria at the school, but from experience, she knew any incident that involved a famous person and possible scandal would spread like wildfire.

It took a few minutes to locate the office, but once inside she knew she was in the right place. While many offices were closed and dark for the night, one office was lit brightly as if it was the height of the school day. Gina approached the room quickly. "Hello, I am Federal Investigator Vincent. I spoke with a Ms. Feld about an hour ago. Is she here?"

A tall woman who looked to be about fifty, with blond hair pulled into a tight, low bun, stepped from behind the desk and extended her hand. "Hi, I am Marissa Feld. I spoke with you earlier. As we discussed, since you called in reference to the senator's daughter, I contacted the dean and president for you to meet with. The faculty takes great pride in the protection of the privacy of our high-profile students. Ashley's privacy is very important to us, and we are very concerned for her welfare. Has she been arrested?"

"No, I assure you Ashley has not been arrested," replied a stunned Gina. She was not used to such efficient and quick cooperation. It occurred to Gina that this seemed like a practiced response to *any* incident involving a high-profile student. The dean's office must have literally practiced their response to any type of situation.

"Thank you very much, Ms. Feld. I appreciate your contacting everyone. Could you make a quick list of Ashley's roommates, sorority sisters, any students that may be able to meet with me to discuss Ashley?"

"Yes, yes, Ms. Vincent. Would you like me to call them in?"

"No, that's not necessary. I will need the list to follow up, but there is no need to contact anyone now."

"Please let me show you to the dean's office. Both he and the president are right through here. Can I get you coffee, water?"

"No, thank you very much, Ms. Feld. I'm fine. Give me a few minutes, and I will be back out to go over that list."

Gina entered the dean's office to find NYU President William Poulsen and Dean Joseph Vallone. "Good evening, gentlemen. I am Federal Investigator Gina Vincent."

They were both dressed corporate casual, wearing Docker-type slacks with collared pullovers in silk or a microfiber material. They looked as if they had just arrived from their yacht or country club. It was difficult for Gina to fight back the inferiority complex creeping into her mind. She had to concentrate to beat back the "out of your league" mantra that was beginning to match the loud beat of her heart.

"Good evening, Agent Vincent. We would like to thank you for meeting us so quickly. What is the nature of your inquiry about Ms. Rydell?" questioned Mr. Poulsen as he turned to look squarely into Gina's eyes.

Gina figured the only way to handle this situation was to hit it head-on.

"I am afraid I have some very bad news for you. A female matching the photo identification of Ashley Rydell was found deceased in an abandoned home in downtown Brooklyn early this evening."

Gina paused to give the men a chance to register the information. From experience she knew they wouldn't hear anything she said beyond the word *deceased* anyway.

William Poulsen sat in his chair and let out a deep sigh followed by a very deep breath. He was physically collecting himself and battling a wave of emotion. Dean Vallone was simply in shock. His hands shook as he grabbed the arms of the deep-cushioned leather chair. President Poulsen spoke first. "Are you sure it was Ashley Rydell?"

Gina took the plastic bag containing the student identification card and placed it on the desk. Speaking softly, she said, "This is the student photo ID we found, and that picture matches the deceased. Of course, she will need to be identified by an immediate family member at the morgue, but her identity is not in question."

"How did this happen? Where? Who?" questioned Dean Vallone in a voice entirely too loud.

President Poulsen responded as he raised his hand to quiet the dean. "Agent Vincent, this is very disturbing news, so we ask that you forgive any inappropriate response. Could you please share the details of this tragedy?"

"At 5:15 p.m. this evening, an anonymous 911 call was made from a payphone across from an abandoned house. The police and ambulance responded by 5:27 p.m. to the house, where the girl was discovered unresponsive in the kitchen. The rescue squad was unable to find a pulse, and the victim was pronounced dead at the scene. Of course, we won't know for sure until the autopsy is complete, but it appears she hemorrhaged to death. The cause of bleeding is probably a failed termination. At this point, it is an assumption we believe the autopsy will confirm. We are investigating the incident fully to find the responsible party. It is very important that we stop the perpetrator from doing this again. I am truly sorry to have to bring you this news."

Dean Vallone pounded the arm of his chair with a white-knuckled fist, and his face reddened. "This is going to devastate the senator! The scandel will be huge. There is no way I am going to be able to hold the media at bay. This place is going to be overrun with news teams by midmorning!"

President Poulsen again raised his hand to calm the dean. "Relax, Joe. We can handle the media. What we need to do is notify the senator. Once he's notified, the senator's office will be directing ours. Agent Vincent, can we notify the senator?"

"I think it's best if we speak to him together. If you contact the senator and his wife now, I will deliver the news with you so I can answer as many of their questions as possible. This will allow me to help stem the media tide as well. Agreed?"

"Agreed," Poulsen replied in almost a whisper as he slumped in his chair and subconsciously massaged his temples. He picked up the student folder that lay in front of him, turned to the first page, and dialed his phone. After a few seconds of silence, he said, "Hello, may I please speak with Cynthia or George Rydell?"

After a few more seconds of silence, he asked, "Is this Cynthia Rydell?"

"Hello, Cynthia. It's William Poulsen. Yes, I'm fine, thank you." He faltered and then said, "Cynthia, I have some very serious news for you. It may be best that you get George."

"Is this about Ashley? I don't need to get George. Is Ashley okay?" Cynthia commanded.

"Very well." Poulsen paused, and his eyes shifted toward the ceiling as he continued. "Ashley has been murdered." Before he could begin to explain Cynthia wailed, "No, not my baby! Not my baby…" The screams that filled the Rydell home in Illinois were all too audible to those standing in New York. What seemed like minutes was actually less than thirty seconds before a man picked up the phone.

"Who in the hell is this?"

"George, it's William Poulsen. I am sorry. I wanted Cynthia to get you, but she was adamant. I know this is devastating, I am here with the federal agent now."

"Are you telling me that my daughter is dead? That I sent her to your school and she died in your care? I want to know every detail right now. You put that Agent and whoever the hell else you have in that room on this phone now."

"Yes, of course."

Poulsen put the call on hold and looked at Gina. "He wants us on speaker. Are you ready?"

Gina nodded, and Poulsen hit the speaker button. "George, can you hear us?"

"Yes, now please tell me what's happened!"

"Senator Rydell, I am Federal Agent Gina Vincent. At roughly 5:27 p.m. Eastern time, your daughter, Ashley Rydell, was found deceased in an abandoned house in downtown Brooklyn by authorities who responded to an anonymous 911 call. We are confident of her identification due to her student photo ID, which we found at the scene."

They could hear Cynthia Rydell sobbing in the background while a flurry of sounds indicated the senator was trying to calm her down.

After a brief pause, Poulsen asked, "Senator, are you there? Would you like me to contact your assistant?"

"No ... I ... uh ... ." He was playing Senator, but the overwhelming grief of a father threatened to overtake him at any second.

"Agent Vincent, how did my daughter die?"

Gina answered readily. "She hemorrhaged to death, sir."

"She *what*?! What do you mean?"

"It appears that your daughter is the victim of an illegal abortion. While this will have to be confirmed by the autopsy, it seems she bled out, sir."

"This is absurd! Ashley would never do such a thing. Do you know who I am, Agent Vincent? Do you really think *my* daughter would do such a thing?" George Rydell was on familiar ground once again. Fury was an emotion he was much better at managing.

"I want a private investigator on this right now! It appears my daughter was murdered, but I can assure you it was *not* because she was having an abortion."

"I understand your anger, but if I am wrong, it will be established by the autopsy results. I must caution you, sir. I am a specialist in this field, and I do believe this is a termination."

"Agent Vincent, I do not doubt your expertise, but you do not know my daughter. If you did, you would understand the absurdity of what you are saying!"

"Senator, it is most important that you come to New York to identify your daughter so the coroner can proceed. We wouldn't want your daughter's identity to be revealed until you are prepared. We are trying to keep it quiet until you arrive."

"Agent Vincent, please leave your number with William. As soon as I have my flight arrangements, my assistant or I will contact you directly. Until that time, I would ask that you refrain from questioning anyone about my daughter. If possible, I would like to keep this quiet until the autopsy is complete and a statement from my office is prepared. Do you think we can do that?"

"Senator, I will try my best, but I have seen these situations break open despite enormous efforts to preserve confidentiality. It would be prudent for your office to prepare a statement in the event we cannot wait for the coroner's report."

"I understand. I will meet you as soon as I can get a flight. Thank you, Agent Vincent. William, please take measures to protect this information until I arrive. I will contact your office upon my arrival." Without further comment, the line went dead.

Gina looked at William Poulsen and saw genuine despair. It looked like the president and the senator were friends—not associates or acquaintances, but actual friends. William Poulsen had to deliver the most devastating news a parent could hear, and he had to deliver it to a friend.

"Mr. Poulsen, Mr. Vallone, thank you. I know this is extremely difficult, and I want to express my appreciation for your cooperation.

I have asked Ms. Feld to prepare a list of students who knew Ashley so I can begin the investigation. I will not start the interviews until I meet with the senator, but I will need the list now. I would like you to review the list for omissions before I leave. I trust you will do everything in your power to maintain confidentiality over the next few hours. I promise I will do the same, but I must warn you to be prepared. The media is very creative in securing newsworthy information. A hot tip can come from anywhere."

"I understand," Poulsen said as he gazed at the wall. "I will prepare a statement for each scenario. When you are ready, you can conduct your interviews right in my office. I will arrange them as soon as I hear from you. Let's review the list right now." He hit another button on the phone and summoned Ms. Feld to the office.

Ms. Feld appeared immediately and directed her complete attention to President Poulsen. In a firm but genuine voice, he told her, "Ms. Feld, Ashley Rydell is deceased. The Rydells are very distraught, as you can imagine. Our cooperation with Agent Vincent is very important to the school, Ashley, and her family. We are going to need to keep all communication confidential until I give further instructions. Ms. Feld, do you understand all that I have said?"

Ms. Feld must have lived for direction and attention from President Poulsen. While she had been concerned and flustered earlier on the phone and again in the office, she was the epitome of efficiency at this moment. Not so much as a gasp exited her lips. She was the perfect assistant when dealing with William Poulsen.

"Yes, sir. I will handle all inquiries and keep all information confidential. You can count on it. I will brief you on any and all developments."

"Thank you, Ms. Feld. Your competency is a great relief to me during this painful situation. Our actions must be measured and calculated to ensure we protect the good name of our students and their families."

Gina sensed that Ms. Feld could be in love with President Poulsen; she seemed to swoon at his every word. In this matter, it appeared to be a great benefit to NYU and the Rydell family. Ms. Feld looked as if she could handle a White House press conference if she had to. "Could we review that list, Ms. Feld?" Gina asked.

"Yes, Agent Vincent. I have it right here."

Joe Vallone, William Poulsen, and Marissa Feld reviewed the interview list and with only two additions submitted it to Gina.

"You will find additional students who should be interviewed from her roommate. Ashley was very popular, a truly lovely girl. We have provided the most obvious names, but we are not aware of all her friends or social circles," warned Poulsen.

"Thank you very much. Mr. Poulsen," Gina replied. "At which number can I reach you?"

He scribbled his cell phone number on a yellow sticky note and gave it to Gina. "This is my personal phone. I will be taking all calls on this phone during this time. In the event you get my voicemail, just leave a message; I will return your call immediately. You will only go to voice mail if I am already on the phone."

"Good enough, sir. Thank you." Gina handed him her card and shook his hand. Joe Vallone was nearly forgotten, which seemed perfectly fine with him. He was clearly just going through the motions. He could not handle this situation, and he looked as if he wanted to disappear. She nodded goodbye to Mr. Vallone, shook Ms. Feld's hand, and caught President Poulsen's gaze one more time. She could see the glassy covering in his eyes as he visibly fought his emotions. Gina found herself sharing his despair. Without anything constructive to add, she quickly left the university.

As she drove toward Midtown, Gina called the Brooklyn precinct to see what information they had collected at the scene. She called the medical examiner to ensure they had received the body, and finally, she called her office to review her messages. It was off to Twenty-Third and Park for a quick shower and a pot of coffee. It was going to be a long night.

Just as she entered her building, her phone buzzed. Robert, her assistant, appeared on her phone image panel and announced, "It's the *Post*. They just called saying they got a tip that a bigwig's daughter is in the morgue. What shall I do?"

"Who called?"

"Charlie Randazzo."

"I'll take care of it," she said.

"Do you need me to do anything else?" he asked. Robert was a great assistant. He made taking care of Gina his personal mission. His partner had died two years earlier after a twenty-five-year battle with AIDS. Robert had been devastated and turned all of his energy to his job and Gina. Initially overwhelmed by his attention, she adapted, quickly realizing she really did need the help. Gina was good at the details of her job, but her organization skills and personal life were, let's just say, underdeveloped. Robert arranged her meetings, paid her bills, and even reminded her to call her mother.

"No, Robert. You've handled everything fine so far. I am going to take a quick shower. Call me if anything comes up." She ended the call and placed the phone in its case on her waist.

Gina waved at the security guard and entered the elevator. She had a beautiful view of Park Avenue from her twenty-third-floor apartment, even if she never did bother to look. Throwing her bag on the floor, flipping her shoes in the air, and flopping onto the couch, she dialed Randazzo's number from her landline. "Is this Charlie Randazzo?"

"Who wants to know?"

"Charlie, it's Agent Vincent. Did you call the office?"

"Hi, Gina. Yes, I called, and you know why. Now, you are either going to confirm the death of Senator George Rydell's daughter, or I will leak this bit of information to every media source in the city."

"Look, Charlie, let's not get ahead of ourselves here. If you are right, this would be some breaking story," she taunted. "You don't want to give up the option of breaking this story any more than I want to confirm your inquiry. If you will just sit on this for a few hours, I promise I will confirm cause of death to you before we release the coroner's report to anyone else. As far as who is in the morgue, you will just have to wait for me to disclose that information."

"Gina, you have a deal! Don't mess me up on this. I have a version without confirmation ready to go. I am going to run it if I don't hear from you."

"Trust me, Charlie. You are not going to run that story." With that, she ended the call and dropped the phone onto the couch. Undoubtedly, it would get lost in the cushions. Gina seemed to page the phone more often than she dialed it.

She ran the water steaming hot and just stood in the shower. After ten minutes, she knew she had to get going, so she ran the water ice-cold. This helped refresh and wake her mind and body. She also had read somewhere that it was supposed to be good for the pores. Just as she turned off the water, her cell rang. Dashing for the phone and counting rings on the way, she caught it just before the fifth tone. "Vincent here."

"Agent Vincent, it's Senator Rydell. My wife and I will be on United Flight 1250 arriving in Newark at 6:50 a.m. Where would you like me to meet you?"

"Would it be possible for you to meet me at the medical examiner's office before going to your hotel?"

"I will meet you anywhere you want as long as we get to see our daughter as quickly as possible. I assume the coroner's office is also the morgue."

"That's correct, sir. You will be providing a positive identification as soon as you arrive."

"Fine. I expect we can be there between eight and nine, depending on traffic."

"Senator, we only need one person to make identification," Gina offered.

"Agent Vincent, my wife will rip the building apart piece by piece until she gets to hold her baby girl."

"Yes, sir, I understand. I will see you in the morning."

Chapter 4

SARAH Louise Harrison felt sick. It had started as a nagging nausea, almost imperceptible until it escalated and broke into her consciousness. Once it was there, it never left. She knew the feeling and knew it well, but she could not believe —would not believe—it was there again. She had had it for each one of her five pregnancies and two miscarriages. It certainly could not be happening again. She loved her five children dearly, but to save and support them she could not have a sixth.

She was a seamstress who took work in to help make ends meet. Her husband, Nate, was a carpenter. They were working class, always had been, but recently it seemed work was harder to come by. The 1932 two-bedroom saltbox cottage was the only housing they could afford. For them it seemed the American Dream was nearly impossible to attain. Nate often did not have any work and took to working part-time at the Home Depot to earn enough money to put food on the table. They had food stamps and state aid when possible, but medical coverage was not available for Sarah and Nate. The minimum wage did not keep up with the rising cost of living, and no matter what they did, they just couldn't make ends meet. Medicare covered the children, but birth control was not available to Sarah. She knew she should have purchased the condoms last month, but food was more important. They practiced the "rhythm method" to ensure she didn't get pregnant, but something must have gone wrong. She knew this feeling better than anyone did, and she *knew* she was pregnant once again.

A visit to the free clinic would confirm her fears, but she would have to wait until the children were in school to go. She couldn't tell Nate just yet. He had a temporary job at the new library installing crown molding and chair rail. His carpentry was a work of art. He could transform any room into a masterpiece with the precision and detail he applied to his work. It wasn't fair. They were good people, and they both worked very hard to take care of their family and make a good living. Why didn't they ever get ahead? As it was, their youngest child was not growing, apparently due to malnutrition. Despite the creativity Sarah applied to making pasta, protein was lacking in their diet. They lived in fear of the state placing their children in foster care if they could not demonstrate the ability to care for them. A sixth child could not be cared for and would severely affect their ability to keep their family together.

She pushed the swirling thoughts and emotions out of her mind. It was Sunday. They would go to church, and she would try to make a nice Sunday dinner with the few potatoes and stew meat she had left from the week. Tomorrow was Monday. She would visit the clinic and have her answer then. It was useless to worry over the matter today. She thought it best to make a nice day for the family and address the issue when she was sure. Of course, addressing the issue would become her worst fear.

Dawn broke on a gray, misty Monday morning. Sarah woke to the sinking feeling in her stomach and the quickening of her heart. Today she would know for sure. Her instinct told her that she already knew, but she pushed herself to get the kids off to school and Nate off to work.

"Morning, honey. What's wrong? Did you sleep well?" Nate asked as he noticed the ashen color of his wife's face.

"I slept fine; just feeling a little sick today. I may be coming down with a touch of the flu. Nothing to worry about. I figured I would drop in to the free clinic after getting the kids off to school."

"When did that start? Were you feeling sick yesterday?"

"No, I'm sure it's nothing. Don't worry about me; you have to start at the library today. Go to work, and make me proud of my husband—the best carpenter in town!" She gave Nate a kiss and realized how much she loved her family. Her husband, her children, they were her life—true blessings from God. She hopped out of bed and began rounding up the troops for breakfast. After the normal commotion that was the morning at her house, she found herself in silence with just the baby, who was still sleeping. She saved the last bit of whole milk for a bottle that she would get her to drink after breakfast was finished. She felt bad about hiding the milk from the others, but the baby needed the milk most. At fourteen months, the child was under the fifth percentile for height and in the first percentile for weight.

She arrived at the clinic just after ten. Already there were at least thirty people in the waiting room. Sarah realized she would be there for most of the day. They served apple juice and shortbread cookies for the children who were waiting, and Sarah was relieved to see her baby wanted the cookies. Nadia was a beautiful baby. She had platinum blond hair and the fairest skin. Sarah felt the child's pallor was due more to her poor nutrition than God-given attributes, but she was striking nonetheless. They had named her Nadia because it was the Slavic name for "hope." Sarah couldn't help but thank God every time she looked at her child. She was breathtaking, and Sarah dreamed her name would bring them happiness in the future. The child was a beacon, a brilliant glowing wisp of heaven—Sarah's littlest angel. As Nadia munched her cookies and sipped the apple juice, she began playing with another little girl at the clinic. They waited four hours before the nurse called Sarah's name.

Sarah entered the examination room and figured there was no point in beating around the bush. "Good afternoon, doctor. I am here for a pregnancy test. I have been feeling sick, and think I may be pregnant with my sixth child. I know the feeling well, and if we could just do the test, I will be on my way."

The doctor did not argue. He knew the patients at the free clinic. Many of them diagnosed themselves and showed up only when they felt their poor health was preventing them from working. Half of the mothers he saw had pneumonia before they would come in for an exam. He figured he would give Sarah what she asked for and save them both time. He had nearly twenty-five more patients waiting.

Sarah quickly provided a urine sample, and the test was conclusive in under a minute. The doctor did a quick pelvic exam and estimated she was six weeks pregnant. He gave her a supply of prenatal vitamins and a quick sermon on nutrition for pregnant women and sent her on her way.

Sarah held Nadia tightly to her chest as she ran from the clinic. Tears stung at her eyes, and her heart was beating wildly in her chest. She had already known, so why was she so afraid? She planned to cry it out right now and collect herself for the evening. Tonight she would have to tell Nate. She went to the park. The park was beautiful at this time of year. The sun broke through the clouds earlier in the day, washing everything in brilliant watercolors. It was late spring, and all the flowers were blooming; the world had come back to life. Spring was a promise from God. She sat on the bench and allowed Nadia to play in the sandbox. It would give her time to relax and think. If she had a plan, then maybe telling Nate would come easier. There was a slight breeze and the unmistakable smell of flowers. Her mind started to float as she took in the beauty of the park. She thought of her childhood, her parents, and her maternal grandmother. Her grandmother loved her—truly loved her—and would tell her stories for hours on end. She began to remember the stories her grandmother had told her about times long past. She told her about women's rights and the movement of the sixties. She told Sarah that she could be or do anything if she just put her mind to it.

Then Sarah remembered a disturbing story her grandmother had told her about the time before the movement—the other time abortion was illegal. Her grandmother said that women could sometimes end their pregnancies themselves. A little help from someone and a sharp object like a hanger would do the job more often than not. Sarah recalled her shock and horror at the time, but now she tried hard to remember the details. The story came rushing back to her in such vivid detail she could almost see her grandmother's kitchen, the white Formica table with silver edging and the white vinyl-covered chairs. They would sit and talk at that table for hours. Her grandmother had died before the overturn of *Roe v. Wade*. Sarah knew her grandmother would have been furious if she had lived to see that. She would tell Sarah about back-alley abortions and the friends she had lost. She told Sarah about the do-it-yourself procedure for those who were too afraid to go anywhere else.

Sarah knew what she had to do. It would be the only way. She gathered Nadia from the sandbox and made her way home. She would collect the items she needed and stop at the library to collect some more information. If she prepared well, she might just be able to convince Nate. She had to do her homework. It would be a hard sell. It would take the performance of a lifetime.

After dinner, Sarah washed the children and put them to bed. By eight o'clock, the house was quiet and Nate was sitting in the well-worn brown plaid recliner. Now was the time. She would have to approach the situation delicately and lay out the plan in perfect order. If she didn't get him to see her point of view early on, he would never agree.

"Nate, I need to talk to you about something very important. I need you to hear me out completely before you answer. Can you promise me you can do that?"

"What's wrong? Are the kids okay? Did something happen today?"

"Settle down. Just listen. The children are fine. It's me. I went to the clinic today to see about that nausea, and I found out I'm pregnant."

"Sarah, how? It was just that once, and we were so careful."

"I know, I know. I have been through it in my mind a thousand times. Trying to figure it out now is senseless. It happened, and here we are. Nate, we cannot have this child. You are not going to like what I have to say, but I cannot think of another way. I am going to need your help. If you refuse, I will find someone else to help me. If you love me, you won't let it come to that. Now just listen."

Sarah told the story that her grandmother had told her. She explained to him the details of the procedure and his role. She laid it out in plain English and begged him to see the necessity. When she was finished, she told him it would have to be *that* night. The longer they waited, the more dangerous it would become.

Nate cried. He could not, would not! He knew they couldn't afford another child. They could not afford the five they had. It was an impossible situation.

"Sarah, please. I can't. How can you expect …" Nate pleaded as he swallowed the lump in his throat.

Sarah did not waver. She saw his anguish and knew she would have to seize the opportunity before he put up a fight.

"Nate, I love you and the kids. I don't want our family compromised. They will take the kids from us. You know they will. I know you can do this for me. I know you won't force me to look at another alternative. Please, Nate, I'm begging you. Do this for me. Do this for our family."

Nate never said yes. He just resigned himself to the fate Sarah had planned. He would do as she asked. He just didn't have the presence of mind to argue, and neither did he have an alternative. They set about her plans immediately. In less than an hour, Sarah lay in her bed resting. Nate sat on the porch long into the night, praying.

Sarah died before sunrise. The children would never know the real reason why their mother died that night. Her death certificate would simply state "miscarriage." Nobody bothered to investigate or prosecute the poor. Their priest presided over the funeral, and the parishioners at their church helped make provisions for the children. Their life would never be the same. Nate would never forgive himself.

Chapter 5

GINA arrived at the morgue a little after six. It would be best to check things out before the senator arrived. She wanted to take a closer look at Ashley, review her case notes, and formulate her questions for her meeting with the Rydells. Gina sensed this would be a difficult encounter, especially for Cynthia Rydell.

As she rounded the corridor, she saw the technician. "Hi, Larry. Are you coming in or going out?"

"I'm coming in. Had to start early; we picked up a student last night. Apparently there is a big rush on it."

"Actually, that's why I am here. The case is mine, and I am waiting for the parents to ID. Did they give you any details?"

"Why does this case necessitate briefing?" he asked.

Gina smiled. Larry was very good at his job, and being a native New Yorker, he wasn't easily impressed. "As a matter of fact, this case *does* necessitate briefing. I am glad I caught you before you started. Can we grab a cup of coffee?"

Larry led Gina to the cafeteria. It was still early, so the staff was just opening up. Breakfast was not yet being served, but the large industrial urns of freshly brewed coffee were ready to go. They grabbed two huge cups and a table by the window overlooking the garden courtyard. It was a beautiful little garden in the middle of a concrete building. Amazing what a little greenery could do for the view.

"Larry, this is going to be a tough one. You will have some notoriety by the end of the day. I would be sure to do a very thorough job."

"Gina, I always do a very thorough job. Now what's it gonna be—you gonna tell me who the girl is, or are we gonna keep playing twenty questions?"

"All right, can't you afford me a little drama? The girl is Ashley Rydell—the daughter of one Senator Rydell of Illinois!"

Larry let out a long whistle. "What happened to her? Mugging? Rape?"

"Well, that's the real clincher. We think she bled out from a termination."

"Whoa! That's going to cause a real scandal. He is way right, isn't he?"

"Not only is he way right, but he is squarely in the prolife movement and sits on the Senate Judiciary Committee," Gina returned with a smugness she really didn't feel. "He and his wife, Cynthia, are expected here within the hour."

"Did you tell him how she died?" Larry whispered.

"I did, and he nearly flipped. He is insisting it was murder and that his daughter would never do such a thing. I figured there was no real reason to argue and that the autopsy would tell the story soon enough. Under the circumstances, you are going to have to be very precise in your work today. Prepare to be disputed by the father on every finding."

"Thanks for the heads-up. I will dot every *i* and cross every *t*, but I tell you, I am getting too old for this crap. I swear, I want to retire to a little unknown town in southern New Jersey."

Gina laughed. "Like there are any little unknown towns left in New Jersey. Good luck with that!"

"Better get started. I think it is going to be a very long day," he sighed.

"Oh, Larry, one more thing—the *Post* already knows. I got a call from Randazzo, who seemed to know more than I did, as usual. I was able to hold him off by promising him confirmation of identity before the public announcement. I figured it was a good trade considering the alternative would really screw us up. Imagine the *Post* running the headline at the same time I was notifying the senator!"

"We would have every news reporter at the front door right now. Thanks, Gina. I appreciate your keeping the media at bay until I can do my job. I am going to close out some paperwork from yesterday's cases while you wait to ID. Have them page me as soon as you and the senator are finished so I can get started."

"You got it, Larry. Talk to you soon."

Gina went to the autopsy room, where Ashley lay on the table with a white sheet covering her. Gina wanted to look the body over one more time before she met with the Rydells, making sure she didn't miss any detail. The girl's lips were blackish blue, and her skin looked very thin, almost translucent. Still, even in death the girl was beautiful—your classic wholesome Miss America, with big, blue eyes and the fairest blond hair. Gina felt the emotion, the sadness, washing over her. She thought it best to take a few moments and let her emotion run its course. From experience, she knew she could not ignore her feelings of sadness and pain. She had learned early on that it was best to allow some "moments of mourning." It helped her to move beyond the experience and work her cases from a factual standpoint. If she did not afford herself the time to be human, she would struggle throughout the case. As she was finishing her inspection, she heard the page summoning her to the front desk. It was time, and Gina was nervous. This was going to be one of the most difficult meetings of Gina's career.

As she approached the reception area, her chest tightened. She slowed her step and breathed deeply. It wasn't the senator who evoked her emotion; it was Cynthia, the girl's mother. There was no mistaking her, not for a second. She had the puffy face, red-rimmed eyes, and disheveled appearance of a heartbroken mother. Gina had come to know the sight well, yet it was never any easier to deal with. Very few parents could function once they actually heard the news they had feared since the day their children were born. Cynthia Rydell just stood quietly while her husband waited impatiently, as if he were a horse at the starting gate. Gina quickly approached them, extended her hand, and introduced herself.

"Yes, Ms. Vincent, thank you for meeting us promptly. Now please take us to our daughter." The senator was not going to give Gina the upper hand. From his tone, she understood that this would be his show on his terms. Gina figured it was best to let him do what he did best: give orders.

"This way, Senator. Mrs. Rydell, may I get you anything?"

"No, Ms. Vincent, just my baby girl." Cynthia Rydell choked out the words in a whisper, unable to speak in an audible volume as she fought a breakdown.

Gina prepared them for what they were about to see and what they might expect. "I will take you directly to your daughter for identification and allow you as much time as necessary. Once you are ready, I will need you to complete some paperwork, and I can then review the details I have collected so far. I have reserved a conference room and some measure of privacy for your convenience. Your daughter's autopsy will take place as soon as identification is complete. Anticipating the media, we would like to get as far ahead of them as possible. Do you have any questions before we proceed?"

Senator Rydell silently shook his head and held his wife gently around the waist. It seemed as if he was actually supporting her weight. Gina led them into the viewing room, which had large glass panels allowing a full view of the autopsy room. Ashley lay covered on the table in the center of the room. As is standard for operating rooms, it was freezing. Gina hesitated and looked at the senator, checking his face for the signal to proceed, ensuring that he and his wife were ready. He nodded ever so slightly, and Gina led them directly to the table. Chatting never seemed appropriate at these times, so Gina stayed quiet and stepped back, allowing the Rydells to approach their daughter together. Cynthia turned the sheet back as if she were setting the covers and tucking her child into bed. She stared down into the face, and the tears streamed.

Not a sound did she make as she kissed her daughter's forehead, eyes, nose, lips, and mouth. She knew it would be the last time she could hold her daughter, and she would not let the cold rob her of her last embrace. Cynthia felt the warmth of her daughter even though the body was icy.

Her husband could not stand the sight. His features were stone, every line and crevice chiseled from rock. He stood tall and resolute as if he were facing an adversary. He would not yield but would turn his pain to the issues at hand. This was unacceptable. Somebody would pay for the murder! Somebody would pay dearly. He gently touched his wife's shoulder as he pulled the sheet up and over his daughter's face. "Cynthia, Ashley is gone, and we must let her go. Let's go inside and get some water," he whispered. The gentle sound of his voice was a stark contradiction to the hard expression on his face. His eyes were steel blue, cold, and determined. He led his wife from the room and motioned to Gina to lead the way.

Gina quickly led them down the hall to the conference room. The only amenities in the room were a table, six chairs, a conference-type telephone, and a television mounted to the wall in one corner. The room was much warmer than the operating room; the walls were painted taupe, and the carpet was various shades of tan with hunter-green flecks. They each took a seat, and Cynthia Rydell completely broke down. She could not control herself as the sobs racked her body. She tightened her body into a ball as if she could disappear into herself. Gina quickly excused herself to allow them some time together. She would bring back coffee, juice, and water. The coffee was more for herself than for anyone else. She scurried from the room, relieved to be away from their grief, even if just for a moment.

Senator Rydell put his arm around his wife and pulled her close to him. She abruptly pulled away and straightened up in her chair. She whirled around to look him directly in the eye. "Don't you touch me!" she snapped. "You killed her as sure as I am sitting here. You took my baby from me, and I will never forgive you!"

"Please, Cyn, don't do this to us. I am as sick about this as you are, but I did not do this to Ashley. Some bad people did this to her, and I am going to find out who."

"Don't give me that crap. You and your ideals, your family values, your wholesome platform. *This* happens every day! *This* is the result of your successful campaign to save the unborn. How does it feel, George? Still feel righteous, like you are the savior? Does it still feel victorious? She couldn't even come to us in her despair." Cynthia spun around, pointed directly into George's face and lowered her voice to a venomous hiss, "Why? Because of you— you and your image, your goals. Well, I don't give a damn about any of it anymore. Don't talk to me about your constituents, the rights of the unborn; all you care about are the votes associated with the right. Make no mistake, George, I will never forgive you. I will never forgive *you*!"

He figured it was the grief. Surely, she didn't blame him for this hideous crime. Surely, she knew his baby girl was gone from his life as well as hers. Still, he felt a sick feeling deep in the pit of his stomach. If this was true, if this was how she died, he couldn't help but feel that his wife might be right—it would be his life's work that had caused his daughter's death. *No*, he would not think this way. He could not think this way. If this was what Ashley had decided to do, then this was the unfortunate consequence of her decision. Still, he felt as if he were drowning, as if he had no control. Just as his despair threatened to overwhelm him completely, Jake Woodward his Chief of Staff walked in.

"Why didn't you call me before you left? I have prepared multiple statements for the press, but I figured I would fly with you."

"Relax, Jake. You can run the show. I needed to get Cynthia here quickly. I knew you would be busy preparing for the media, and I needed to get down here. I am not sure what we are going to do. It seems she may have died due to an illegal abortion. We won't know for sure until the autopsy results are back."

"George … Cynthia, I am so sorry. We *will* handle this. I will do everything I can to get you through this. What is the chance of the autopsy results being inconclusive?"

"The agent handling the case is Gina Vincent. She seems to believe it is open-and-shut. She will be back shortly, and you can discuss this with her then. In the meantime, I am taking Cynthia to the hotel. We both need some time. Release whatever statements you think are appropriate; I can't say I really care what the response is at this point."

"Listen, George, I can appreciate how you are feeling right now, but this is a delicate situation. It is no time to act recklessly. We need to choose our words carefully and consider the consequences." Jake appeared to be a little pale and was increasingly nervous. He was the senator's right-hand man, in charge of everything. This was his career, and he refused to watch it disappear. "Let me see if I can get Agent Vincent. We will speak to her together, and then you can take Cynthia to the hotel. I'll be right back."

Cynthia Rydell didn't even glance in Jake's direction. She sensed George was reeling, but as soon as "boy wonder" showed up, she knew the old George would return. Jake would ensure the senator was acting "appropriately" and moving in "accordance with the plan." It made her sick to see politics at work. Even worse was seeing them at work with the body of her only daughter in the next room. She knew she would never truly smile again. Her life had ended when she turned over that sheet. She saw them speaking around her in the room. Jake and her husband were speaking, not to her, but speaking nonetheless. She couldn't hear them. It was as if she were moving in slow motion while everything continued to go on around her at a normal pace. She was there, present, yet completely detached from her surroundings. Her brain was no longer screaming; it was very quiet. She heard only Ashley's voice playing in her mind. *I'm a little teapot, short and stout. Here is my handle, here is my spout.*

Gina and Jake entered the room and sat at the table. Cynthia sat in the chair but was completely withdrawn. George spoke first. "I would like to take my wife to the hotel. What papers do I need to sign?"

"Senator, I truly am very sorry for your loss. I just need you to sign the identification form. I expect the autopsy results will be ready by the end of the day. Where would you like me to contact you?"

Jake spoke firmly, looking directly into Gina's eyes. "Agent Vincent, you will contact me, and I will relay all matters to the senator. I will give you my cell phone number and my secretary's number to ensure you can get us live as soon as you need us. I am sure you can appreciate the senator's need for privacy. I will handle all press inquiries and updates."

Gina was fine with that. Jake seemed like a driven, self-centered little twerp, but she wasn't going to let that stand between her and this mess. He seemed extremely proficient, and if he wanted to take this on, then she was all too eager to let him do so.

"I understand completely, Mr. Woodward. I will contact you directly with all updates. I have a preliminary list of Ashley's friends that I will be interviewing after you have released your statement to the press. I will give you a copy. If you would, review it with the Rydells whenever appropriate, just to ensure I am not overlooking anyone. In the meantime, please feel free to contact me for any assistance you may require."

Jake seemed relieved. "Agent Vincent, is there any chance the autopsy will be inconclusive?"

Gina knew it! She could always tell an asshole when she saw one! "No, Mr. Woodward," she flatly replied. "I really don't think that's possible."

Shocked by her snippy response, he replied, "Well, let's just see how it goes."

Gina once again offered her condolences to the Rydells, and then she left. She could breathe once again. She hated the maneuvering, positioning, the overall political game. Why couldn't they just deal with the truth and act accordingly? She knew Jake would work the morgue all day to see if he could manipulate the results. If he could keep the truth from coming out, he would be able to spin the situation completely—truly amazing and utterly disgusting.

Gina didn't really care what information would be released to the public. It had no bearing on her case. She already had enough information to proceed. She needed to know who did it. By finding whoever it was, she would save others. That was her objective, the sole purpose of her job. Satisfying the political needs of the senator and his staff was not, at the end of the day, her concern.

There wasn't much left for her to do until the autopsy was finalized. Working on just a few hours of sleep, she figured it was best to go home. She would catch a few hours of sleep to prepare her for the end-of-day circus. Once they issued the statements to the press, she could begin interviewing Ashley's friends.

It was time to call Robert and check in. He answered on the first ring, as always. "Yes, dear."

"Hi, it's Gina. Got anything pressing for me?"

"Let's just say Charlie Randazzo must have this office on speed dial! He called three times asking if you were back from the morgue. Your grandmother called to remind you about dinner at her house tomorrow night. Otherwise, everything is quiet."

"That would be the quiet before the storm. Be ready Robert. Call Charlie back for me, and tell him he will hear from me before five o'clock tonight. He should have his story ready to go, and I will be able to confirm identity. In the meantime, I'm taking a few hours to wash up and get a quick nap."

"Lovely idea! I didn't even have to force you to think of it yourself. Gina, we may be making progress!"

"Don't be a smartass, Robert. I will call you in a few hours."

Chapter 6

THE call from the morgue came just as she was getting dressed—perfect timing. When did that ever happen? "Hello."

"Gina, it's Larry. I just finished up. We are going to modify things a little."

"Oh, Jeez, Larry! Did that idiot Jake work you all day?"

"Listen, Gina, it's not important enough to fight this one. She was pregnant; she miscarried and hemorrhaged. That much I am releasing as fact. As far as why she miscarried, that is inconclusive."

"Unbelievable! Look, Larry, I don't give a damn about the politics! I have a murderer out there who is going to cause more deaths. I need a reason to investigate, and you are not giving me one."

"Relax, Gina. The autopsy is inconclusive. There still are enough questionable circumstances for you to continue the investigation. We are just saying there is no medical proof it was a termination. Gina, it is going to be difficult enough for them to handle the fact that she was pregnant and now she is dead. Let's leave this last little tidbit out if we can."

"Fine, Larry. But don't be surprised if you find yourself in a courtroom on this one."

"No problem. We'll cross that bridge when we come to it. In the meantime, let's have the big boys play this out and give the family time to bury the girl."

"I am going to call Charlie like I promised. He may still choose to run the story his way. I don't know his source, but everyone should be prepared. Charlie loves a good scandal, and I don't think we will be able to keep this one under wraps." Gina was exasperated.

She couldn't believe the way the system could be manipulated by those in powerful positions.

"I will let Mr. Woodward know about the *Post*. I have put a copy of the autopsy in your electronic file. Take care, Gina."

"Talk to you later, Larry."

It was inconceivable to think Charlie Randazzo was going to take this lightly. She had to call him right away: best to face the worst. Charlie would definitely run the story his way, and it would be completely out of Jake Woodward's hands. Media backlash is a real bitch! Maybe Larry was right: maybe it was their affair. Gina didn't care how they battled it out. She needed to continue her investigation regardless of the senator's stature.

"Charlie? It's Gina."

"Thank God. Gina, I have been waiting to hear from you. Is it a go? I have deadlines. Am I running the senator's daughter dying of a botched termination or not?"

"Hold up, Charlie. The autopsy report is final, and she was definitely pregnant and she definitely hemorrhaged. However, there is no conclusive medical evidence it was due to a termination."

"Bullshit, Gina! You know where you found her. Did she just drive to downtown Brooklyn and enter an abandoned house so she could rest for a while?"

"Charlie, I know. But this is the official autopsy report. These are the findings. If you feel confident with your original source, run what you want. Be careful though. These boys are playing for keeps. Jake Woodward is running the show for the senator, and he is extremely good at his job! Either way, I've kept my promise. You are the first to know."

"Thanks, Gina. Can't say I like it, but I've seen it before. I am going to run it my way, but I'll tone it down a bit. I'll just insinuate why she hemorrhaged." Charlie already rewrote the article in his mind.

"Good luck, Charlie. I am still looking for leads on who may have done this. My investigation is moving forward, so if you hear or know anything, please keep me posted."

"You got it. Be careful out there."

As Gina hung up, she felt a little better. Maybe her fears were wrong. It would be great if it didn't turn into a media feeding frenzy, especially for Cynthia Rydell. Gina saw grief often, but a mother's grief was always the worst. Mothers who lost children looked vacant. They had a lost look in their eyes, as if they weren't sure why they were still here. It was heartbreaking. For Cynthia's sake, Gina was relieved Larry had caved in to Jake's pressure.

It was time she were available to the press. After the official press release, she would start interviewing Ashley's friends. She still had a case, and it was important to find some leads. She knew she needed to track the abortionist. He or she had displayed a total disregard for human life, which was a good indication the person would strike again. With the exception of the phone call to 911, the person had done nothing to preserve Ashley's health. The conditions were filthy, the location remote, and there wasn't even running water available. Gina wondered how desperate a well-educated, beautiful, young girl could be to actually enter some dump and go forward with the procedure. Was her fear of her father, the public, or the press so great that she would overlook her own well-being?

Gina knew two things: there was a father, and she needed to find him. There was a killer, and she would have to move quickly before he or she killed again.

Gina selected her navy blue suit, cream blouse, Enzo Angiolini navy loafers, and a pearl choker—the perfect outfit to meet the press. She was pretty—dark brown hair, green eyes, average height and build. While not overly athletic, she had a toned body. By the way she dressed, she would not turn heads, but in her field, which was dominated by men, she still stood out. Most attractive was the fact that she didn't think she was. She overlooked her femininity completely, which explained her lack of dates and steady boyfriends. Her job was truly her life. The thought of a husband and family was there, but it seemed like a plan for the future, not for the present.

Except for her grandmother constantly trying to fix her up, she really didn't think about it at all. She felt her job allowed her to accomplish a greater good. She really believed she was saving women and children. She never felt good about prosecuting and convicting mothers, but she always knew the life of the child must be the top priority. So strong was her conviction that polite dinner conversation could become an all-out argument if someone disagreed.

As she pulled up to the morgue, the media barrage hit her. "Agent Vincent, is it true Senator Rydell's daughter died from an abortion?" "Who was the father?" "Where was she found?" "Do you have any suspects?"

Gina took a deep breath and put on her game face. "One at a time, please. Unfortunately, we did recover the body of Ashley Rydell, Senator George Rydell's only daughter. We do know she was pregnant and she miscarried. She died from excessive bleeding, and that is the *official* finding of the autopsy. We do not have any evidence that a termination was involved, nor do we have any details as to who the father was. I will continue the investigation, but as it stands right now, it seems this is a very unfortunate and painful situation for the Rydell family. If anything criminal is uncovered, we will, as always, release a statement. For now, I would hope that you all try to consider the task ahead of the senator and his wife."

"Agent Vincent, the *Post* is reporting death due to termination. What is your response to that?"

"The autopsy results indicate that there is no conclusive evidence of a termination. I need to continue my investigation, so if you will excuse me … ."

As she turned, she completely shut off the fifty or so questions simultaneously thrown at her. They would ask you the same questions eighty-eight different ways if you gave them the chance. She didn't think that it went too badly, and she was feeling pretty good. Now she could get down to work, doing her job, her way. She always felt best when she was in charge.

As she arrived at the campus, it was evident the news was fresh and raw. A memorial was already outside Ashley's dorm, with flowers, teddy bears, candles, and letters. This was the hard part.

Ashley's roommate was Indigo Violet, truly the antithesis of Ashley. While Ashley was raised in a strict, right-wing, conservative home, Indigo was the daughter of artists. Expression and form took precedence in her household. Starting with her name, Indigo had learned to express her feelings, look into her heart, and find her soul. She had dark black hair, deep blue eyes, and very fair skin. Her light skin and dark hair caused her eyes to stand out. It was difficult to focus on any other part of her face. Her eyes seemed to be windows to her soul in every sense of the cliché. She was quiet yet confident. She met Gina's gaze head-on and firmly shook her hand.

"I am Indigo. You must be Agent Vincent. The dean's office told me to expect you."

"Hello, Indigo. I am very sorry about Ashley. I can appreciate how painful this must be for you. I only have a few questions, and I will try to keep this as brief as possible." Indigo motioned for Gina to join her on the couch. They were sitting side by side.

"I knew what Ashley was going to do. We didn't keep any secrets from one another. Nobody else knows, but I do. I know the news reports have been hinting that she had an abortion, but it doesn't seem like they know for sure. I do, but I do not want the world to know. The only thing I can do now is to try to protect her memory. I failed miserably at trying to protect her life." Indigo spoke evenly and with great despair as if she could have prevented this tragedy. This girl was heartbroken, and worse yet, she was blaming herself.

"Let's just take this one step at a time. First of all, everything you say to me is highly confidential. My primary objective is to find out what happened, determine if a criminal act occurred, and then find the perpetrator. I am not interested in a scandal or any political platform. I do need to know what you know about the events leading up to Ashley's death." Gina stared intently at

Indigo, trying to make her see and sense her sincerity. Gina knew she needed trust before she could get the story. Indigo believed Gina and seemed to welcome her presence.

"She found out she was pregnant a few weeks ago. She was only six weeks along, but she knew she couldn't have the baby. She went on and on about the scandal, her father, how it would kill him. She refused to tell Richard. He didn't even know." Her calm exterior began to crack, and tears were streaming down her face. Indigo was not only sad, but she also seemed afraid.

"Let's just stop for a second. Can I get you a glass of water? Do you want to rest for a moment? When you feel you are ready, continue by telling me about Richard." Gina held Indigo's hand.

"Richard Barton III was Ashley's boyfriend. He is a junior studying political science. They have been dating since the fall. He is just like her father, and he would never have agreed to this. He would have arranged a wedding immediately. He is very upset. He called here yelling at me, blaming me. He said I should have told him, he would have stopped her, that I could have saved her!" Indigo completely broke down. Gina realized this was far too much pressure for this young girl to take. Her best friend was dead, the boyfriend was blaming her, and one of the most affluent political families in the country was about to bear down on her.

"Indigo, you have to stop blaming yourself. If Richard would like to blame someone, he should blame himself. Ashley did not create her pregnancy by herself. I need to know where Ashley went and whom she contacted to make the arrangements. Do you know any of this?"

"That's the problem. I tried to talk Ashley out of it! I tried to have her think about it and give herself some time. She wouldn't even consider it. She was so afraid of what the world would say. She felt it would ruin her father completely. The morning she left, she didn't know where she was going. She promised me she would tell me once she figured it out. I never expected her to go through with it on the same day. I thought I would be able to take her and make sure she was okay. She never even called me. I thought she was in class. It wasn't until Richard called later that night that I started to worry."

"Do you know any sources on campus where one might go to find out about an abortion?"

"This is only our first year. I am still scouting the best coffee shop. I really don't know where she was going. She didn't even go to a clinic to find out she was pregnant. She took a home pregnancy test."

Gina felt sorry for the girl. She would replay the series of events for the rest of her life. "Thank you, Indigo. If you find out anything or remember something you left out, please call me. A telephone number, a friend, anything that might give me some indication of where Ashley went that day would really help. I want to make sure that whoever did this doesn't do it again." Gina handed Indigo her card and gave her a hug. "One last thing: where can I find Richard now?"

It took Gina only three minutes to reach Richard's dorm. She walked one block over and two houses down—a real frat house. She rang the doorbell, and a young boy, likely a freshman, answered. "May I help you?"

"I'm Agent Vincent, Federal Bureau of Life Investigation. I need to speak with Richard Barton."

Before the boy could answer, a 6'2" sandy-haired fellow stepped into the doorway and replied, "I've got it, Wietz. I'm Richard Barton. I guess you're here to talk about Ashley. Please come in." He led Gina into the dining room. "Have a seat."

"Thank you, Mr. Barton. Yes, I am here to talk about Ashley. I understand you were her boyfriend, and I would first like to offer my condolences."

"Look, Agent Vincent, spare me your sympathy. I was Ashley's boyfriend, and if she was pregnant, then I am the father. However, I did not know she was pregnant, nor did I know of her plan to terminate. My values are definitive. I plan to serve this country in political office. I share the values of Senator Rydell, and I absolutely never would have agreed to Ashley's actions."

Gina was stunned. Not only was he cold, but he didn't even seem to care she was dead. His only concern was himself. He acted as if he had absolutely nothing to do with the situation. Gina was furious, but she needed to maintain control. She took a deep breath and smiled. She had learned early on in her career that it is very hard to be furious when you are smiling, not to mention that it's completely unnerving to the other person.

"Yes, Mr. Barton, I can certainly understand how you must be feeling. She didn't even tell you about the pregnancy. Then for her to continue without even consulting you … well, I can appreciate how upsetting this must be for you. Not to mention the scandal she knew it could cause. Let me see … were you sexually active with Ms. Rydell?"

"Yes, I told you I do not doubt I was the father."

"Did you take precautions that would ensure you would not conceive?"

"Well, that was Ashley's responsibility, not mine. I assumed she had everything under control." For the first time he looked at Gina a little less forcefully.

"Ah, I see," Gina replied. "Did you know what form of birth control Ashley used?"

"No. She took care of it. It was not my concern. I didn't even know she was pregnant as I have already told you."

"Yes, Mr. Barton, you told me. Let's see … you *did* have sex with her, it *was* unprotected, and you do not doubt you *were* the father, but *none* of this was *your* affair. Did I capture that correctly?"

"Look, Agent Vincent, if I need to contact my attorney, I will. Otherwise, I do not have anything to add. Now if you will excuse me, I am meeting with Senator Rydell shortly."

"Well, Mr. Barton, that will certainly require the political performance of a lifetime. In my world, you would be the root cause of their daughter's death. I do wish you well in your meeting. Good day."

As she turned to leave, her anger nearly overwhelmed her. Just a few more steps out the door, and she could breathe again. The cool mist of a rainy spring night hit her face and immediately calmed her. She could see it all now. Senator Rydell would probably meet with Richard and hammer out his career path! They would discuss how to "handle" the situation. They would share notes and ideas, but never once would they discuss Richard's role in Ashley's death. No, that would be *inappropriate*. Ashley should have known better. The important thing now was simply how to proceed for the greater cause. Gina hated politicians and their inability to speak the truth or own up to their own faults.

As Gina finished her campus interviews, she knew she had hit a wall. She had uncovered nothing. Even if there were a lead, it would have come from Indigo or Richard. Indigo had shared everything she had, and Richard was incapable of identifying the truth, let alone speaking it. She would have to go back to the scene—the call to 911. Maybe that would take her somewhere.

Her cell rang. "Vincent here."

"Gina, its Grandma. I just heard about Senator Rydell's daughter: terrible, just terrible. Do you know who is handling the case, dear?"

"Yes, Grandma, I'm handling the case, but you know I can't discuss it with you. I got your message, and I will be over tomorrow night for dinner." Gina never understood how her grandmother seemed to have a pulse on everything.

"Oh, that's wonderful, honey. Please be delicate with Cynthia Rydell. This must be just horrible for her. I will see you around six o'clock tomorrow."

"See you then, Grandma."

Chapter 7

AFTER a completely uneventful day, Gina was relieved to be driving to the country. Her grandmother lived in Colts Neck, New Jersey, a town that seemed to be untouched by time. In an area once comprising mostly horse farms, strict zoning combined with farmland preservation had created a picturesque vista with gentle rolling hills. Huge mansions, four golf courses, and a variety of farms in an area of only thirty-one square miles made an impressive statement in the overbuilt, overpopulated East Coast area. Stress disappeared when she found herself stopping her car to allow ducks to cross the road. She felt like the intruder when faced with earth's natural beauty. Gina decided to take her time and enjoy the view. Each home was prettier than the last. She especially loved the grounds of the municipal buildings and police station. The buildings seemed to fade into the landscape, complete with a lake, park, and walking trails. The area was completely unlike any of the precincts Gina found herself in on a daily basis.

Her grandmother was an icon: a strong-willed, active woman who worked, built a business, raised a family, and continually gave back to humanity. She was born Sophia Renato in Brooklyn, New York, in 1954. Married twice, she divorced her first husband before finding the love of her life, Sean Cavanaugh. As an American of Italian descent, she always found it humorous that Sophia Cavanaugh sounded so proper, so "un-Italian." Sean and Sophia were a perfect match. She was outspoken, liberal, and headstrong, while he was conservative, quiet, and deliberate. They were a true balance for one another as they built their family and lives together.

They had three children, Sean Jr., Julia, and Anna. Anna was Gina's mother. They were a close family, but both Anna and Julia found Sophia to be a little overbearing. Sophia knew this and was content to give them a little room. The grandchildren, however, flocked to Sophia. They loved her unconditionally. She was "Grandma," and she would tell them everything about everything all the time. Grandpa would tease them that if they stayed around too long, Sophia would have each of them building an empire. Grandma Sophia believed a person could accomplish anything in this world. Desire combined with research and practice created results. Both Sean and Sophia enjoyed a happy and successful life. All of their children and their families were together frequently, and they truly seemed to enjoy each other's company. Gina loved going to her grandmother's and couldn't wait to see her. The house was a beautiful brick colonial with soaring ceilings and huge windows. From the library, they could see the forest with rabbits, deer, and possum frolicking in plain sight. Sophia said it was that view that had prompted them to purchase the property before the allure of Colts Neck reached the wealthy in the late 1990s. She stood on that ground and said, "The library should be right here," and so it was. She always accomplished what she set out to do. It was her way. She would come up with an idea, develop a plan, and work it to completion. Grandpa Sean must have found it completely frustrating, yet he loved her, admiring her strength and conviction. They were a great team and were wonderful together. Sophia felt that worth should not be measured by money, but rather by the number of lives one could touch in a positive fashion while on this earth. Gina loved them both dearly.

She arrived to find Sophia in the library and her grandfather out playing golf. He loved the game and would play as often as possible. Sophia was busy on her computer checking news stories and reviewing stock prices. The television monitors displayed three different news channels. Sophia spent her days "in touch" with the world.

"Gina, how are you? Give me a kiss!" Sophia hugged Gina tightly and kissed her on the cheek and on the top of her head.

"Grandma, I'm fine. The ride out was great. Everything is so green and beautiful."

"Spring is the best time here. Everything is alive and colorful. Come, sit down; I have so much to ask you." Sophia sat at her desk. It was a partner desk, with one side for her and the other side for Sean. It was at this desk that they would work together to build their life. Gina sat in her grandfather's chair. "Grandma, the Rydell case is terrible. Ashley was so beautiful. It's a tragedy, and at such a young age."

"Now, Gina, I know you don't want me to get started, but if it were my time, Ashley would simply have gone to a clinic and been home for the six o'clock news. She would not be dead, and you would not be looking for a murderer. This whole business is very upsetting. Sets women's rights back sixty years!" As usual, Sophia just hit the issue head-on and held back nothing.

"Grandma, it is important we protect human life. We must save the children. You know my position on this." Gina pleaded with her grandmother for what seemed like the millionth time.

"Gina, let's not make our visit about this. I do hope you find whomever or whatever you are looking for on this case. I saw on the news today that her boyfriend is devastated and didn't have any knowledge of the pregnancy. He made a joint statement with the senator, although I noticed Cynthia wasn't there. I think the news said the funeral is set for Saturday. They are not coming down on the senator just yet, but if it is confirmed that she had a termination, his career is as good as over."

"Grandma, his career should be the least of his problems. He lost his only daughter in a terrible fashion, along with his first grandchild. I hardly think he should be worried about the next election." Gina couldn't believe the complexity people added to life. It seemed so simple to her. Ashley was dead; she had made a mistake and paid with her life. Her family should focus on that and nothing else.

"Okay, dear, let's just move on. I wanted to see you because I am hosting a fundraiser in two weeks for juvenile diabetes, and I was hoping you could attend. Many of my doctor friends will be here, but there is one doctor in particular that I would like you to meet." It was more like Sophia announced this to Gina than asked her.

"Grandma, we have been through this: *no* blind dates. My work keeps me very busy, and I don't have time for this right now."

"Now, Gina, settle down. That's why I want you to come to the fundraiser. You could see him in a casual, unattached setting, and things could progress naturally from there. Besides, I want to show off my beautiful granddaughter to my friends. His name is Dr. Nicholas DePaolo, and he is an OB/GYN. He is very successful, young, and handsome. I think he is perfect for you. Gina, you must join us." Now Sophia was pleading, and Gina found it humorous because Sophia always got what she wanted anyway.

"Yes, I will come to the fundraiser. I will meet all of your friends, but no dates and no pushing. I am not making any promises about the doctor, but I will be here for the event," Gina said firmly.

"Excellent! Thank you, Gina. You'll see. Grandma is right. You are going to love him."

Just then, Gina noticed someone was working in the library. He was installing new crown molding above the bookcases.

"Forgive me. Where are my manners? Gina, this is Nate. He is updating the woodwork and adding a few more bookcases for me. He is an absolute artist. His work rivals the craftsmen of the 1800's. Nate, this is my granddaughter, Gina."

"Pleased to meet you, Gina," he answered. Nate was a soft-spoken man who looked up briefly to meet Gina's gaze. He seemed sad and distant. Gina had to fight the urge to console him. It seemed as if the weight of the world were on his shoulders.

"Dinner is ready. Nate, would you like to join us?" Once again, Sophia announced this more than asked.

"Thank you, Mrs. Cavanaugh—I mean, Sophia—but I really do need to get home. The children are expecting me. I will be back tomorrow. I should be finished by then."

"Thank you, Nate. It really is coming out lovely. I will see you in the morning."

Sophia led Gina to the kitchen. Gina loved when they ate in the kitchen instead of the dining room. There was a big table, surrounded by two walls of windows with a fifteen-foot tray ceiling. A person could sit at the table or at the kitchen counter and be a part of everything that was going on.

"So, Grandma, we are eating in the kitchen. What plans do you have for me? It's always serious business when we eat in the kitchen."

"Don't be silly, Gina. I have no plans for you other than what I have already told you. I would like you to reconsider your career choice, but sitting in the kitchen will hardly change that." Sophia hated Gina's job.

"Grandma, you know my job is important to me." "Gina, I don't want to fight, but women should be allowed to make their own choices. Abortion is a terrible outcome, but it is hardly the affair of the government."

"I am saving lives. I am the child advocate, Grandma: the protector of those who cannot defend themselves."

"Gina, motherhood is a lifelong commitment that should not be imposed. Besides, abortion and the legality of it is not the real issue anyway. We should have put programs in place to avoid the unwanted pregnancy. Abortion is just a symptom, not the problem."

"Be that as it may, the law is clear, and I uphold the law. Now, Grandma, is there a point to this discussion, because we have been over this a million times already."

"Imprisonment of women is absurd. Women do not rejoice in terminating their pregnancies. They are tormented, sad, and afraid.

It is incomprehensible what a woman faces today if she finds herself pregnant."

"A woman would find herself having a baby—a very natural, normal process for the female of the human race."

"You're right, Gina. We get nowhere with this. I have a favor to ask. My friend Millie Stone: her granddaughter who works for that big law firm in the city was pregnant. They arrested her for trying to abort. Millie says she was up for partner in the firm but would be passed over if they found out she was pregnant. To make matters worse, Millie says the father was the senior partner, who happens to be married. Do you think there is anything you could do to help her, Gina?"

"Why didn't she come to you before she tried to abort? I can help them before, but once they make the decision to break the law, it's very difficult for me, Grandma. Think about it—you shouldn't even be telling me this."

"I know, I know, but she is so upset. The girl worked so hard to become partner, and she is going to lose it all."

"Would she testify against the father?"

"No, that would be political suicide!"

"Will she give us the name of the doctor who performed the procedure?"

"Well, see, that's just it: turns out her friend helped her do it. That's when she ran into problems and they called an ambulance."

"Grandma, what do you expect me to do with this? It just gets worse as you go on. I will see who is on the case, and if there is something I can do, I will. I can't promise you anything," Gina counseled.

"Thank you … I know … thank you, baby. Doesn't it feel better to help these women than it does to arrest them?"

"Grandma, please, let's just leave it alone. I love my job. I like to look at it as if I am saving lives. To listen to you, Grandma, one would never know you are a Republican."

"I am a Republican because it suits my cause, Gina. Make no mistake about it—Grandma does what Grandma has to do. Anyway, what harm is there in my beliefs? I simply want to educate children about their sexuality, counsel them, and if the situation arises, allow them to secure a safe abortion. I want them to know that abortion is a terrible thing than can be avoided."

"Abortion is murder. Period."

"Gina, we have implemented these laws and have done nothing to fix the problem."

"That's not true, Grandma. We no longer kill six million babies a year!"

"You're right, Gina. Now we kill three million babies and three million mothers at the same time through illegal terminations in horrendous conditions. Our problem was not six million abortions—it was six million unwanted pregnancies. Stop the unwanted pregnancy, and the need for the abortion goes away on its own. Apply all the money, resources, and energy to avoiding the unwanted pregnancy. Then we would have a real solution."

"Grandma, I do not make the laws; I enforce them. I happen to think I do a very good job at it."

"You're right, Gina. Forgive me for going off on my soapbox. You do a very good job, dear. Now eat your peas. Francesca has been cooking for you all day."

Francesca had been Sophia's housekeeper for the last twenty years. Sophia had spent most of her life cooking, cleaning, and taking care of the house herself in addition to her job and family. She should have had a housekeeper back then; instead, she hired Francesca after her kids were grown and out of the house.

"Thank you, Mrs. Sophia. Dessert has been prepared and is on the counter. I will be leaving now. May I please have a word with you in private before I go?" Francesca seemed nervous. She didn't usually request to see Sophia in private.

Sophia seemed fine with it. "Yes, Francesca, let's go to the library. Gina, you will excuse us, won't you?"

Francesca followed Sophia into the library and as Sophia sat down, Francesca stood staring at the floor nervously shifting her weight from one foot to the other. "Francesca, what's the matter? Is something wrong?" Sophia was genuinely concerned and dropped the nonchalant façade she put on in the kitchen.

"No, no, Mrs. Sophia. Nothing is wrong. I need your help. My friend … she is in a bad way. She is the housekeeper for a very important man, but she is in a bad way. She does not know what to do. I don't want her to get hurt. She is the daughter of my cousin, and I do not know who to ask for help." Francesca spoke very fast and became increasingly nervous, wringing her skirt tightly in her hands.

"Francesca, is the girl pregnant?"

"Yes."

"Did the important man make her pregnant?"

"Yes."

"Will she leave their household?"

"I don't know."

"Does she want the baby?"

"No, she has no home, and if she has the baby, she will have no job."

"Francesca, tell her I can get her a home and I can arrange for employment. If she still feels the same, then I will still help her. However, I want her assurance she will allow me to approach her boss to discuss the circumstances. I do not want this situation to repeat itself." Sophia spoke slowly as she stared directly into Francesca's eyes to ensure she understood.

Francesca nodded vehemently. "Yes, thank you. Thank you. I will talk to her tonight and tell you tomorrow. Thank you."

Sophia entered the kitchen and gave Gina a hug. "Gina, it's so good to see you, my beautiful granddaughter. Have you spoken to your mom?"

"Oh, Grandma, she is so busy. Between my work and her schedule, we never seem to touch base. I did speak with her last week, briefly, and I think she and Dad are planning a trip to Paris this fall."

"Yes, as a matter of fact she did mention it to me. It sounded more like *she* wanted to go to Paris in the fall, not so much your father." Sophia looked preoccupied, as if she suddenly had something on her mind. Gina saw it but chose to ignore it.

"Grandma, where did you find Nate? He really does such a beautiful job."

Sophia brightened immediately. "Yes, doesn't he? He is wonderful. So sad though. He has five children, and his poor wife died unexpectedly. He is raising the children all by himself. I met him through my church group, a very good man. The church has formed a tight support group around him, helping with meals and watching the kids. The baby—she was so young to lose her mother. Sometimes you have to wonder about the master plan."

"I know what you mean. That's how I feel about Ashley Rydell. She was so young. What could God's plan be? Why? I try not to think about it because—" Gina choked up; she couldn't push the ball in her throat down, and finally she broke down.

Sophia ran to hold her. "I know, baby. I know. So much sadness. Tragedy. You must cry, Gina. Let it out. It's normal for you to feel this way." Sophia gently rocked Gina back and forth as the sobs racked her body. It was just too much for her. In the comfort of the kitchen, in the quiet of the country, in the arms of her grandma, she needed to be a child, if just for a moment.

Chapter 8

PATTI couldn't do it anymore. He was her ex-husband; why didn't he just disappear? She never asked him for child support. She didn't ask him for anything. She just wanted him out of her life. With four boys under six and two jobs, she was just barely holding it together. The kids went to daycare while she worked at Walmart during the day, and her neighbor watched them while she waited tables at the local diner during the evening rush. When he wasn't around, she could fall into a routine and at least enjoy Saturday and Sunday with the kids. It was hectic Monday through Friday, but the weekends made it all worthwhile.

She could lie in bed with the kids piled in her bed. They would cuddle until late in the morning, watching cartoons. These were her most precious moments. They would jump on her, hug her, kiss her, and love her. It was like having a long, cool drink on a hot summer day; she just couldn't hug them enough on their Saturday morning snuggles. On Sunday, it was off to church and then the park. They would play, run, and laugh. She loved Saturday and Sunday. The weekend rejuvenated her and made her ready to face the week.

Unless, of course, *he* showed up—he would be drunk, or high, and *always* mean. He would throw the kids around as if they were rag dolls. He didn't care about them, didn't even seem to notice them unless they were directly in his way. No, he was not there to see the kids. He was there for her. She didn't know how she could have ever loved him. He was evil. She hated the sight and especially the smell of him. Cigarettes, sweat, and alcohol—it was enough to make her gag. She couldn't yell, scream, or fight. He would threaten her with the kids. He would grab one of them by the hair if she didn't do exactly as he asked. He hadn't been around for a few months, and then about four weeks ago he had shown up. It was a Saturday morning, and he just barged in the front door. He was drunk from the night before.

She made the kids run and hide. She didn't want him to touch them. "Quick, in the closet, boys! Don't come out now. Don't let him know you are here. Hurry! Hurry! Shh," she pleaded as he pushed his way into the bedroom.

It was over quickly. She knew not to fight. She knew not to talk. He didn't want to hear her voice. He just wanted her, and he would take her whenever and however he pleased. He was merciful this day, because he staggered out after only thirty minutes, giving her only one black eye.

She washed and washed, but the smell would not leave her body. She couldn't get rid of him. He would always be back. He would always shatter her world.

At first, she ignored the feeling, but after the fourth day, she knew. She had been there four times before. She was most certainly pregnant. It wasn't until today, nearly five weeks later, that she knew for sure. The clinic confirmed her worst fear. The sick feeling in the pit of her stomach was not from morning sickness. She could not have another child. She could not work seventy hours a week, take care of the kids, and have a fifth child. There was no way. It didn't take long for her to work out a plan. This was survival, and she was going to make it.

Before she left the clinic, she carefully looked around to see if she could find the answer to her problem. She knew the answer would be in the vicinity. As she left the building, she spotted what she was looking for. Two men were standing on the corner. She knew why they were there. She went to them and asked, "Can you help me?"

"That depends," said the dark-haired man.

"On what?" she pleaded.

"On how much you are willing to pay to make your problem go away." He sang the words as if they were a chant.

"I can pay six hundred dollars. No more. It is all I have," she begged.

"It's enough," he said.

He handed her an address, and then he and his friend walked away, just like that. They got in their blue Buick and drove away.

She would not wait. It was only 10:00 a.m., and she had the whole day off. She could get it done today and then be back to work in the morning. By the time dinner rolled around, it would all be over and behind her.

The address was not far, and her neighbor would be picking the kids up from daycare. She needed to move quickly, so she went to the bank and withdrew the cash. She drove to the address to find a one-story, white, warehouse-type building. There was no sign on the building, just a gray, metal door. She opened the door and saw abandoned offices with a reception area. Beyond the reception area, before an open warehouse space, was a small vestibule. She slowly approached and saw a single green door. The place was musty, the paint on the door was peeling, and she was starting to worry. She had known it would be bad, but she hadn't expected this. She had to fight the overwhelming urge to run, but she knew she had to be strong. This had to be resolved—today. Just as she was about to turn away, a young woman came through the green door.

"May I help you?" the woman asked.

Patti just handed her the paper with the address that the men at the clinic had given her.

"Are you ready now?"

"Yes," Patti answered.

"Follow me. You will need to give me your payment."

She took Patti down the staircase. They were old wooden steps with open spaces between them. Cobwebs were on either side, and a thick smell permeated the air. Patti was starting to feel sick, but she continued to follow the woman. She led her into a basement room with a wooden bench and laundry baskets lining the wall.

"Take your clothes off, and place them in one of the baskets. Take a gown, and put it on. Take two of these pills right now. I will be back for you in ten minutes. Now, may I please have the money?"

Patti handed her six one hundred–dollar bills. It was her whole savings. Now the whole thing was gone, and all because of *him*! He was truly evil. Patti closed her eyes and prayed for strength.

She chewed the pills and didn't take water. She wanted them to work right away. She knew it was going to hurt, and she was afraid. The woman returned and took Patti down the hall to another basement room. As they walked down the hall, Patti heard moaning and crying. She peeked into one of the rooms and saw bunk beds—rows of them. No sheets were on the mattresses, and there were girls everywhere. She had known there were others because she had seen the other laundry baskets with clothes in them. She hadn't expected to see so many.

A chill ran through her as she entered the operating room. There was a single table in the middle of the room with a hanging light over the table. Not a surgical light—just an old hanging light with a single bulb. A sink with a small counter was in the corner with a variety of instruments laid out on a white towel. There were roaches scurrying across the floor. She knew there must be hundreds of them because they usually didn't come out in the light unless there were too many of them. She sat on the table and couldn't help but shake. Her body was rebelling. Then a warmth started to flood her body. It started in her head and spread throughout her limbs. The pills were taking effect. She was no longer cold or shaking. She felt fine, almost peaceful.

He entered the room briskly. He was overweight, with curly, black, greasy hair. He didn't hide his face. He was wearing gray polyester pants, worn and stained, with a white button-down shirt. He rolled up his sleeves, revealing thick hairy arms. He wore black wire-rimmed glasses, and his feet were bursting out of the sides of his shoes. His breathing was heavy as he looked at Patti and asked, "How far along?"

"Four weeks," she croaked.

"Look, I have no time for the crying. I will be finished here in ten minutes. I am going to leave this room as soon as I am done. You may rest for a while on this table, retrieve your clothes, and dress in one of the recovery rooms. Stay in recovery as long as you like, but be out of here before dark."

Patti just stared at him. She couldn't believe this was happening. It was as if she were watching the scene as a spectator and not a participant. She was out of her body and could see him talking to her while she lay on the table. She watched him tie her legs to the table. He didn't even wash his hands. He selected two instruments, pushed all his weight onto her left leg as his right hand performed the procedure. Patti swallowed a scream so that only a little yelp escaped.

The sight of them made him furious. They all looked at him in the same way—like *he* was responsible for their condition, as if he was doing this to them. Their crying, sobbing, and fearful faces always accused him! It never ceased to amaze him how they played the role of the victim. They had an active hand in their fate, and he would not lose a wink of sleep over it. It had become a great business for him. On a busy day he could perform as many as twenty-five by himself. His prices varied with the client's ability to pay. Those with money paid more than those without. Never did he accept anything under five hundred dollars. On a good day he could clear as much as thirty-five thousand. Not bad for a day's work! As far as the mishaps went, well, he never really heard about them if there were any. The women were discreet. They had to be—they were committing a crime. He was in the perfect business. He didn't bother maintaining a regular practice anymore. The insurance, supplies, rent, salaries, and general overhead, coupled with managed care and set pricing, left him completely disenchanted with the medical profession. He worked less and made far more than any of his legitimate counterparts. Yes, his was the perfect arrangement.

"All done," he announced as he threw the instruments into the sink and abruptly left the room. It had taken under two minutes.

Patti passed out. She wasn't sure how long she laid on the table, but when she awoke, she knew she had to get going. She changed as quickly as she could and left without ever entering any of the recovery rooms. As soon as she was outside, she knew it was close to six. The sun was starting to drop in the sky. She hurried home, but the cramps were increasingly worse, forcing her to stop and catch her breath every couple of minutes.

She picked the boys up from her neighbor's and took them home. It felt good to hold them. She needed to rest, the pain was so bad. She decided to make a game of dinner. She called it "breakfast at night." The kids could pick their favorite cereal, and they would eat breakfast for dinner. The kids thought it was so much fun, and she could sit while they made their cereal. As soon as they finished, she put them to bed and mercifully laid down herself. She tried not to think about the day. She thought of her boys, she imagined their Saturday morning antics, she felt their bodies hugging her, their kisses on her face as she gently, softly, peacefully faded away.

Gina's phone rang, and it startled her. She was on her way back to the city, and her thoughts had her far away. Her heart beat furiously in her chest. What the hell was the matter with her today anyway? "Vincent here. What can I do for you?"

"It's Robert. Another possible termination. You need to get to Cabrini Medical Center and ask for Patti Darby's room."

"Why didn't they call me directly?" She didn't understand why Robert was calling her.

"They did. They got your voice mail, so they called me."

Gina looked at her phone and saw that she had indeed missed a call. She had never heard it ring. "I'll be there in forty minutes. Thanks, Robert."

"Have a good night. I'll see you in the morning." He hung up before she could say goodbye.

The sinking feeling returned. Not another one. She just hoped the woman would make it. Another death, so soon after Ashley, would certainly push Gina over the edge. She used the rest of the drive to pull herself together. She could not cry; she had to focus and put her game face on. If this was the same bastard, she needed to find him quickly. Racking up dead women was not on her agenda for the week. By the time she reached the hospital, there was no trace of Gina the granddaughter; it was just Agent Vincent, and she was ready to work.

"Hi, I am Agent Vincent, and I need Patti Darby's room," she announced to the receptionist, flashing her badge.

"That would be 312A in the intensive care unit. Use the elevators on the right just past the lobby."

"Thanks." Gina had known the woman would be in bad shape, yet she was still shocked to hear she was in intensive care. She started to worry she wouldn't be able to get the information she needed.

Patti Darby had tubes running from her body to every machine imaginable. Her heart, her brain, everything was being monitored. A nurse welcomed Gina.

"Hi, I am Agent Vincent, and I was called to investigate. Could you tell me what happened?'

"Hello, I am Rosemary Squire, the evening nurse. From what I understand, her neighbor watched her kids today. When she picked them up, she looked pretty pale and sick. She took the kids home at about 6:30 p.m. The neighbor didn't like the way she had looked, so at about 10:00 p.m. she went to check on her. She found her unconscious in her bed in a pool of blood. We have signs of a perforated uterus, which is consistent with a termination. We gave her eleven pints of blood, and she's comatose. We don't know if she will come out of it. It's too soon to tell."

"Did the neighbor have any idea how it happened?"

"No chance. She was definitely upset. She took the kids home with her but really couldn't give us any information. She didn't even know Patti was pregnant."

"Thanks so much, Ms. Squire. Take my card. If her situation changes or if she wakes, please call me directly. There is no need for an officer, as I do not see her as a flight risk. She cannot, however, be discharged by anyone other than myself. Where can I get the name of her neighbor?"

"It's all in the admitting report. I'll get you a copy."

Gina took the copy and left the hospital. This day was way too long, and she needed it to end. Her apartment and her bed were the only things on her mind as she left Patti Darby's room.

Chapter 9

"GOOD morning, Robert," Gina announced as she entered her office.

"Well, well, so thoughtful of you to visit your office," he jabbed as he raised his eyes above his magnifying glasses. Robert complained he could no longer see the computer screen, and he kept his magnifying glasses on most of the day. Gina would never tell him that she saw him peering over the top of them more often than she ever saw him looking through them.

"Robert, I have a good feeling today. I think it is going to be a good day. I slept through the night for a change, and I really feel great!"

"I am very glad to hear that since you will be meeting with Senator Rydell this morning at 10:30 a.m."

"What do you mean? I didn't schedule an appointment. How did this happen?" Her good mood vanished in an instant. Her normal feeling of dread returned immediately.

"Easy, Gina. Apparently the senator doesn't need to compare calendars. I tried to explain that we would need to check your schedule, but I think a Mr. Woodward—yes, Mr. Woodward—just said they would be here at 10:30 and that I should contact you to make the arrangements. Senator Rydell is leaving the city today, and he wanted to speak with you before he left."

"That's just freakin' great! I do need to speak with him, but you would think, under the circumstances, they would drop the whole 'high and mighty' approach."

No use fighting them today, Gina thought. *Might as well roll
with it.*

"Robert, do me a favor and order in some fresh juice, coffee,
and pastries. Arrange everything in the conference room, and buzz
me when they get here. I am going to try to get through my pile
of messages."

"Your wish, madam, is my command." Robert didn't even look
up from the screen as he spoke. He could be quite the comedian.

Gina was surprised at her irritation with the senator, especially
when he was on her list of contacts for the day anyway. She
reviewed her calls for the day and realized the schedule was actually
light. She would meet with the senator and have enough time to
interview Patti Darby's neighbor and meet her girlfriend Lisa for
lunch. She didn't dream of canceling Lisa's lunch date, considering
Lisa had made her swear two weeks ago that she would be there
no matter what. Lisa could be so dramatic. Nonetheless, Gina was
looking forward to seeing her. They had met in grammar school
and remained friends all these years. Lisa was her oldest and best
friend.

The morning went surprisingly well. She completed all of her
paperwork, finished the report on the Rydell case, and still had
some time left for web research. She always saved her web research
for last because it always took longer than she planned. The web
was an amazing repository of information, but Gina always drilled
too far down and went off on tangents, no matter how hard she
tried to stay on the issues at hand. She had just finished viewing a
report on the most common causes of death during termination
when Robert buzzed in. "Milady, the lord has arrived."

"Robert, I hope they can't hear you!"

"Not to worry, darling. They are already seated in the conference
room, enjoying your muffins!"

Gina grabbed her notes and strode confidently into the
conference room. There was no use in making them wait, and
truth be told, she just wanted to get it over with.

The senator's camp didn't want the case solved, so Gina really didn't have much to cover with them. She was unable to secure any leads from the body or from the crime scene itself. All of Ashley's friends were distraught and unaware of her situation. Only Indigo knew what had happened, and she had no details. Gina still had a nagging feeling about Richard Barton, Ashley's boyfriend. Besides the fact that he was self-centered, driven, and already on the political campaign trail, she still found his callousness difficult to accept. His girlfriend was dead, and he didn't show any sign of grief, just fear that his illustrious career might end before it had even started. Gina still had the 911 call but it hadn't turned up anything so far. Her real lead was Patti Darby, and she wasn't talking.

"Good morning, gentlemen."

"Agent Vincent, thanks for seeing us on such short notice," Jake Woodward said as he put out his hand.

Gina looked him in the eye and firmly shook his hand. "No problem. As a matter of fact, I was hoping to catch up with the senator today."

The senator seemed exhausted. There were dark circles under his eyes, and his face just seemed to sag. He was there, but only because Jake had brought him. The senator did not seem to be doing very well at all. For the first time, Gina truly felt sorry for him.

Jake continued, "Agent Vincent, we are returning home today. The funeral is set for Saturday, and we wanted to make sure there weren't any loose ends. We know you interviewed Ashley's friends and wanted to see if you were able to uncover any new information."

"As you know, Mr. Woodward, the autopsy was inconclusive as to the cause of the miscarriage. While I have my own theories about that, I was unable to find any information to the contrary. Ashley's friends were unaware of her situation, and that includes her boyfriend." Gina would not let them know about Indigo. The last thing Indigo needed was this group breathing down her neck.

Gina continued, "He does not deny, however, that he was the father. I am not sure I completely believe him, but there is no indication that he was with Ashley that day, and we know the 911 call was not his voice. This leaves me with the 911 call and who might have placed it. I am not optimistic it will give me what I am looking for. Combine this with your desire to have the case closed, and I imagine my report will be complete by next week."

Jake Woodward looked ecstatic. She could see a gleam in his eye as he tried to maintain his austere expression. "Please, Agent Vincent, don't misunderstand me. I just want to maintain some privacy for the Rydell family. The sooner we can move forward and put this behind us, the better it will be for everyone. Mrs. Rydell is having a terribly difficult time, and the media hasn't given her a break."

Senator Rydell looked up at the mention of his wife's name. Up until this time, he had not said a word. Gina wasn't even sure he was listening to their conversation. He looked confused as he stared at Gina. "I love my wife, and I miss my daughter. I do not know how or why this has happened. Please do not let my position dissuade you from your job. I know you expected different autopsy results, but please investigate the case. It is important to my wife." He paused and stared at the floor. "And it is important to me that I know who did this to Ashley."

Jake Woodward looked as if he were going to throw an embolism. "Senator, please let me handle this. Agent Vincent, I am sure you can appreciate what a difficult time the senator is going through. Of course we want you to investigate the case; we just want to maintain as much privacy and confidentiality as possible. If there is anything you uncover, or if there is anything we can do to help you gain additional information, please know that we will do it. We all want to know how this happened, and an expedient outcome would be beneficial to all who are involved."

Jake was very good on his feet, and Gina almost laughed out loud. She maintained her composure, mostly for the senator's sake. He was visibly distraught, and it was apparent that Jake didn't care one damn bit about anything but their political image.

"Please, gentlemen. I completely understand the sensitivity involved in this case. I plan to find out what happened, but I may be able to do that through a different venue. I do not want this to turn into a circus any more than you do. I harbor no political agenda or desire to ruffle anybody's feathers. For the sake of Ashley, and other women like her, I will find out what happened. If I find anything conclusive, I will be sure to contact you directly."

Jake breathed a sigh of relief and looked at Gina with a look of respect, glad that she would purposefully protect the family. The senator simply stood, shook Gina's hand, and left the room.

Gina stared at them as they walked away. A minute later, she slumped in a chair and poured a cup of coffee. The meeting had gone much better than she thought it would. Still, the whole situation was very unfortunate, and she found herself once again fighting back the grief that threatened to overwhelm her.

Usually she tried to maintain a detachment from the family, the victim, and the case itself. For some reason it was different this time; from the moment she arrived at the scene she had felt an attachment. She couldn't dwell on it—she needed to move forward. Jake Woodward believed she would protect their interests, and now she could investigate without any of them hawking her. As she poured cream into her coffee, she yelled, "Hey, Robert, come join me for a Danish!"

Patti Darby lived on the Lower East Side in a rent-controlled apartment. The buildings were directly across from the East River, with a full view of FDR Drive. Her neighbor Ginny Lui lived two apartments down the hall on the same floor. Gina checked the address one more time and hit the buzzer. A very even "Who is it?" came through the speaker. "Ms. Lui, my name is Agent Vincent, and I need to ask you a few questions about Patti Darby. May I come up for a minute?"

There was no response for at least ten seconds, and then she replied, "Yes, just give me a minute to get the kids settled." Less than a minute later, the door buzzed and Gina entered the building. The elevator reeked of a variety of odors from cooking, smoking, and who knew what else. She knocked on the door and heard children running and yelling. Ginny Lui was a petite woman of Japanese descent with jet-black hair and a slim figure. She spoke in an even tone and did not seem excited or nervous. She handled the children well and invited Gina into the kitchen to have a seat. "Agent Vincent, would you like some tea?"

"No, thank you, Ms. Lui. I just have a couple of questions. I know you must have your hands full with Ms. Darby's children in addition to your own."

"Please, call me Ginny. The children are not a problem at all. Her boys are great, and when they are together with my children, they behave even better. Besides, I only have the youngest home today. The others are in school and won't be home until three. I just hope she gets well; the boys will be devastated without her." Ginny's eyes were full. She tipped her head back slightly, focused on the ceiling, and continued to make the tea. Not one teardrop escaped her eyes. Gina had never seen such self-control. From what she had seen in under a minute, Ginny Lui appeared to be a very special person.

"Ms., uh, Ginny, I know it is in the report, but can you tell me in your own words what happened?"

"I am not really sure. I usually watch the boys in the evening after they get home from school. Patti works at Walmart during the day. They all meet at home, and then she brings me the kids. Once the boys are settled, she goes to the diner to work the dinner shift. That day she said she needed to go to the doctor. She asked if I would watch the boys after school and said that she would come and get them before dinner. She didn't seem upset or preoccupied or anything. When she came to get the boys, she did not look well at all. She was pale and looked like she had severe pains in her stomach. I asked her what was wrong, but she said she just needed to rest and everything would be fine. I really didn't like how she looked. She seemed very sick, but she insisted on taking the boys. About three hours later, before I went to bed, I thought I would check in on her just to make sure she was okay. I knocked, but she didn't answer the door. I didn't want to wake the boys, so I used my key. We each have a key to the other's apartment since we help one another out. When I went into her bedroom, I found her. I called 911 and tried to wake her up. I couldn't."

At this, Ginny once again looked at the ceiling and took slow, even breaths.

"Take your time, Ginny. Make sure you're not forgetting anything," Gina prodded.

A few moments later she continued, "Agent Vincent, those are the facts exactly as I remember them. What I am going to tell you now is my opinion, with no proof or fact behind it. You can take it for what it's worth. Patti's ex-husband is abusive. He comes around every so often and beats her. I know he has raped her, and she never calls the cops because he threatens to hurt her boys. If she was pregnant, he did it against her will. If she tried to terminate, it was because she is trying to survive."

Ginny's hand swept the small room, "Look at us. We just scrape by. If I didn't have her, or vice versa, we wouldn't make it at all. We live a paycheck away from homelessness. Our children are our lives, and we live in fear of losing them, or worse, not being able to feed them. I know you have a job to do, but Patti is a great woman. I pray she makes it, and if she does, I hope she will be allowed to keep her boys." Ginny finished her plea as she slowly stirred cream into her tea.

"Ginny, I want to find out who hurt Patti. I need to find the person and stop him from hurting others. My only interest in speaking with Patti is to find out who and where. I will ensure her cooperation allows her to stay with her boys."

Ginny, relieved by Gina's response, sat with her at the table.

"Ginny, did Patti's ex-husband know about her pregnancy?"

"No way! He didn't even speak to her when he showed up. He did his thing and left. I would know about the pregnancy before he did. He is a drunk, an addict, and a rapist."

"What's his name, and where can I find him?"

"Joe Darby. I don't know where you can find him. He scores his drugs at the park, drinks at Mulligans, and lives all over. He won't be able to help you find out who hurt Patti."

"Oh, I am not looking for his help. I'm going to have the police find him and see if we can bring him in on the rape or the beatings. Even if we can't hold him, we can scare him. Do you know where Patti may have gone to take care of the pregnancy?"

"I really don't know. I didn't even know she was pregnant. I thought she was just going to the clinic."

Gina closed her notebook and placed her card on the table.

"Ginny, you have been a big help. If you remember anything else or discover something I should know, please give me a call. Have you called the hospital today?"

"I did. There is no change. She is still unconscious." Ginny started her self-composure routine again.

"Are you okay taking care of the boys? Does Patti have any family?"

"Oh, no, I am her family. I have papers Patti drew up naming me the legal guardian if anything ever happened. The only person who could contest them would be Joe, and he doesn't care one bit about the boys." Ginny's words tumbled out of her mouth as she glanced at the baby, Sean.

"I didn't mean ... that is not why I was asking," Gina added quickly. "I just wanted to make sure you could handle all the children. I know how difficult it must be as a single parent."

"No, I'm fine. My relief is knowing I can take care of them and that they will not be put in the system," Ginny explained.

"I hope that Patti recovers soon. The social worker will be visiting and will probably want to look at those papers. In the meantime, call me if you need anything."

Gina stood and shook Ginny's hand. Gina wanted to tell her what a great person and friend she was. Gina wanted her to know that she was a rare breed indeed, but she couldn't. Agent Vincent was in professional form, and she would not let her emotions play a part in the day.

Her timing was perfect. She hit the street at 12:45 and would be right on time for lunch with Lisa.

Lisa Talbot was twenty-nine, blond, and beautiful. She was a highly successful pharmaceutical sales rep and made a small fortune. Every male doctor had time to see her, and every female doctor preferred a female rep to a male. Lisa was meticulous in her work. She knew her products well, had a thorough understanding of medicine, and was definitely a force in the pharmaceutical sales industry. Gina loved being with her. Everything in Lisa's world was matter-of-fact, with no gray areas, just black or white. She made decisions quickly, spoke her mind freely, and was confident in all she did. It was hard not to envy her strength and success.

As always, Lisa was at the table sipping a white wine spritzer as she pondered the menu while waiting for Gina to arrive.

"I thought you were going to call and cancel," she said as soon as Gina reached the table.

Gina kissed her on the cheek and feigned a hurt look. "Me? Why would I cancel? I told you I would be here."

Lisa laughed. "Sure, you only cancelled the last three times. Anyway, I am so glad to see you. Sit down. Are you hungry?'

"Starving! I know you don't believe me, but I have been looking forward to this lunch. I have missed you," Gina said, trying to look serious.

"Oh, please, spare me the dramatics. What are you having? I have a three o'clock, and we have a lot to talk about," Lisa replied.

"Chicken Caesar with an iced tea. And you?"

"I think I am going to have the spiedini appetizer and the whole wheat rotini filetto pomodoro."

Gina's jaw dropped. "What are you eating? I have never actually seen you eat anything but a few pieces of lettuce!"

"Please, stop it. Can't a girl eat a healthy, wholesome lunch?"

"Most girls—but you? You haven't eaten that much at one sitting in all the years I've known you."

"Well, then this will really send you—I plan to eat dessert as well! The zabaglione is to die for, and I am going to enjoy every last bit of it." Lisa answered as she disappeared behind her menu.

"That's it. Who are you, and what have you done with my friend Lisa Talbot?"

"Oh, Gina, it's me. That's why I needed to see you. I'm pregnant! Three months already. I haven't told a soul, and I just couldn't be alone with it anymore."

Gina was shocked. She didn't know what to say or do. Lisa wasn't married. Hell, she wasn't even dating! Gina couldn't form an intelligent sentence.

"*Well*, say something!"

"How did it happen?" Gina stammered.

"What do you mean? How it always happens," Lisa answered.

"No, what I mean is, who, when … who is the father?"

"See, that's the problem. The father is the regional director for Northeast operations at my company. We hit it off and have been carrying on a little love affair for the last six months."

"Lisa, that's great. Tell me about him. Do you love him? What does he look like?" Gina was excited for her friend.

"Not so fast. He's a great guy, and I do have strong feelings for him; however, so does his wife." Gina deflated in her chair.

"Gina, don't look so disappointed. I'm pregnant, and I am going to have a baby. I am very excited about it, considering I am not getting any younger. It's really good news. I just haven't been able to share it at work because of the circumstances. I broke off the relationship, not that it was hard after he realized my condition."

"What do you mean? He doesn't want a part in the baby's life?" Gina asked.

"Gina, really, you would think you lived under a rock. You, of all people. You see this every day. This baby is not his problem; it's mine, and I don't consider it a problem at all."

Gina went blank. She looked at her friend, but she couldn't find words appropriate to the situation. Her mind was racing, and it felt as if an hour passed as opposed to a painfully silent twenty seconds.

Finally she mustered, "That's great, Lisa, and I really am happy for you, especially if that's what you want. I just feel he needs to take responsibility too. I can help you obtain paternity. I can make him at least support the baby financially if not morally." Agent Vincent kicked in and was prepared to take the Northeast regional sales whatever-he-was directly to task.

"Easy there, tiger. I don't want his involvement. It would only make things more difficult. I would have to worry about his wife, last names, uncomfortable situations, and the possibility of problems at work. No, I don't want any part of him. I want to have my baby, give the baby my last name, and go back to work. I do very well for myself and will be able to share a very full life with this little bundle of joy," Lisa beamed as she patted her belly.

Gina was in awe. Her friend never ceased to amaze her. Lisa always saw the positive side of every situation. She had it all planned and was truly excited!

Gina completely relented. "Congratulations, Lisa! I am happy for you, really." Gina jumped up and gave her friend a hug. Everything would be fine. Gina knew Lisa was capable of anything. "You are going to make a *great* mom! When are you due?"

"Mid-November. I am hoping before Thanksgiving. It would be so nice to have the baby here for the holidays."

Gina and Lisa enjoyed having lunch and planning for the baby's arrival. Gina agreed to be Lisa's birthing coach and promised to try to attend at least one or two classes. They would see one another once a month so Gina could see Lisa's progress. Lisa still needed to fill her parents in, and Gina promised she would go with her to Boston to tell them in person. Gina figured she would *definitely* need moral support during that visit. By the time lunch was over, Gina was happy. She was even a little envious. She always thought she would be a mom, but she was always too busy establishing her career. At the very least, she would enjoy Lisa's pregnancy and her new baby.

They made plans for the trip to Boston, hugged, laughed, and left. It was 2:30, and Gina headed back to the office.

She realized she was *truly* thrilled for her friend.

Chapter 10

JENNIFER Annapolis stared at the purple line until her vision blurred. She was in the girls' locker room and had been staring at the white stick for what seemed like hours. She was sixteen years old, and the purple line had just told her she was pregnant. She wanted to die. There was no other way. As soon as her mind tried to think of what she would do next, she would arrive at the same conclusion: she wanted to die. There would not be a solution to this. She wouldn't be able to talk her way out of it, bat her eyes, or pout. There wasn't a person on earth who could fix her problem. She just had to die.

She had thought she might be pregnant for over a week, but she kept pushing the thought out of her mind. Her best friend kept telling her not to worry, that she could get it taken care of if she was pregnant. She even gave her the telephone number of a place she could go to get it fixed. The thought of calling the number made her ill. She could not do it. She just wanted to die. This was too much. She had ruined her life. What a stupid, stupid decision! Everything ruined in a minute! A stupid, stinkin' minute!

Adam was so cute and popular. Every girl in school dreamed of dating him, so when he asked Jennifer out, she thought he was kidding. At first, she was so self-conscious it was difficult to even have a conversation; she kept thinking she wasn't good enough to be with him. She finally became comfortable with him as he continued to date her. It seemed as if he genuinely cared about her, calling all the time and wanting to be with her constantly. Still, every day Jennifer thought how lucky *she* was to be dating Adam.

When he made his first advance, she let it go, just kind of brushed it off. He backed off immediately, and Jennifer figured he understood. Yet, after that, he kept trying every time they were together. He told her how much he wanted to be with her, how beautiful she was, how he couldn't keep his eyes and hands off her. He told her she was just driving him crazy. She *wanted* to believe him. He was *the* guy, the hottest boy in school, and she wanted to believe everything he said.

Finally, one night, she gave in. He whispered in her ear, "I love you, baby. It will be wonderful. You'll see. I need you. I promise I won't hurt you. I love you—I would never hurt you."

She squirmed as he pressed up against her. She felt dizzy and flushed, but he continued, "I won't make you pregnant. Don't worry, Jen. I'll take care of you. We are meant to be together."

She tried to pull away again, but he just pressed harder. "Jen, it will be perfect. Just relax. I would never do anything to hurt you."

She tried to relax, tried to feel what he was feeling. He seemed consumed with passion, but she felt nothing but fear—a heart-gripping, sick-to-your-stomach, room-spinning fear.

She didn't understand why he wanted to do it. It hurt her terribly! Oh, God, he was panting, sweating, and pushing on her, *in* her, so hard! Why would anyone want to do this? She didn't understand. Then, in a flash, it was over. She wasn't even sure what had happened. It was not wonderful. It was not beautiful. It was not passionate. It was ugly, sweaty, and painful.

She cried most of the night. She didn't even know why she was crying. She would never do it again. Never! Not with Adam, not with anyone.

Not that she had to worry about it. Once it was over, Adam lost interest in her almost immediately. It seemed that once he got what he wanted, he didn't want or need her anymore. He just moved on. Jennifer thought he might be trying to conquer every girl in the school. She would not have been surprised to see him keeping a scorecard. She was miserable. Her mother had talked to her about sex, told her all the details, how it should be with someone you love, at the right time, the right place. As always, her mother was right, and she had done everything wrong!

Why did she do it? Why did she let him? Part of her just didn't want to hear about sex anymore. She was sick of thinking about it, hearing about it, talking about it. Enough was enough! What was the big deal? Why was it on everyone's mind?

Now she had done it, and she had absolutely no idea what all the fuss was about. Truth be told, it was disgusting!

It was nearly four o'clock. She had to get home; her mother needed to know where she was at all times; she was a real worrywart. The thought made her cringe. For all her mother's fretting and fussing, here was her daughter, pregnant! In spite of the healthy, caring, loving home life her mother and father gave her, she was pregnant.

She arrived home and couldn't even remember getting there. She mumbled a greeting to her mother and went to her room. She closed the door and lay on her bed, wishing she could stay there forever—just shut the door and live in her pink room with hand-painted furniture and rose-covered quilt all her life. Her room was so pretty. She loved her fuzzy, white phone and Beanie Babies that stared at her from baskets on the floor.

If only she could turn back the clock to that moment and make a different decision. If she had just said no.

It didn't matter anymore. It was all over.

It wasn't a plan. It wasn't a fully formed thought. It didn't go through a thought process of any kind. She moved as if on autopilot. She simply went to her mother's bathroom and moved the cold medicines, aspirin, and Tums out of the way to retrieve the prescription bottle pushed way in the back. It was a full bottle. It took three swallows and two full glasses of water to wash them all down.

She curled up in her bed and pulled her blush-colored quilt tighter around her. She cuddled her favorite chenille teddy bear and simply went to sleep.

Chapter 11

WHY did the calls always come in the evening? They should have just called it second shift and made her workday start at four o'clock and go until midnight. They never called her to an emergency early in the day and, it seemed, never in the morning. Gina had to move quickly; the precinct that called in felt they had a lead for her and wanted her on-site right away.

She was getting that feeling again, the nagging little flutter in the pit of her stomach that was almost imperceptible but was consistent enough to break into her conscious mind. She had learned to pay attention to what most would call her intuition. Her heart would quicken, her senses would become alert, and her mind would methodically review every fact collected. It was like a puzzle, and every shred of evidence was a piece. Her job was to collect the pieces and fit them together. Sometimes the fit was in front of her all along, yet she couldn't see it. A break, a diversion, a new piece of information would allow her to see the pieces differently and uncover what had been there all along.

The call was in Staten Island, Todt Hill to be exact. The details were sketchy: sixteen-year-old female, suspected suicide, possible pregnancy. She knew this information wasn't enough to call her in, especially with such urgency. There would be more, and she would have to get there to find out.

It took her nearly an hour to get from the Gowanus over the Verrazano Bridge. During rush hour, she wished she could just take a helicopter. The truth was, she *could* have taken a helicopter but was deathly afraid of them. When she was nineteen, she had watched them pull a female traffic reporter from the East River. Despite attempts to resuscitate her—on camera, no less—she had died. Initial footage showed the woman, bare-chested, being worked on by the EMT. Gina was horrified for a variety of reasons. The woman was dying, and the media (her own kind) would air the footage of her body pulled from the river, shirt ripped open, and heart shocked for the whole world to see! This was not a nameless victim! Anybody who commuted to Manhattan listened to this woman's voice on a daily basis. She told you what roads to take, which to avoid, the quickest way in, the fastest exit out. The whole city felt as if they lost a friend—a person they never actually met, yet still a friend. Gina remembered the incident clearly, as if it had just happened yesterday. As a result, Gina would drive, traffic or no.

The address was located two-thirds up Todt Hill. The least expensive homes (not cheap by any means) were located at the bottom, and as you drove up the hill, the homes became larger and more expensive.

The home of Jean and Rich Annapolis was a fifty-year-old center hall colonial on a highly manicured stamp of property. You never had acreage in the city, but the houses on the hill did manage to carve out nice pieces of land to hold the majestic structures. The house was on a dead-end street, as many of the homes were. Todt Hill Road went up the hill, and dead-end streets branching off the main road held the homes. The scene was surreal; the coroner's van and police cruisers created an eerie contrast to the beautiful home on the quiet street beneath the mature pink cherry blossoms.

Gina parked at the end of the block, somewhat in the forest. She wondered if she was trying to hide her vehicle and not add to the already ugly scene. She saw the coroner first as he paced, speaking into his phone. She worked with Bennie often when he was assigned to Manhattan.

As soon as he recognized her, he ended the call. "Gina, you're here fast, during rush hour, no less."

"Bennie, it's been a while. How've you been?" Gina gave him a hug. They had worked together on a variety of cases in the past and were good friends.

"Pretty good. I'm enjoying being on the island; it's not as hectic as the city. I actually make it home by seven—most nights, anyway."

Bennie was relieved to see Gina on this case. He knew she had a heart and would be sensitive to the strain on the family. Suicides were never easy, and this one was tragic.

"What do we have?" she asked.

"Sixteen-year-old female, overdose sedatives. Her mother found her unresponsive in bed and called EMT, but it was too late. The parents are completely distraught. Not that I blame them, but you know how we see varying degrees of grief: these people are done! The mother is sedated, and the father appears to be in shock."

"Dispatch told me she was pregnant and that it was related." Gina was still wondering why they had called her.

"The officers found a positive EPT, but there are no other visible signs. I won't be able to confirm a pregnancy until I can examine her. I am sure they have more for you. They've been waiting patiently for you to arrive." Bennie was being mildly sarcastic; they both knew the cops were never patient.

"It's good seeing you, Bennie. I'd better get inside." Gina walked briskly to the front door, where one of the officers greeted her.

"Hi, I'm Agent Vincent. I was called by your precinct," she announced.

"Yes, we've been waiting for you. Please, right this way." Without introduction he cut her off and escorted her up the stairs to the girl's bedroom.

Gina had to fight the wave of emotion that threatened her composure. It was a little girl's room, fit for a princess. *Stay focused, Gina. Look for the clues. Collect the pieces.* Her mind was willing her to maintain a professional appearance. They had moved the girl's body, but the infamous chalk line brutally invaded the space of the room. Aside from that, it was the picture of innocence and childhood. The mix of mementos from Daddy's little girl to hip teenager told the story of her life. *How did this happen? This child grew up in a caring and loving home.* "What's going on? What do you have for me?" she asked.

"Agent Vincent, I am Detective Giannelli. The girl returned home at about 4:30 this afternoon and went to her bedroom. Her mother went up to get her at about 6:30 for dinner and found her unconscious. She called 911, but the girl was dead. We found the mother's empty bottle of Xanax and *this* in the bathroom." He held up the white EPT test stick with the now-faded purple lines in the window. "Her mother hasn't been able to help us much. The father claims they had no idea she was pregnant. She was dating a boy at school, but it was nothing serious as far as they could tell. We wouldn't have called you without the medical examiner confirming the pregnancy, except that we found this candy wrapper with the test stick in her belt pack. The candy wrapper has a note and number scribbled on it."

The officer handed Gina the note, which read, "Don't worry. Just call if it's positive. 917-483-3733."

Gina couldn't believe what she was reading. This was too easy. She decided to take it slowly and save her excitement for later.

"Well, what do you think it means?" she asked as she tried to read Giannelli's expression.

"At first I thought it might be the number for whoever fathered the child, especially if he was an adult. We were about to run it down when it hit me it could be a termination. With the recent Rydell case, we thought it best to call you. It could be something; it could be nothing. It's your call. Just tell us how you want to proceed."

Giannelli was genuine. He was a seasoned professional. He had no desire to crack the case or be the hero; all he wanted was a resolution, and he knew how to call in help.

"Detective Giannelli, I have to thank you. I am not sure if I were in your position that I would have had the same foresight. I agree there is the possibility that it could be the baby's father. It is more likely, however, that someone close to her, maybe the father, gave her the number to take care of her problem. I have to believe she would know how to contact the baby's father without having his number written down. We need to test the wrapper for prints and get a list of her friends. We'll start with the boyfriend and any close girlfriends. Do not call the number; just run it and see if we can get a name and address. If it is what we think it is, calling at this point would be a huge mistake."

Gina hated sounding so authoritative. No matter how hard she tried to project a calm, calculated attitude, she always felt she came off too assertive. She realized it was far more powerful to listen than to speak, yet putting that into practice did not come easily.

Detective Giannelli compiled the list of names for Gina. He asked if Gina wanted to rule out the girl's own father, Rich Annapolis. It was common to find incest as the cause of many underage pregnancies.

"At this point I would not take that path. Just ask for DNA samples from both parents so we can separate them from their daughter. That will easily clear the father, and we don't have to add to their stress. It would be inhumane to approach him at this point. Let's run down these other leads first."

Gina decided she would stay in Staten Island and interview the best friend, Christina Galindo. Detective Giannelli was going to see Adam Winter, Jennifer's boyfriend, and collect the necessary material for paternity testing. Gina was having much better luck with the best friends these days anyway.

Gina arrived at the Galindo home to find the girl surrounded by her parents and crying uncontrollably. Her parents stayed in the room the entire time Gina was there. Not that it mattered: Christina Galindo was not holding anything back. She told Gina everything.

"It was Adam! He used her. He forced her to have sex with him, and then he dumped her! I hate him!" she screamed as sobs racked her small frame.

Gina began slowly. "Christina, we found a telephone number in Jennifer's things—"

"I gave it to her! It's a place that would take care of the pregnancy. I know it's illegal, but a friend of a friend told me about it. She was only sixteen, and she was my best friend. She *couldn't* have a baby! I wanted to help her. That's all. I never thought she would kill herself. *Never!* I would never have left her. Not for a minute!"

"I know, Christina. I know you would have helped her. You did the right thing. You tried to help her," Gina offered, although her soothing voice sounded awkward and patronizing.

This girl was very confident and comfortable speaking in front of her parents. She was hiding nothing and wanted—no, *needed*—to tell Gina everything. Christina's parents, Doreen and Gerry Galindo, were worried about their daughter. The child was distraught, and Gina's presence seemed to make her even more excited.

Gerry motioned for Gina to join him in the kitchen.

"Agent Vincent, I know we need to help you find out what happened, but Christina has been through a lot today. If you could continue this at a later date, my wife and I would be truly grateful." He was sincere and had only his daughter's interest at heart.

"Mr. Galindo, I completely understand. Your daughter is a very strong girl. She has given me more information than I expected. Take my card. If she remembers anything else or if you need to speak with me, please do not hesitate to call." She shook his hand as she handed him her card.

Gina left the house bewildered. The case was completely running itself. She contacted Giannelli and told him where the telephone number had come from. This was the break Gina needed. She would take over from here. Giannelli would be in charge of the boyfriend and confirming his paternity. The telephone number was Gina's responsibility. She would call in her team immediately.

Gina dialed Robert's cell phone. "Sorry to bother you. It's me."

"Yes and of what service may I be, m'lady," Robert drawled.

"Look, I know it's late, but I need you to make a few calls for me. We need to pull the team together. I have to go in."

Robert dropped the nonchalant attitude and was all business. "Are you sure you need to go in? Why don't you wait until you meet with the team and explore your alternatives?"

"Robert, I have a lead that is critical to possibly all three cases. It just dropped in my lap, and I am not wasting any time! I want to meet with everyone at 7:00 a.m. I'm going in as soon as tomorrow morning."

"Done. I will see you in the morning," he announced as he hung up. Robert would make sure everyone was present in the morning. When he was in form, he was a powerhouse. A bureau field detective, surveillance unit, A/V guys, and two undercover field agents would undoubtedly be in the conference room by 6:30 a.m.

Gina was going undercover. As a rule, they usually avoided it whenever possible, but under the current circumstances, she had to do it. She was female, and she didn't need to be briefed. She wouldn't have to memorize lines of questioning like a female officer would. Gina knew what information she would need, and she knew how to get it. She just had to work on her appearance a little.

Before she went to sleep, she transformed herself from a brunette with pin-straight hair to a platinum blond with curls. She used a box of L'Oreal hair dye and an Orly home perm, the $75.00 extreme makeover. Her own mother wouldn't know it was her.

Chapter 12

GINA was up by 5:00 a.m. She didn't sleep a wink and figured she might as well get ready for work. She brewed a pot of coffee and poured herself a mug while rummaging through her closet for a suit to wear with her new blond hair. The team would meet this morning, and Gina needed to review her case notes.

She showered quickly and tried to finesse her new look but to no avail. She would definitely shock them with her appearance. She arrived at the office by six o'clock and sat in the conference room waiting. They would be there soon, and she was getting excited. So far, this was the first lead that looked like it could take them somewhere.

Robert showed up first, which was absolutely no surprise to Gina.

"Oh, my Lord! What have you done? You look like Madonna on the Blond Ambition Tour!"

"Robert, please. First of all, Madonna is old enough to be my grandmother! Second, the Blond Ambition Tour happened before I was born," she said as she stifled a laugh.

"Grandmother or not, that's who you look like. You will definitely not be recognized, my dear. Now please tell me why you couldn't just buy a wig," he asked.

"Robert, this is serious. I may have a lead directly to an abortionist. If I go undercover, it has to be genuine. I can't risk being made."

Immediately sobered by her response, he mumbled something about everyone being there shortly and went to make some coffee.

Gina felt bad for turning things so serious so quickly. Robert usually joked with her to ease the strain, and she had jumped on him for no reason. She found him at the sink and asked, "Who is assigned?"

"Winthrop is the assigned bureau detective. The field agents are Lister and Addison. They couldn't confirm for sure last night, but I think Curt Conroy may be the A/V," he answered.

"I hope it is Curt. A little weird but the best damn tech weenie I've ever met." she joked in an effort to make up for her terse response earlier.

"I don't think he would appreciate the 'tech weenie' title, but I definitely know what you mean," he said with a laugh.

By 6:45 the team was assembled in the conference room. John Winthrop, the team leader, Sally Lister, a loyal and tenacious field agent, Ben Addison, a "by the book" agent and Sally's partner along with Curt Conroy, the information technology and security genius were the members of Gina's team. She was pleased. Robert had managed to pull together the best team the bureau had to offer in less than twelve hours. She didn't know what she would do if she didn't have Robert.

John Winthrop spoke first. "What do we have, Gina?"

"I have a sixteen-year-old girl who committed suicide. The precinct contacted me because they found her with a positive pregnancy test and a note." Gina laid the note, wrapped in plastic, on the table for them to read.

Gina continued. "I believe the number could lead us to an abortionist. It may not lead us anywhere, as I cannot confirm the source. Her best friend, who refuses to tell me where she obtained the number, gave the paper to her. The girl says she got it from a friend she can't name."

Sally Lister jumped in, asking, "Did you confirm the child was pregnant? The EPT could have belonged to any one of her friends."

"The medical examiner promised to confirm today, but the best friend corroborated the pregnancy."

Ben Addison, ever the diplomat, asked, "Gina, I know you have more than this to call us in on such short notice. What's the story?"

"I have what I believe is one girl dead due to a termination, a second in a coma due to a termination, and finally a third, while not dead from a termination, has left behind a note that could lead me to the person responsible for the others."

"Whoa, Gina. That's a leap, even for you," Winthrop said. "Let's just slow down a minute and review the facts. No conjecture, please."

"I know Ashley Rydell died from a termination. I don't care what the autopsy said, she bled out. Period. My second case, Patti Darby, is in a coma in Cabrini Medical Center due to a perforated uterus that caused her to lose eleven pints of blood. You're right; they could be totally unrelated. I could have any number of abortionists running around this city. But I have a telephone number that could lead me to a murderer. Related or not, it is important to this office."

"I agree this is an important lead. I also agree we have to be careful, especially with the media attention we are getting due to the Rydell case. However, we cannot jump to conclusions," Winthrop replied.

"You're right, John. I simply want to go in, and I need a team to do it. All I have to do is call the number and pretend I am a pregnant woman in need of help. If it pans out, then we are ready to move. If not, no harm done. I just want to move quickly. Today if possible."

Ben nearly jumped out of his seat. "Today? Gina, you're a high-profile player in this office, and you want to go undercover, risk being found out, on nothing but a gum wrapper? Come on, you just finished a press conference the other day!" "Have you looked at me today? With the right clothes and makeup, nobody will know it's me."

"Fine, let's assume we go with you on this. You are no longer field personnel. You have to follow specific guidelines in order to gain a conviction. Do you even remember the entrapment law code?" Winthrop asked.

"I can create a favorable opportunity for a person to commit a crime they are willing to commit, but I cannot *persuade* or *induce* a person to commit a crime," Gina answered.

"Good for you. But can you remember that when your heart is pounding in your ears? When you hope your perspiration doesn't drip down your face? Gina, going undercover is serious business, and you haven't done it for quite some time now," Winthrop cautioned.

"I need to see with my own eyes and run this down personally. I feel strongly about this, John. I am the only one with all the facts. I know what to look for. You guys are the best, and you will be with me all the way. Please, can we just work it my way this one time?" Gina pleaded.

"What do you have in mind?" John asked.

"My name would be Gina Janssen. This way, we don't have to worry that I may not respond to my name under pressure. See, I'm being cautious," she joked.

Robert rolled his eyes as Gina continued. "I'll need a few audio/video feeds, and we'll need a surveillance van. We set up the trace phones, and I call the number. If it is an abortion source, then I try to secure the earliest appointment possible. After that, we simply move in."

"I can have the van, phones, and feeds set by eleven o'clock," Curt said.

"Now that's what I'm talking about! Thank you Curt."

Ben quickly added, "Sally and I will work the perimeter, and John can call the shots from the van."

"Well, I guess the team has decided. Gina, you'd better listen to everything I tell you from this point forward," John warned. John Winthrop was not a man to play with, and Gina knew it.

"I promise. Starting now, this show is yours," she said. True to form, Curt had the audio and video surveillance devices ready by 10:00 a.m. Gina would make the call from the A/V van. Curt had at least fifty telephone numbers reserved for their private use and could broadcast whatever caller ID they needed. John was notorious for being thorough. He ran over the details with the team for what seemed to be the hundredth time.

The plan was simple. Gina would call the number and try to arrange for an immediate procedure. She would be distraught and adamant about wanting her procedure done right away. She would offer twenty-five hundred dollars for the service, and the cash was already in a purse prepared for her by Curt. There would be a camera on the clasp of the purse. She would also have a small camera and audio feed located in a pair of diamond stud earrings. In the event they made her remove her jewelry, she would have to use the audio feed located in the fake nails Curt put on her.

Gina would be wearing ten beautiful pink nails with a microscopic camera in the nail of each index finger. Once they had enough information, Ben and Sally, in close proximity to Gina, would take the building on Winthrop's command. Until Gina could get the address, they would not know if they could pull it off.

By 10:30 a.m. everything was in place. Gina was nervous but anxious to get started. The team was in the van together so they could all hear the call.

She took a deep breath and dialed.

A male voice answered. "Yeah."

"Uh, hello. I need some help. Badly," Gina stammered.

"What kind of help?" the male responded nonchalantly.

"I … um … I think … no … no … I know … I'm pregnant," Gina continued

"How much help do you need?"

Gina was unsure how to continue but said, "Please, mister, I need help. I need help right away, today! I can pay! Please, I can pay." Gina pleaded as she started to cry.

That did it.

"How much can you pay?" he asked, entirely too interested.

"I have two thousand," she whispered.

"Twenty-five hundred," he countered.

After a brief hesitation she said, "I don't know—"

He cut her off before she could finish.

"Look, lady, I'm busy. Twenty-five hundred."

"Okay, okay. I need it done right away. Please," she begged.

"Is now too soon for you?" he asked in a taunting tone.

"Where do I go?" she asked.

"You have to meet me in Brooklyn."

Gina's heart jumped. This was good. No, this was great! Ashley Rydell was found in Brooklyn. Her spirits soared. This could be the link!

"Yes, I can meet you in Brooklyn."

He gave her a different address than the location where Ashley was found, but that didn't dampen her enthusiasm in the least. She didn't expect him to continue to use the same house, but his using the same general neighborhood was very promising. The abandoned buildings would allow the surveillance units to operate without issue. He was going to meet her at 2:00 p.m. Everyone would be in place by noon.

The man hung up and smiled. He was taking this one for himself. Just like the other high-paying chicky, this one would be for him. He would have to call in the idiot to help him, but it didn't matter. Two hundred fifty to the idiot, and he would be thrilled. Too bad the other chicky had died. He would have to try to keep this one alive. He didn't really want another death on his conscience. He just wanted the cash. Why should the good doctor make all the money? He had been bringing women to the doctor for nearly three years. For what? He would get nothing but a pittance. He knew the cash the good doctor was bringing in. No, he was going to get paid for his effort. Five thousand from the last one, twenty-five hundred today—this was starting to work out very, very well. It wasn't even that hard. He had watched the doctor a thousand times. Less than five minutes worth of work, and they never screamed. They were so scared, they would either whimper or bite their cheeks until they bled. He didn't know why the last one had died. He had called 911—damn city, probably took too long to dispatch the ambulance. He would try to be careful today. He dialed the idiot and then started the car. As the blue Buick pulled away from the curb, the driver grinned ear to ear.

Gina was trying hard to hide her excitement. They could wrap the whole thing up before dinner. She had to fight her optimism, another shortcoming she was working on. Her optimism could cloud her vision of the case. As far as she was concerned, this case was practically in the bag. Gina was elated, but she knew from experience to hide her enthusiasm from the rest of them.

The address given to Gina was a white, single-level warehouse located on a corner not two blocks away from the brownstone where Ashley's body had been found. This location was better for the team because they could put cops in buildings across the street on two sides. Winthrop was taking care of all the details; Gina didn't have a say. He decided the number of cops and where the agents would be located, and *everyone* would be listening to him.

John Winthrop was in his mid-fifties and had been with the FBI since he was twenty-five. He had accepted a job with the FBLI because, similar to Gina, it represented a promotion. He welcomed the opportunity to stop abortionists. He never got involved with pressing charges against the female "mothers" because that job usually went to the local police or to Gina. He took care of the larger operations: the manhunts. Today he would keep Gina alive. If he was lucky, he would also arrest an abortionist and save countless other lives. He planned to have a good day.

Gina would be driving a tan Nissan Altima that Winthrop selected from the yard because it was nondescript and appropriate to Gina's age. He wanted her to be able to drive through the neighborhood without drawing attention. She would go to a café on Third Avenue in the seventies and wait until 1:45. The others would be in place at the address.

At 1:55 a blue Buick arrived at the warehouse and parked on the side street behind a dumpster.

Winthrop radioed Gina. "It's time. Proceed to the site. Gina, drive slow and don't worry about being nervous; they will expect you to be flustered when you arrive. Remember, we hear anything we don't like, we're coming in."

Gina's hands were shaking as she pressed the button to respond, "I hear you. I'm on my way." Gina envied his calm, cool approach to the situation, especially because she felt like a wreck.

Two men got out of the Buick. Both were dark—Italian, Spanish, or possibly Middle Eastern, but they couldn't tell for certain. The driver was taller, maybe six feet, with black, curly hair, dark sunglasses, jeans, a black T-shirt, and a denim jacket. The passenger was about 5'10" and nearly bald, with black-rimmed eyeglasses. He wore tan khaki pants with a plaid button-down shirt. He didn't appear to be as confident as the driver. He followed the driver into the building.

At 2:02 p.m., Gina arrived. She parked the car in front of the building on the main street, checked the address, and got out of the car. As she approached the door, she could hear the thumping of her heart in her ears. Once she stepped inside, she fought to overcome a wave of nausea. It was a filthy, abandoned warehouse that reeked of mildew. She could see the rattraps set in the corners and the roaches scurrying up the wall. There was an office in the rear to the right. Gina assumed this was where she needed to go. She proceeded to the door and knocked.

The man who was the driver opened the door and asked her to have a seat. It was a small office, maybe ten by twelve feet. There were two file cabinets, a bookcase, and a large metal desk. There were two chairs for visitors and one chair behind the desk.

"Do you have the money?" he asked

Gina stammered, "Uh, yes."

"Let me have it," he demanded.

"Sure, mister. Here it is. Look, can you just tell me how this will work? I've never done this before. Please—" she rattled on as he cut her off.

"Look, give me the money, and then we will proceed. My assistant is preparing the instruments. I will do the procedure in this room. You will lie on the desk. There is a small bathroom through that door." He motioned to a small wooden door behind the desk in the left corner of the room.

"Once my assistant is done, you can go in there and strip from the waist down. The procedure will only take a few minutes. We will leave before you do. You can stay and rest as long as you like. You will need to take Tylenol for the next few days. Bleeding should be light but is to be expected," he explained.

The bald man came out of the bathroom with a sheet, some silver surgical instruments, latex gloves, and a black plastic garbage bag. Gina knew she couldn't go to the bathroom just yet. They had not actually said what the procedure was. She knew she was getting good video, especially of the items the bald one had brought out from the bathroom.

Gina feigned her most timid persona and pleaded, "Mister, I think I am about eight weeks along. I realized I missed a period after about six weeks, so I am guessing it is about eight. Will it hurt?"

The driver, clearly agitated by her statement, replied, "I already told you what the plan is and how long it will take. Take the Tylenol for pain, and you will be fine!"

Gina pressed further, "Are you sure you will be successful? I mean … uh … there isn't any chance I will still be pregnant when you are done, is there?"

The driver went ballistic. "You will be terminated in as little as ten minutes as long as you shut up, go in the bathroom, and change!"

She had it. Perfect! She would go in the bathroom, and they would be in there before she had time to close the door. Gina was thrilled!

As soon as Winthrop heard the words "you will be terminated," he gave the command. They stormed the building before the two men knew what happened. They did not remove Gina from the bathroom until the suspects were on their way to the precinct.

They would keep Gina's name out of the papers, and the men would not know whether she had been involved—until the trial. Winthrop was pleased: everything went off without a hitch. Today was definitely a good day.

Chapter 13

SOPHIA was up early. Everything had to be perfect. The fundraiser would allow the group to meet privately to discuss their plan. They had reached a critical juncture, their momentum growing, and Sophia knew today would represent their single most critical session.

The auction portion of the fundraiser would take place on the patio. It was a huge flagstone patio with marble balusters and planters attached to the rear of the house, raised three steps above the pool and gardens. The tent, which already had been erected, would provide ample room for the one hundred guests. They would serve the food buffet style, but she wanted at least three food stations. She hated it when people were lined up to get food. She had discovered that if she had food stations placed in various locations, everyone would get their food quickly and without the dreaded lines forming. There would be a full food station on the patio, one in the kitchen, and another in the two-story entranceway, which was more like a ballroom than an entrance hall. They would serve the hors d'oeuvres on silver platters. Sophia wanted each platter mixed and servers assigned to areas of the house. This was just another common problem of catering that Sophia had solved. If they put all the filet mignon over toast points on one platter, then the guests would have to have access to that one server to have some filet mignon. If each server had a mixed platter, then the server could stay in a smaller area and each guest would have access to a variety of appetizers at once, thus eliminating the hunt for the server. She hosted excellent parties, anticipating the needs of every guest. As a result, her events received a huge turnout and were the talk of the town.

Speaking of her town, it was Republican—*completely* Republican. In local elections, the Republican candidate had *no* opposing candidate. It had been this way for at least a hundred years, and there was no sign it was going to change. Still, Sophia, a registered Republican, refused to vote for the local candidate. She considered it an insult to have to pull the lever for a person who had absolutely no opposition. It was just ridiculous. Sophia knew how to pick her battles, and fighting for an opposing candidate in her small town was a waste of her time. Today she would make a difference. The tide was turning in their favor, and today was critical.

Sophia was very excited. In addition to the fundraiser and meeting, she planned to introduce Gina to Dr. Nick DePaolo. Sophia really thought they would be perfect for each other, and she was looking forward to showing off her granddaughter to her friends. She knew Gina had uncovered the alleged abortion operation that was plastered all over the news in recent days, and Sophia was hoping she would be able to relax. Sophia was worried about Gina; she had been so distraught the last time she visited. She was really hoping Gina and the doctor would hit it off. There was nothing like a good romance to distract one from the stress of a job.

Gina certainly had a stressful week following the arrests. The press hinted that the abortionists could have been responsible for Ashley Rydell's death despite the lack of information officially linking the two incidents. The backlash toward the media was swift and strong. Public support for the Rydell family was so overwhelming that even the press decided not to fight it. The constituents did not care how Ashley had died; they just cared that she had died and a well-respected family was torn to pieces. Sophia knew that Ashley Rydell's death would forever be classified as an accident. There was nothing to solve, and even if there were,

Jake Woodward would ensure it never saw the light of day. Gina, of course, still didn't accept this. Sophia felt bad for her in a way. Gina was an altruist in every sense of the word. She believed in truth and justice and that ultimately both would prevail. Sophia had lived on this earth long enough to know that justice wasn't served very frequently, and truth would have to be pursued—vehemently. It wasn't that Sophia didn't believe there was good in humanity; she just wasn't naïve enough to overlook the overwhelming propensity for evil.

The staff began to arrive to take over the house and grounds. Sophia knew this was her cue to leave and begin to dress. This was the hardest part of the day for her. Her inclination was to stay and help everyone prepare, but the servants would shoo her out of the way. They knew how to do their jobs, and Sophia would just have to learn to accept it. As the linens and flowers were being unloaded, she went to her bedroom.

She loved her bedroom. She had designed and decorated the room herself, and it addressed their every need. One corner held an overstuffed chair with an ottoman for Sean to watch television. He never watched TV in bed because he claimed he would just fall asleep. Sophia never bothered to tell him he slept in the chair just as easily. There was a writing corner completely stocked with elaborately covered journals and writing instruments. She would make notes to herself, write to her children, plan events, and manage her lists. Her writing corner was her favorite place, offering her solitude and a break from the commitments of her life. She could organize her thoughts, meditate, reflect, and plan. Because she was worried by her propensity to forget, her journal writing and note taking had become more copious in recent years.

The furniture was massive in size, French Provincial in design, and off-white in finish, with brown marble surfaces and carved edges rubbed in silver and gold. The draperies, bedding, and linens were a rich taupe with blush and cream accents in satin and silk. The room, decorated in light colors, had four huge palladium windows covered with thick satin curtains that heavily filtered the light, lending a darker, more private feeling to the room.

Sophia needed to think carefully and plan her speech. She made a list of the items she needed to discuss with the group and the order in which she would present them. Success was in sight; they were getting very close to their objective, and Sophia wanted to step up the pace.

It had all started out innocently enough. After one of her parties, a few of her closest friends stayed late. They were drinking, laughing, and talking, just generally enjoying the end of the party and the intimate size of the group. The discussion became very open—whether it was the friendship or the alcohol or a little of both, one could not be sure. They each lamented the outcome of the *Roe v. Wade* overturn. The same politicians who had fought most of their lives to have the decision overturned were admitting to their unhappiness with the outcome.

Everyone in public life knew the strain the decision was placing on the government, law enforcement, social services, and ultimately the well-being of women and children. Homelessness, poverty, crime, and the numbers of female convicts all skyrocketed. There was also strong evidence indicating the decision had not eliminated abortion at all. It simply stressed the system and caused as many deaths—only now it was the deaths of the mothers as well as the fetuses. By the end of the evening, they all felt better after voicing their darkest feelings. They carried a burden they could not share. They had played a major role in creating the current system, and it was very difficult to be human and admit to having changed their minds.

Sophia was quick to berate them. Never accepting the overturn, Sophia was initially furious with the decision. She figured repeal was in order. Never did she think it would last! Just like prohibition, she expected the public would force the issue. After *fifteen* years, though, abortion was still illegal, and the situation continued to get worse. As far as she was concerned, it was a fight that never had focused on the root of the issue. Education, affordable day care, student mother programs, housing, and birth control should have been overhauled and addressed with all the resources they had poured into the overturn of *Roe v. Wade*.

Finally, Sophia pushed them into action. While she never had supported the overturn of *Roe v. Wade*, these people were her friends, and she would not get into political arguments with them. She saw an opportunity on this one night to spur them into action. "You managed to overturn *Roe v. Wade* with *Mather v. Tutola*. Why don't you simply work to overturn *Mather v. Tutola*? You did it once—why not do it again?" She smiled as she remembered her words and the shocked looks on their faces. She could still see them looking at her as if she were crazy. "Our constituents ... the votes ... we have an obligation ... ." They went on and on. She acted as if she didn't even hear them.

"You each helped to create this situation, and now you see it may not have yielded you the intended outcome. We each make choices and decisions that give us a result. If we do not like the result, we must change the situation." She continued to persuade each of them. By the end of the night they agreed: secretly, they would capitalize on situations and begin to build a case. They were mostly conservative or considered "hard right" by their public, so it would not be obvious that they were working covertly on a plan to overturn *Mather v. Tutola*. They were in a strong position, with an inside track on the conservative Republican agenda.

Sophia was elated! She would be working on something that truly mattered. It was important to leave a mark on the world, and Sophia saw this as her chance to make a difference. It was not that she wanted women to have abortions—she just didn't think that making it illegal stopped them. In fact, she knew it did not.

Over the years, she had helped so many girls. She would help them do what they needed to do in their heart. She would give them money and arrange for housing, medical care, adoption, you name it. There were times that these women could not, would not go through with their pregnancies. Sophia helped them arrange a safe termination. She might burn in the depths of hell for her actions, but she would rather see these girls alive than dead.

The way Sophia saw it was she didn't think she would see Jesus picketing an abortion clinic if he walked the earth *she* lived in. Never judge a person—just try to help. That was the message he sent, and it was one that Sophia lived by. Sophia helped as many women as she could, but ultimately they had to make their own decisions.

Over the period of a year, their secret little group had grown. It seemed that many were unhappy with the outcome of the overturn. Each member harbored a secret reason for wanting to participate, whether it was the death of a loved one due to an unsafe abortion, an accidental pregnancy they had caused, or the inability to provide justice. The women offenders were persecuted easily enough, but not the men. Whatever the reason, they believed there needed to be a choice, a better way, and so they organized and planned. Publicly they would focus on the open political agenda; privately they would posture and position for the cause.

Today would be a huge day for them. Associate Justice Thomas Chesterfield had died, and the country would need a new nominee to the Supreme Court. The president would make his nomination, and the Senate Judiciary Committee would have to approve it. The group strongly believed they could have a hand in choosing the nominee. The president would try to recommend a candidate he knew would have a chance of being approved by the Senate, and therefore he was likely to solicit input before a formal nomination was made. This was where the team would come in: they would work the Senate Judiciary Committee, ensuring they had overwhelming support for their candidate. They would not select a candidate based upon his or her pro-life beliefs, but rather on their work history and qualifications. They had four candidates and would need to select one tonight. A new justice could bring them a five-to-four majority: just what they needed.

Sophia would wear her cream silk pantsuit with ivory tank and a single strand of pearls. She put gel in her hair and pulled it back into a tight bun and secured it at the nape of her neck. Her hair was curly, but she preferred a more sophisticated look for this event. Her skin was tan, which caused more wrinkles than she cared to count, but she lived her life repeating the mantra "life is always better with a tan."

As Sophia descended the stairs, she was pleased with the accoutrements of the affair. Huge Grecian urns filled with fresh flowers were arranged throughout the house and rear deck. Gas lamps glowing amber framed the patio around the tent, lending an ethereal atmosphere. The faint springtime aroma of peonies and wisteria filled the air, while piano music played softly in the background. Sean arrived home from the club later than he had planned, but he was already dressed in his evening attire. At sixty-nine years of age, Sophia's husband was still extremely handsome, with light green eyes, a golfer's tan, and dimples that stole people's hearts each time he smiled.

Kissing Sophia on the cheek, he said, "Place looks great. Is everything ready?"

"Yes, honey, everything is ready. How was your game?"

"Good, as always. Do you need to me to do anything before everyone arrives?"

"No, Sean, everything is ready. I will need you later on. Once the auction begins, I want you to ask the team to join me in the library. I expect auctioneering will take at least forty-five minutes, and they will not be missed," she said as she twisted the pearls around her neck.

"I can do that. Who's coming—Dave, Al, Gerard, Domenic, Anita, Rita, and Nicole?" he asked.

"Don't forget Jane. She will be key this evening," Sophia replied.

The "team" consisted of three senators, all of whom were on the Senate Judiciary Committee, one U.S. Supreme Court justice, three state supreme court justices, and the mayor of New York,

Nicole Huerta. Judge Al Benazir (New York Supreme Court), Judge David Chabin (Florida Supreme Court), and Judge Rita Conover (Rhode Island Supreme Court) were possible candidates to replace Associate Justice Thomas Chesterfield. Patrick Graham (California Supreme Court) was also a candidate. He was not on the team, but he was openly pro-choice and would be an excellent selection. Senator Gerard Schuman (Pennsylvania), Senator Domenic Dispenza (New York), and Senator Anita Hyde (New Jersey) were the Judiciary Committee members who were critical in ensuring the selection of the proposed candidate.

Jane Letterer was the U.S. Supreme Court justice and a key member to the team and their strategy. She represented one of the four justices who had voted to uphold *Roe v. Wade*. She was well aware of the personalities that sat on the U.S. Supreme Court and would be instrumental in selecting a candidate who would "work well" with the others. Jane was easygoing yet concise and exacting in her opinions. She would arrive with her selection in mind, and Sophia didn't doubt for a moment that the group would be in alignment within minutes.

Nicole Huerta, the dynamic force on the team, was not only female but Hispanic as well. She was the first female Hispanic mayor in the history of New York and was completely dedicated to its welfare. The problem of illegal abortions and underground termination rings had reached epidemic proportions in the city. She could not ignore the reality of the situation, and she knew the pace of the political machine She just did not have the time. The team represented a chance to help her cut through the red tape. The posturing, politicking, promises, and tradeoffs would be for other issues—not this one. She needed help, and she needed it quickly. Funding for housing, daycare, medical benefits, birth control, and family planning would come from the exorbitant costs used to investigate, capture, and house female offenders under the current law.

Nearly one hundred socialites were attending the event, creating an electric atmosphere. The auction included paintings and sculptures from some of the most promising young artists. It was a great idea: the artists would donate their work in order to gain exposure, and the money would directly benefit the charity event. Tonight there were twenty-five paintings along with three sculptures, which had a starting bid of fifty thousand dollars each. The event would raise nearly two-and-a-half million dollars before the night's end, and undoubtedly one new artist would rise to notoriety, especially if a bidding war took place. The beneficiary of the event was the Juvenile Diabetes Research Foundation, which continually strived for a cure for the disease. Near the turn of the century, it had been believed that a cure was close at hand. The ability to implant healthy eyelet cells into a diabetic pancreas had eliminated the need for insulin in many patients. The problem was supply: there just weren't enough healthy cells available to cure the number of diabetics. Stem cell research could have allowed the possible growth of eyelet cells, but government funding for this research had been eliminated due to political and religious pressures in 2002. Certain groups felt stem cell research could result in human cloning and was unethical. It was now nearly twenty years later, and a cure still eluded the top researchers in the world. Private fundraising could help overcome the lack of government funding, and that was Sophia's main objective.

Sophia and Sean welcomed their guests and circulated throughout the party. Sophia spotted Gina and quickly scanned the room for Dr. DePaolo. She saw him by the ice sculpture and glided over to him. "Dr. DePaolo, how are you enjoying the evening?" Sophia cooed.

"Sophia, we've been through this a hundred times: call me Nick. I'm too young to be 'Dr. DePaolo'!" he said with a smile as he kissed her cheek.

"I have been dying for you to meet my granddaughter. She just arrived; would you do me the pleasure?" she asked, slightly batting her eyes.

"It would be an honor to meet her, Sophia. You wouldn't be playing matchmaker, would you?" he asked with a mischievous gleam in his eyes.

"Why, Nick, of course … I … well … oh, hell, maybe a little," she said, laughing. "Just humor me. I think you two would at least be great friends."

"Lead on, Sophia," he said as he looped his arm through hers.

Sophia gently urged him through clusters of guests and brought him directly to Gina, who was standing inconspicuously by the bar in the corner of the tent.

"Gina, I was worried you may have forgotten. When did you arrive, dear?" she asked as she gave her a hug.

"Grandma, I would never forget one of your affairs. I've only been here a few minutes; the traffic was heavy out of the city."

"Well, your timing is wonderful! I was just speaking with my good friend Dr. DePaolo, and I wanted to introduce you. Nick, this is my granddaughter, Gina. She works for the FBLI and was responsible for the recent arrests in Brooklyn," Sophia said in a very proud, grandmotherly bragging sort of way.

"It is excellent to meet you, Gina. Congratulations! I heard the arrests were critical to recent investigations," Nick said as he locked his eyes on hers.

"I am very pleased to meet you, but my role in the recent arrests was truly minor. Mine is a life of paperwork and interviews, but I thank you for the compliment anyway," she answered.

Gina liked Nick immediately. She wasn't sure if it was the way he looked directly at her, his self-assured manner, or the twinkle in his eyes, but he gave the impression of young boy who had played a prank and only he knew when the mischievous event would play out. Sophia noticed the attraction and disappeared in a flash. Neither Gina nor Nick noticed. They became heavily involved in conversation, and it was quickly evident that they weren't interested in anyone or anything else.

"So, how long have you known my grandmother?" Gina asked.

"I have been friends with Sophia for some time now. Your grandmother is a very special woman. We met at an event for unwed mothers. I sometimes offer free prenatal care, and Sophia offers time, money, and moral support. She really cares about people, and I think she is a very special person." Nick clearly liked and respected Sophia.

"I agree. She is wonderful, although I must admit we don't always see eye to eye."

"Why is that? She seems so open-minded," he asked.

"That's exactly the problem. I think she is too open-minded. I work for the FBLI. It is my job to uphold the law and to preserve life. Sophia feels strongly that abortion should be legal; I do not agree, and I have committed my life, my career to that vein." Gina spilled these words out a little too fast and with a definite edge in her voice.

"Easy there, Gina. I completely understand your frustration, but I must say I can also see Sophia's point. I am an obstetrician, as I am sure your grandmother has told you. There is nothing more precious than bringing a life into this world, but I can also tell you that there are times I wish I could abort a pregnancy. Severe drug use, deformities, danger to the mother's health, rape, incest, and a variety of other reasons to terminate in the first eight to twelve weeks are causes I would support," he explained.

His response didn't incite her to argue as her grandmother's comments often did. Instead, she listened with interest to a man who delivered babies for a living, a man who witnessed the miracle of birth on a daily basis yet supported legalization. She wasn't sure if she liked him too much or if his words truly had merit. In either case she didn't care: Dr. Nick DePaolo was definitely fascinating.

As the buffet wound down, the guests began to take their seats in the tent where the auction was about to start. Gina and Nick were in the gardens and returned to the tent at the announcement of the auction. It became crowded quickly on the patio as the guests streamed in from the house, the gardens, and the foyer. The auctioneer began, and his voice carried in the thick night air. The first painting, *Innocence Lost* by Leonora Duvan, depicted a young child crying in a hallway, clutching a blanket as war was evident outside a window. It was a very moving piece and reached two hundred thousand very quickly. Nick excused himself from the auction as Gina settled into a chair to view the bidding action.

As the masses moved into the tent, a string of stragglers discreetly worked their way through the crowded patio and into the house, ostensibly to visit the bar, the bathroom—any reason they could think of to excuse themselves. Silently they entered the library and milled about until their host arrived.

Sophia walked swiftly through the living room entrance to the library and closed the double doors behind her. The library was dark mahogany with custom-built units housing books from the floor to the twelve-foot ceilings. Despite the size of the room, it seemed cozy and quiet, with a variety of seating options.

"Welcome. I am very glad to see you could all make it tonight," Sophia began. "We need to get started right away, as we have only about thirty minutes before we will be missed. We need to decide our nominee to replace Chesterfield. Pushing our candidate to the forefront of the president's agenda is paramount to our position. We will review our candidates and speak openly about their strengths and weaknesses. Associate Justice Letterer will share her opinion, and we will leave this meeting with our selection. Regardless of whom we select, we must keep our objective clear and refrain from personal initiatives. Agreed?" Sophia looked at each of them intently.

They each agreed, and Sophia continued,."Our candidates are Al, Dave, Rita, and Patrick. Patrick is not part of this team, but his objectives align with ours. This puts you in competition with each other for selection. How do you feel about that?" Sophia asked them directly.

Rita Conover, a brilliant woman of fifty-two with dark blond hair and strong Slavic features, responded first. "I do not want to be considered. My nomination would tip the scales. I would represent the fourth female justice, which we all know will *not* fly, so I suggest we not even try it."

Everyone nodded or grunted an acknowledgement without actually responding to the statement. David Chabin spoke next. "I nominate Al Benazir. He is a New Yorker, an American, and of Middle Eastern descent. I believe the president would welcome his nomination, and I think he would be a true asset to the Supreme Court. I personally would recommend him regardless of this committee's agenda." David was the judge from Florida, and he felt that certain states held more status than others did, New York being the most significant.

Al responded quickly. "Thank you, David. I appreciate your comments, but I am afraid my descent may cause an issue. I am not sure this country is ready for a Palestinian associate justice. A brilliant Jew from Florida would be a much safer recommendation," he mused as he winked at David.

Jane Letterer continued to observe the interaction among the candidates, but she didn't speak. Sophia kept glancing at her and expecting her to interject, but Jane was quiet.

Nicole paced as she listened and finally announced, "It is wonderful that you all love one another! Such respect and admiration in one room may kill me. I do think it's time to move forward. I agree with David: Al is the best choice. Patrick Graham is strong, and I would consider him a second, but he does not sit on this team, and I would prefer an insider. If Al could work his way up to supreme court judge in the State of New York being of Middle Eastern descent, then he could win any election anywhere. I don't think it will hinder us, and I think he is an excellent candidate. Let's wrap this up."

New York City women—you had to love them! They assess a situation and sum it up in a few short but brutally honest statements. Sophia quickly took her cue. "Do we have any other input?"

There was silence. Sophia announced, "Al Benazir, New York, is our choice. What are your thoughts, Jane?"

Silence hung over the room as all eyes turned to Jane. Jane Letterer looked at them and simply stated, "My choice exactly."

Sighs of relief filled the room. Gerard Schuman of Pennsylvania spoke next. "Do we have a rundown of Judiciary support for the nomination?"

Sophia was prepared for this and quickly answered. "Prior to last week we had the support of Margaret White of South Carolina, Lindsey Cole of Georgia, Joseph Kennedy of Massachusetts, Priscilla Wiltz of North Carolina, and John Lavin of Arizona, along with Domenic, Anita, and you, Gerard. As you can all count, this leaves us two short of our majority. It seems our own senator from New Jersey, Joseph Flanagan, has recently run into a little problem of his own and has committed his support to our nominee. I have every reason to believe his vote is assured, as I have arranged to help him with his problem." Sophia paused, allowing the group time to draw their own conclusions. She continued, "Finally, I believe Senator George Rydell will support our nominee."

There were gasps from everyone in the room as they chattered their disbelief. "It's true. I spoke with him to offer my condolences, and he brought it up to me. He told me he knew my agenda and was ready to support it fully. He was very solemn; it was truly heart-wrenching," Sophia urged as she tried to accurately convey the Senator's sadness and need to do something.

Nicole jumped all over it. "How do you know this is not his way of sandbagging us? He could offer support and then simply vote the other way. He is a staunch pro-life supporter. There is no way he will go with us on this!"

Anita Hyde spoke for the first time all evening. "I agree with Sophia. Rydell is devastated over Ashley. Cynthia blames him for

Ashley's death, and I think this will help him vindicate himself. I think this is bigger than his political campaign. He has ghosts that he needs to beat down, and I think he sees this as something he must do."

David had been scribbling notes and counting tick marks for the last five minutes. He interjected, "Look, we have eleven with Rydell. That's our majority, since the others are not looking at this from a pro-choice platform. I think Al will get at least one or two votes from the eight other senators. We will win the nomination even if Rydell *does* sandbag us. Once the committee supports the nomination, the floor will simply follow suit. It's just window dressing at that point."

David closed the deal. Sophia put it to a vote for the last time. "Al Benazir, New York. Any opposition?"

Silence.

"Al Benazir, New York, will be nominated to the U.S. Supreme Court as long as everyone does their job. The key to our success will be execution and follow-through," Sophia warned.

The meeting lasted twenty-five minutes, after which they quickly returned to their places at the auction. The auctioneer was only halfway through the items when the absentees jumped right into the bidding. By the time the auction ended, they had bid on so many items it seemed as if they were there the entire time.

The event was a complete success. They raised five million dollars, which was nearly a half-million more than expected, all while the team moved significantly closer to their objective.

Sophia saw Gina and Nick talking in the rose garden and swelled. It was a wonderful night, and *everything* was working according to plan.

Chapter 14

GINA awoke before the alarm went off and stared at the ceiling. She replayed the fundraiser in her mind and could not control the beating of her heart. Her face flushed, and she thought she might be getting sick. What could be wrong with her? Nothing was wrong with her. She was in love. Afraid to even think such thoughts, especially after one brief encounter, she scolded herself for acting like a schoolgirl. *You are thirty years old, for God's sake. Cut it out!* She could not help herself as she imagined his hair, his lips, his smile, and his eyes. His eyes were beautiful, with a twinkle that made them seem like they were laughing. Sophia had finally succeeded. Nick DePaolo was definitely "all that," and Gina was thrilled.

After the party, they had exchanged numbers, and he promised they would make plans to go out. She would not think about him anymore until he called—then she would know where she stood. They always promise to call, but mysteriously you never hear from them again. It would definitely be best to put him out of her mind. She would get dressed and go to work. With three open cases, an interrogation, and a variety of paperwork to catch up on, she had more than enough to keep herself occupied.

Gina added a string of pearls and earrings to her olive silk suit with cream silk chemise. She applied her makeup carefully and decided to put on lipstick. She usually hated lipstick, believing it a complete nuisance and constantly wiping it off drinking glasses, clothing, and faces. This was a long-wearing brand guaranteed not to rub off, so she figured she would try it. She studied herself in the mirror: she looked great. This was going to be a good day.

She bounded into the office to find Robert standing in the doorway.

"Well, what news have we forgotten to share with our assistant today?" he drawled.

"What are you talking about? I have no news. I just woke up and came to work. What's going on?" she casually asked.

"Look, Gina, I've known you too long and too well. Come clean!" he pressed.

"Robert, you're crazy. Why are you carrying on?" she asked as she cut off her own sentence.

Just past Robert, sitting on her desk, was the most beautiful, huge, breathtaking bunch of white roses she had ever seen.

"Who sent those?" she breathed.

"My question exactly! Let's start with who, what, when, and where," he sang.

"When did they come?" she asked. She didn't want to get too excited. She paused in an effort to measure her response, as she didn't want to jump to conclusions.

"*Gina*, snap out of it! They arrived at 8:15 this morning. There is a card. Of course, I didn't open the card, although I *wanted* to open the card. You know I would *never* violate your privacy, but I am dying to know what that card says!" he stated in a most animated and flamboyant manner.

"Robert, stop it! My grandmother introduced me to a friend of hers last night, and we seemed to hit it off. It's still a little too early to tell whether it will go anywhere." She maintained a nonchalant attitude, sat at her desk, and started ruffling through her messages while Robert nearly had a stroke.

"Will you please open the damn card?" he yelled, half-joking and half–dead serious.

She couldn't maintain her composure anymore and laughed as she grabbed the card and tore open the envelope.

"For a lovely lady. Thank you for a pleasurable evening."

Robert whistled. "It must have been soooome evening; there are two dozen of them! Tell me *everything.*"

"There really isn't anything to tell. My grandmother introduced us, we talked, and I went home. No kisses, no romance, no hot, torrid love affair."

"Gina, can't you just lie to me? Fabricate a story, my dear. The roses deserve a juicier tale than that."

"I'm sorry. It was nice. He is handsome. I do like him, but there is really nothing else to tell."

"Fine. I guess we will just have to play twenty questions. What does he do? What does he look like? Where does he live? How old is he?" Robert rattled off the questions, dramatically counting on his fingers.

"He is a doctor. Tall, dark, and handsome. Lives in Rumson. I am not sure how old he is, but he looks late thirties, early forties," she answered.

"He sounds perfect—for me! I swear, you girls have all the luck." Robert said in his best drag queen impersonation. Robert was genuinely excited for Gina because he didn't think it was natural for a young, attractive woman to be without companionship, and he never missed an opportunity to tell her so.

"I am trying to take it slow, Robert. I really like him, but it's too soon to have strong feelings. I am way too insecure, and I need to see how this is going to play out."

"Honey, I completely understand, and I will give you a little room here. But as soon as I think this is showing promise, I am going to force you to drop the 'hard to get' routine. You hear me?"

"Yes, Robert, I hear you."

"What's his name, and when do I get to meet him?"

"His name is Dr. Nick DePaolo. If he calls—and *if* is a big little word—maybe he can stop here and we can go to lunch. But I don't know if he is going to call, so don't get your hopes up."

"Gina, he sent you two dozen of the largest white roses I have ever seen. I am sure he will be calling. Sometimes I just don't understand you women."

"I have to get to work. I have a backlog of paperwork threatening to topple my desk." Gina went to her desk and started to organize her messages and piles of correspondence.

"I will just be out here, by my desk. Shall I screen your calls?"

"Yes, Robert, you can answer my phone. By the way, did the DA call back on the inquiry I made?"

"Your grandmother's friend's daughter?"

"Yes, the lawyer," Gina corrected.

"The DA did call, and the message is in your pile. If she agrees to take a few pro bono cases, he's sure he can make a deal on her behalf," Robert said.

"Did he mention if he can get it thrown out? I would prefer she come out clean."

"No, we didn't discuss it. He just mentioned her agreeing to the pro bono work," he answered.

"Excellent. Thanks, Robert."

Gina called the hospital and checked on Patti Darby's status—still no change. She called Winthrop to get an update on the arrests.

"Hi, John. It's Gina."

"Gina, I was getting worried about you. I thought you would be down here all over these guys by now."

"I know you have everything covered. Do you have their profiles completed?"

"It has taken a little longer than planned. They wouldn't cooperate and called in their lawyers immediately. We have their names, addresses, and fingerprint profiles. Only one has a prior, and it's a misdemeanor. Their bail hearing is set for this afternoon. I think they'll make bail," he said with little emotion.

"Can we search their apartments?" she asked.

"I've requested the warrant, but I won't hear back until later this morning."

"John, I do not like how this is sounding. I need something. I thought they would at least want to deal."

"I hear you, Gina. Let's wait to hear back on the warrant. I don't want to approach their lawyer until we have something to bargain with. Don't panic just yet."

"I need photos. I need to do a little digging myself. What did the DA have to say?" she asked.

"He's a little skittish. I had to ensure him entrapment was carefully avoided during the arrest. He's listening to the recordings this morning. He wants to draw his own conclusions."

"Thanks, John. Look, upload a copy of the photo file into Robert's file drawer, and I'll call you later on. Call my cell if the warrant is granted."

"You got it, Gina. I'll talk to you later."

Gina's good mood evaporated with that little update. She needed a concrete link between the Rydell or Darby case; otherwise, she didn't really have a strong case against the two of them. The truth was, Jennifer Annapolis *never* called the number—only Gina did. She didn't have proof that they had ever performed abortions before. If they built their defense on the premise that this was their first time, then Gina would have them on very little. Their arrest took place before they actually did anything to her. Reasonable doubt could be established, and Gina did not want to lose these guys. Now she was on the clock, and she had to move fast.

Robert printed the full-color photos of Tony Arabia and Joe Primak. Gina stared at their faces and felt sick. On the day of the arrests, she never had a chance to react to the situation. Her adrenaline pumping, senses sharp, she just wanted to make sure she had enough evidence. When it was over, the excitement, the media, propelled her forward, affording her little time for reflection. Now, as she stared at the digital prints with their dark brown eyes staring back, she was overwhelmed. The thought of what could have happened, what did happen every day to countless others, consumed her. Robert saw her reaction immediately. Like a parent who senses when a child is sick, he gently pressed her into a chair.

"Gina, honey, let's sit for a minute," he said.

Robert knew the fallout; he knew it was hitting home for her. It had been a few days, and she was doing so well he thought she might have a handle on it. But deep down he knew it would happen. Inevitably, the human mind must have a chance to respond to events both joyful and tragic.

"Robert, I don't know what happened. I just feel overwhelmed."

"It's fine. Just take a minute. A lot has happened in the last few weeks."

"I'll be okay. I am going to need a few copies of the photos, and I am going to visit Ginny Lui and check on the Darby boys. Maybe she will recognize them."

"Gina, I think you should take it easy. Make this an office day. Finish your paperwork, return calls, but stay in. You can check on them later."

"I wish I could. I just spoke with John, and the bail hearing is soon. We are going to need more than what we have. I need to tie these two back to Ashley or Patti."

"Then do me a favor. Take Sally or Ben with you. It's their case, too," he pleaded.

"If either is available, I'll meet them at Ginny's apartment."

Robert didn't need to hear that twice. He was on the phone with Sally before Gina reached her office.

"It's all set. Sally will meet you there at eleven o'clock," he announced.

Gina kept replaying the facts in her mind. Ashley Rydell had died from an illegal termination. She didn't give a damn what the autopsy said: this she knew to be true. Someone had illegally aborted Patti Darby's pregnancy, but until Patti could talk, Gina didn't have any facts. Jennifer Annapolis, on the other hand, took her own life. The only link was Jennifer's friend Christina, who had uncovered a termination source that led Gina to the arrests.

Looking at it in black-and-white, it created a bleak picture. She did not have one shred of evidence to tie these guys to the other cases. She was still sure she had enough to convict them with the surveillance video, but if the judge threw out the video for any reason, they would be set free. She needed to charge them with at least one of the abortions.

Gina dialed tentatively. She knew they wanted to protect their daughter, but Christina Galindo was the only lead that could talk.

"Mr. Galindo, hi, it's Agent Vincent. I know Christina is still very upset, and I didn't want to make matters worse. I'm calling because I need to know where she got the telephone number. I know she was clear on not wanting to tell me that, but I need to work backward."

"Agent Vincent, my wife and I have been expecting this call. We have spoken with Christina about this very issue. Christina's friend, who we will not name, got the number from another friend who was in trouble and received help from a source she met outside the free clinic on Bay Street. It seems to me they stand outside and market their services," he said.

"I won't press the issue, Mr. Galindo, but I do need to stress how important these unnamed friends could be to this case," Gina said.

"Agent Vincent, we completely understand your plight, and we have gone out of our way to give you additional information. These unnamed sources are protected under the Fifth Amendment; their participation could incriminate them. The government cannot have it both ways."

"Mr. Galindo, I assure you they would be protected from any and all indictment. I simply need to speak with them," she pleaded.

"I'm sorry. I cannot help you." Gerry Galindo gently hung up the phone.

"That didn't go very well," she said aloud to herself. She felt like the enemy. She sensed that the Galindos blamed her in some way for Jennifer's suicide. Those who supported legalization blamed the authorities for every death. Why didn't they understand that she was trying to help, that she was doing her job? She was trying to catch criminals who were killing babies and women, yet the public had a way of making her feel like a criminal.

Gina headed to Ginny Liu's apartment. Sally was waiting outside pacing, looking genuinely conspicuous in the project housing.

"Hi, Sally. Thanks for meeting me," she said.

"Gina, how ya doing? Do you have something?" Sally asked

"No, Robert thought I should have help today. I was feeling a little overwhelmed this morning. Anyway, I do have something on the source of our guys. Turns out they were waiting outside the free clinic on Bay Street. Maybe when we're done here, you could take a drive out to the Island."

"Not a problem. I've been circulating the photos in Brooklyn. Came up with nothin'."

They entered the building and buzzed Ginny's apartment. "It's Agent Vincent," she announced through the static on the intercom.

Ginny buzzed them in immediately.

"Hi, Ginny. This is Agent Sally Lister. She is working with me on this case. I just wanted to check in on you and the boys."

Ginny let them in and shook Sally's hand.

"Pleased to meet you, Agent Lister."

"Call me Sally."

Ginny looked tired. Just the two younger children were home, but it looked like taking care of all the kids definitely was taking its toll.

"Ginny, how are you feeling?" Gina asked.

"I'm worried. Patti hasn't shown much change, and the boys are having a hard time. Michael, the baby, cries for her every night. I hold him in his bed, and his body just shakes. My heart is breaking," Ginny whispered, making sure Michael didn't hear her.

This woman was amazing—not a single complaint, just complete concern for her best friend's children.

"Has there been any update from the doctors?" Gina inquired.

"They say there is brain activity, but she is still in a coma. They say it's possible that she will just wake up. In the meantime I am trying to give the boys hope, but it's difficult."

"I have some photos I need you to look at." Gina placed both pictures on the kitchen table. "Have you ever seen these men before?" Gina asked.

Ginny looked at the photos and immediately responded, "No, I have never seen them before. Who are they?"

"We think they could be related to Patti, but we don't know. We're just running down our leads," Gina answered.

"I'm sorry I couldn't be of assistance. Were those the men arrested the other day?" Ginny asked.

"I'm not at liberty to say, Ginny. We're working on it, though. Baby steps," Gina responded.

Gina promised to check in on Ginny in a few days. "I call the hospital daily, but if you hear of any change, please call me right away."

Ginny promised, and the agents left.

Once they were out on the street, Gina walked Sally to her car. "Have you had any luck finding Joe Darby?" Gina asked Sally.

"No, but we've put the word out. Something will come up," she answered.

"In the meantime take a ride to the clinic and see if you come up with anything. Keep me posted," Gina said.

"You got it, boss."

Sally was a little rough around the edges, but she was dedicated, and Gina knew Sally would be in Staten Island within the hour. The team was excellent.

Gina was about to head to the hospital to see Patti Darby for herself when her phone rang.

Robert was on the other end, and he spoke in a mocking and distinguished English accent. "Juliet, I have Romeo on the phone. Shall I transfer?"

"Nick called?"

"Gina, he is on the line. Pull yourself together. He's coming through."

With an audible click, the switch was made.

"Gina, Gina, are you there? Can you hear me?" Nick was yelling into the phone.

Stammering, she answered, "Y-yes, I'm here. I'm sorry. I'm on the FDR, and it's difficult to hear."

"I had a great time last night. Really," he said.

Gina heard him, and her heart squeezed like she were riding an express elevator and it just descended twenty floors.

"I did too. Thank you for the roses; they are exquisite."

"Roses. What roses?" he deadpanned.

Gina panicked. Her mind raced. What if he hadn't sent the roses? Who had? She must sound like an idiot. What should she say? In the silence that transpired as these thoughts ran through her head, Nick realized she didn't get the joke.

He quickly added, "Just kidding. I'm sorry. I'm in a really good mood today."

"Very funny. It's just that in my line of work, you have to be very careful. Actually, it was quite funny. I don't know why I am so serious."

She recovered quickly, and her mood soared. God, she really liked this guy!

"Gina, I was wondering if you are free for lunch," he started to suggest.

"What day?" she asked as she shuffled through her bag for her day planner. Gina was all business, and her social skills seemed nonexistent. Throw in a handsome doctor, schoolgirl flutters, and two dozen roses, and she was a complete mess.

"Today. I thought maybe if you are free, I could meet you. I'm in the city, and was just wondering, thought I'd give you a call ...." He rambled on trying to justify what apparently was an absurd request.

"Yes! Yes, I can meet you for lunch. I am so sorry. I am just not thinking today. I thought you needed to schedule a time. I'm free right now. I just finished a meeting, and I'm on the East Side," she said, recovering quickly.

"Would you like to meet me at The Plaza? I was planning to have lunch in the Oak Room."

"Great. I'll meet you there in twenty minutes," she answered.

"I'll have a table ready. See you soon," he said as he clicked off the call.

She would definitely have to pull herself together. What reduces an otherwise intelligent female to a bumbling idiot? She wasn't really sure she wanted an answer to that question—not yet, at least. She would have to call Robert and let him know; it was only fair. She pictured him sitting at his desk, drumming his fingers and looking at the phone while rolling his eyes. He would be totally unproductive if she didn't fill him in.

"Hi, Robert. It's me."

"Well? What happened?"

"Nothing really. He needed the telephone number of a mutual friend that I promised I would get for him," she said in her best monotone.

After what seemed like a minute of silence, he responded, "Oh."

"He also wanted to know if I could meet him for lunch at the Oak Room."

"Gina, you wench! You are on your way, right?"

"Of course I'm on my way. Robert, I sound like a driveling idiot when I talk to him. Whyyyy?" she whined.

"Gina, you've met someone with potential. There's a spark. You are going to sound like an idiot. It's a prerequisite to the real deal. I'm so excited," he said.

"Look, I'll call you after lunch and fill you in. Let's not make too much of this, Robert. I don't want you to be disappointed," she teased.

"Gina, just be your charming self. Don't talk about work," he warned.

"Why not?"

"Gina, just enjoy lunch and avoid any 'change the world' discussions."

"What do you mean?" she pressed.

"We all know you're passionate about your work. Just don't chomp his head off trying to make a point."

"I don't do that."

"Yes, Gina, you do. Don't worry about it. Just have a nice lunch. Toodles!" Robert hung up. He had learned early on that with Gina you just had to state your case and run. She would argue her point until you just plain relented out of sheer exhaustion.

It took Gina only a few minutes to get uptown. That was New York City for you—the FDR would get you from the thirties to the fifties in a few minutes, but trying to get from First Avenue to Fifth could take the better part of a day. Traffic was light, and she was in front of The Plaza in no time. She loved it when things went smoothly—it was divine intervention. There was no other explanation for it. A valet took her car and parked it to the left of the entrance right in the courtyard. Because she was a law enforcement official, everyone accommodated her parking needs throughout the city. This benefit alone made her love her job. The fact that she also got a salary was a bonus.

The Plaza Hotel was by far the most beautiful landmark hotel in the city. Fairmont Properties, which had owned it for the last thirty years, did a great job refurbishing the guest rooms and maintaining the common areas in their original splendor. Overlooking Central Park South and GM Plaza, the hotel offered breathtaking views of the city. The Oak Room, which had opened in 1907, had twenty-four-foot ceilings, walls paneled in sable oak, and fluted columns. It had remained unchanged since its original design, affording visitors a nostalgic experience. A patron could sit at the table where their great-grandfather proposed to their grandmother or where John D.

Rockefeller may have sat when conducting business. Initially, the Oak Room was for men only. Women were allowed to dine only after three in the afternoon. In 1974 the restaurant had changed its policy, welcoming both men and women. Gina loved teasing Sophia about this little fact, knowing her grandmother had been incensed that women could not dine with the men for "power lunches."

He was sitting at a table tucked in the corner, reading the paper. She took a moment to stare at him from across the room, wanting to create a reference in her mind. He was very handsome but welcoming, not at all conceited or self-absorbed. She felt he was too good to be true, too perfect; something had to be wrong with him. He smiled and stood as soon as he saw her walking toward him. He gave her a kiss on the cheek and pulled out her chair—*definitely too good to be true.*

"That was quick. I'm so glad you could meet me. I wasn't sure how hectic your day would be …," he started rambling.

Gina noticed his speech was clumsy also. "I just finished up an interview and was heading to the hospital when you called. I needed to eat lunch, so your call was very timely," she said, pleased with her ability to produce a coherent sentence.

"Do you have office hours today?" she continued.

"No, Tuesdays and Thursdays are my days in the city. Mondays, Wednesdays, and Fridays, if needed, are in New Jersey. I try to keep Fridays free if I can."

"So what brings you in today?"

"Charity work. I sometimes donate hours at the free clinic, and I had a meeting with the administrator this morning."

A high-profile, wealthy, handsome doctor who donated large amounts of money to charity *and* worked at the free clinic in his spare time. She was starting to look for the Candid Camera.

"How is the case going?" he asked.

"Actually, I am working on a few cases, and unfortunately I've run into a series of dead ends. Let's not talk about work. Tell me about you." She would never tell Robert she actually took his advice.

They enjoyed lunch with easy conversation, sharing stories of their childhood, education, careers, and interests. He fascinated her. He loved coin collecting, fine art, and all forms of sports. She thought it odd that he was a coin collector, but his grandmother had willed him her collection of U.S. proof sets from 1950 to 2000. When he was a young boy, she had taught him her hobby, and he loved it, just as he loved her. When he explained that she had died when he was nineteen, it seemed as if he was fighting tears. Gina thought she could marry him right then and there. They each felt familiar with the other, as if they had been friends for years. They made plans to go to the Monmouth Racetrack on Saturday afternoon, followed by dinner at a little bistro in Red Bank. They were both looking forward to it a little more than they wanted to admit. She kissed him on the cheek and left him staring after her in the lobby.

Gina jumped into her car and headed back toward Cabrini Medical to check in on Patti as she had planned earlier. Her mind replayed lunch repeatedly in her head, and she caught herself smiling in the rearview mirror. She was pathetic, and she loved it. She just wished she could stop that nagging dread that would creep in to ruin her thoughts. Was he too good to be true? Was there such a thing as true happiness? Truth be told, she didn't care; she was having fun and was loving every minute of being with him.

She called Robert and filled him in on the details of her lunch date. He was waiting patiently for her call, and she couldn't disappoint him. Robert was genuinely happy for her. He had been pushing her to date for as long as she could remember. He was relentless, nearly as bad as her grandmother. Gina would soon have to figure out a way for Robert to meet Nick. Robert would be impossible to work with until he had a chance to grill Nick firsthand. Of course, it would be the emotional equivalent of a father meeting his daughter's first date. Gina smiled at the thought.

Gina stared at Patti Darby, searching her face for something, anything that would indicate thought. She saw nothing. Patti had the standard variety of tubes, equipment, LCD displays, and monitors attached to her body. Gina had no idea what each monitor did, but in spite of the equipment, she thought Patti looked well. She had good color in her face and appeared to be sleeping. Flashes of Patti's four boys ran through Gina's mind, and her earlier euphoria disappeared. Standing in the room, looking at this young mother, seeing her young sons, wondering if she would ever wake to see their little faces again overwhelmed her. Tears streamed down Gina's cheeks.

The nurse unknowingly interrupted her reverie. "Can I get you anything?"

"Uh, no, thank you. I, um … I am Agent Vincent with the FBLI. I was just wondering if I could get an update on her condition," Gina stammered.

"Sure. Let's see. Her vitals are good; her heart is strong. We are just hoping she will come out of it," the nurse answered as she flipped through the patient chart.

"Is she out of immediate danger?"

"Yes, but she could stay like this for years. If she does wake, we won't know what neurological damage, if any, is present. At this point, it's just a waiting game. Her blood volume is good, and she is healing well from the hysterectomy."

Gina thanked the nurse and decided to stay with Patti a little longer. Thoughts and emotions were swirling through her mind, and she needed a chance to sort them out. Gina liked her job and thought she was doing a noble task. Saving lives, preventing death—she could feel good about her life's work. However, looking at Patti, she felt sad and confused. Gina would never be able to arrest Patti for terminating. How could she? Gina saw firsthand how hard this woman worked to keep her boys together and maintain a family life. She worked double shifts and supported four boys on a meager income. For the first time ever, Gina could understand why she had done it, why she had made a decision to terminate her pregnancy. For Patti Darby, it was a matter of survival. It was a world that enforced the ideals of some at the expense of others. Patti did not have affordable day care options, the authorities were unable to keep her ex-husband from beating and raping her, and her housing costs, although controlled, still equaled her entire first income. She needed a second job just to put food on the table.

Gina was afraid. She was afraid of her thoughts. They were all wrong! Patti Darby had had her unborn child killed! That was murder. Patti was a criminal, plain and simple. The problem was she just didn't look like one.

Gina felt like a schizophrenic manic-depressive. She spent the early part of her day euphoric, the afternoon melancholy and confused. She wondered at times if she was losing her grasp on reality and her place in it. The best thing to do was to go back to the office and work. Stick to the facts; isolate and review them. This was not a time for ideological debate. This was her job, and she needed to get to it.

Just as she was leaving the hospital, Winthrop called. "Gina, we have the warrant. We're searching their apartments right now. Bail was set at five hundred thousand, and we expect they will make it. In any case, we'll be done with the search long before they're out."

"Excellent! I want to meet with you as soon as they're done. We need to go over everything."

"Sure, Gina. We'll meet at your office. Have them bring in dinner. I'll bring Sally and Ben."

Gina called Robert. "Hi. Can you order Chinese for six o'clock tonight?"

"Why, your every wish is my command," he answered.

"John, Ben, and Sally are coming in. Can you stay until about seven tonight? I want you to sit in on the review. The judge issued the warrant, and they are searching the apartments as we speak."

"This is a busy day for you, Gina. A big break and a big date," he joked.

"It's not a big break yet. It would be nice to find something concrete. I'm heading back. I'll see you in a few minutes."

She ended the call, and not a second later, her phone was ringing. Gina thought it was Robert calling back because he forgot something. "Yeah, Robert."

Nothing.

"Hello. Can you hear me? Hello," Gina yelled into the phone.

She heard sobbing, inaudible at first, and then louder as the person tried to catch her breath.

"Hello, who is this?" she yelled.

The sobbing was louder, yet there were still no words.

Gina clicked caller ID: last caller, unknown.

"Please tell me who you are," Gina pleaded.

Finally, "G, it's me. Lisa."

"Lisa, what's wrong? Are you okay? Where are you?" Gina panicked. She had never known Lisa to cry, and now she was hysterical.

"I'm in Starbucks on Forty-First and Madison. I'm using a stranger's cell phone," she said, sobbing. Her words were barely audible.

"I'll be there in a minute."

Gina hit the gas, threw on her emergency siren, and careened toward midtown. Her heart was pounding, and her mind was racing. Lisa never lost her composure. She was a rock, always confident and sure, never wasting energy on tears. Gina was weaving in and out of cars. A cabbie was close behind trying to capitalize on her run through the late-day traffic. She pulled up in front of the Starbucks, left the car half on the sidewalk, and ran into the coffeehouse. Lisa was in an overstuffed armchair in the corner, hunched over with sunglasses on, wiping at her face with shredded napkins.

Gina rushed to her. "What happened?"

"G, I'm sorry to call. I'm sorry to bother you. I didn't know what to do. I can't—" She burst into sobs. Tears were streaming down her face, and she was having difficulty catching her breath.

"Lisa, stop it. I don't want you to talk. Just try to breathe—long, deep breaths through your nose." Gina held Lisa's hands tightly and was breathing with her. Lisa was hysterical. Gina thought she might have lost the baby, but she was afraid to ask. She needed to calm her.

"Lisa, do I need to take you to the hospital?" Gina asked.

She was breathing much better and seemed to be settling down a bit. "It's nothing like that. I'm fine, really. The baby is fine."

Gina let out her breath. "Then what's wrong?"

"It's my parents. They came to town on a surprise visit, and I told them."

"So, what's the problem?" she asked.

"They were furious. G, they wanted me to … I can't even say it," she shouted as she once again burst into tears. Her whole body was shaking, and she lost her breathing once again.

"They want me to abort the baby. My baby, their grandchild! Can you imagine? I thought they would be happy for me! I thought they would be excited!" She nearly screamed the words, then stopped. She took a deep breath, wiped her face, and looked at Gina. "Do you believe it? They would rather I commit murder than have my baby. They would rather me be a convict than an unwed mother!"

Gina didn't know what to say. She couldn't believe Lisa's parents would respond like they did. She would never have expected it— she thought they'd be a little shocked, maybe, but never this.

"Lisa, you have to calm down and think about this. Look at it from their point of view. It's a big shock. They didn't even know you were dating. They were just coming for a surprise visit," Gina reasoned.

"Guess the surprise was on them," Lisa said as she managed a little laugh.

"You got that right. Give them time. Once they see that beautiful baby of yours, they'll come around. In the meantime, I am here for you. I promise I will help you with everything. Let's go back to your place and get you cleaned up."

"I just thought they would be excited. It's my baby."

Gina knew Lisa was hurt deeply, the kind of hurt people don't rebound from. Lisa never needed emotional support from anyone, but having her parents attack her had just put her over the edge. Gina worried Lisa might never forgive her parents.

"Lisa, we are going to be fine. Did your parents leave?"

"Yes. It was ugly. I am not sure exactly when, but I know they were going home," she answered.

"In a few days I will give them a call. In the meantime, let's go make a huge, fattening hot fudge sundae. By the way, I have big news: I think I have a new boyfriend."

Gina was able to take Lisa home and settle her down. As soon as Lisa heard about Gina's date, she wanted to know everything. It was a good diversion for Lisa, and it felt good for Gina to talk about it. She really liked Nick but was afraid to rush into a relationship. Whatever happened, Gina would indulge every inquiry Lisa made. The more Gina talked about herself, the better Lisa began to feel. Gina thought about Ginny Lui and Patti Darby. Everybody needed a best friend.

By the time Gina left Lisa, it was after five, and she needed to meet everyone at the office by six. It was a roller coaster of a day, and Gina didn't think she would be able to live through many more like it. She made it to the office by 5:30 and answered all of her calls. Robert was busy arranging everything for their meeting, so he left her alone to do her work.

John, Ben, and Sally arrived together and were digging into the Chinese food by the time Gina went into the conference room.

"So, guys, what've we got?" Gina asked.

John moved his food aside, took out his notepad, and flipped through a few pages before he answered.

"I'm afraid the search came up empty. I spoke with the DA. They feel they have enough for intent; murder, of course, is not an option. They are not willing to deal; their lawyer is confident she can beat all charges."

Gina had that sick feeling you get when your worst fears are confirmed. "You didn't find *anything* in their apartments?"

"Nothing incriminating, nothing tying them to Darby or Rydell. We did find a box of rubber gloves that matched the gloves they had in their bag. It only proves that the bag in their possession was theirs," John answered.

"Let's talk worst-case scenario. If we get a conviction on intent to murder, they will get at least two years. If we uncover additional evidence, then we can prosecute a second time for murder," Gina said.

"That's not the worst case. The worst scenario, which is what will probably happen, is that they beat all charges and we never uncover any additional evidence," Sally interjected.

"Let's not jump to conclusions. There is still a chance Patti Darby will recover, and if they allow the jury to view the videotape of Gina, we absolutely will have intent. Beyond any reasonable doubt," John said.

"I thought for sure they would have given us something during interrogation. Who is their lawyer?" Gina asked.

"They have Dendrite," Ben answered.

"Dendrite! How the hell can they afford her?" Gina was shocked.

Robyn Dendrite was an excellent and extremely expensive criminal lawyer. Gina couldn't believe they had enough money to afford one of the top New York City criminal attorneys.

"Abortion is big business. You know that," Sally replied.

"Did anything in their apartments suggest their operation is that lucrative?" Gina asked.

After a brief silence, John answered. "No. We found nothing extravagant, just the typical audio/video paradise, wall screen, multicomponent theatre, and integrated stereo. Clothing is common, nothing custom. Not a lot of furniture, just the usual. No expensive jewelry or watches."

"There is definitely more to this. We are missing something critical. There is a reason they have the most expensive lawyer in the city. Sally, did you find anything at the Bay Street clinic?" Gina asked.

"I circulated the photos among the staff and some of the clients. Nothin'. Nobody knew them," Sally answered.

The team spent the better part of an hour reviewing the facts and their strategy.

Sally would take the photos and hit all the free clinics in Brooklyn, Staten Island, and the city. Ben would try to track the money trail—there might be someone funding their lawyer. John would stay close to the pending case, making sure all their ducks were in a row for trial. Gina would monitor Darby, their only hope in the matter.

Gina prayed Patti Darby would wake up.

Chapter 15

THE girl considered herself lucky, even though she couldn't stop crying. She was afraid, but Francesca was with her, and she wouldn't be alone. Francesca's good boss was helping her. She needed their help, and she was very grateful, but she was still afraid. Francesca promised everything would be all right, that Ms. Sophia was a good person and she would help them take care of things. The tears just streamed down her face; she wished it had never happened. If only she could have done something to stop it. She played it through in her mind for the millionth time.

She had been cleaning the master bathroom and had just finished scrubbing the tub when he came in. She apologized for being in his way, excused herself, and hurried to leave. He told her to stay, said that she wasn't in his way. She didn't know what to do. Should she keep cleaning the bathroom while he was there? She was only sixteen, and she needed her job. She didn't want to go back to Mexico; she wanted to stay in America, and so she went back to scrubbing the tub. He unzipped his pants and peed in the toilet, with her right there in the bathroom! Her heart started to beat fast; she knew this was bad, but she didn't know what to do. He didn't say anything to her at all. He zipped his pants, and she thought for a second that he was leaving. She almost let out a sigh of relief when she felt his hand on her lower back. He said, "Let me help you with that." He took her hand with the sponge and started to scrub the tub. His other hand grabbed her breast. She was so afraid she couldn't breathe. She couldn't scream, she couldn't think, everything was foggy, and the rest seemed like it didn't really happen. He pushed his way in from behind as he squeezed her breast even harder. He grunted in her ear with every thrust as he slammed his body into hers. It all seemed so unreal, like it was happening to someone else. When he finished, he left as quickly and quietly as he had arrived. She didn't know what to do, so she just straightened herself and finished cleaning the bathroom.

She didn't discover her problem until a few weeks later. She missed her period and was feeling very sick. She went to the clinic, thinking she needed medicine so she could continue to work. She could not miss work! She needed to do a good job. She was afraid of him, but she was more afraid of losing her job. The doctor told her she was pregnant and gave her vitamins and a little book in Spanish on having babies. Francesca was her mother's cousin; she knew Francesca would help her, so she told her everything. Now they were on their way, and she was so afraid.

She prayed the rosary in her head. She knew she would not be forgiven; she knew she was going to hell. She didn't need rosary beads. Ever since she was a young girl, she would pray the rosary and keep count on her fingers. Ten Hail Marys, one for each of her fingers, one Our Father, begin again, repeat five times, end with the Glory Be, Our Father, three Hail Marys, a last Our Father. She ended with the Act of Contrition and repeated it over and over again. The tears would not stop. The train pulled into the Red Bank station, and Francesca gently took her hand.

It was a white row house two blocks from the station. Each house looked alike, although they were different colors—one pink, one green, one blue, all with small front yards. It was on a quiet dead-end street with a limousine company parking lot at the end. They rang the doorbell, and a young, blond woman answered and escorted them into what would have been the living room if the house were a residence. They sat in comfortable armchairs facing the couch, with a glass coffee table in the center. The young blonde sat on the sofa and introduced herself as Angela. She explained that she would be the nursing assistant as well as the patient advocate.

Francesca did all the talking. That was fine with Rosetta; she was too afraid to speak. Angela insisted that Francesca allow the girl to answer the questions herself.

"What is your name?" Angela asked.

"Rosetta Gonzales," she whispered, staring at her hands in her lap.

"Rosetta, do you know we can help you to have the baby if you want? We can find you a place to live and help you pay your bills. Do you understand?" she asked as she searched for a response in Rosetta's eyes.

"Si."

"Do you still want to end your pregnancy?" Angela asked.

"Si."

"Rosetta, can you tell me why?" Angela pressed as she reached over to touch Rosetta's hand.

The tears flowed down her face, and she choked back sobs. She frantically looked at Francesca and didn't know what to say. Francesca hugged her tightly and kissed the top of her head.

"Rosetta, tell Angela what happened," Francesca urged.

"He made me … he just did it! I couldn't stop him … I don't want a baby. I don't want *his* baby," Rosetta sobbed as her body seemed to crumple even further into a ball.

Angela looked at Francesca and realized this was too painful for the girl. She took Francesca into the dining room, which separated the living room from an immaculate white kitchen.

Rosetta could hear every word they said.

"I don't think she should do this while she is so upset," Angela said.

"Please! I beg you. Her boss did this, Senator Flanagan. Ms. Sophia said you would help. Rosetta cannot wait any longer. She is very sad. She just wants it over," Francesca pleaded.

Senator Joseph Flanagan. It made Angela sick! A strictly conservative right-wing Republican was responsible for impregnating a minor. Angela finally understood the urgency of the matter, but she still didn't like Rosetta's emotional state. It was her job to make sure each woman was confident in her decision and fully aware of her options.

"What is to stop him from doing it again?" Angela asked.

"He promised Ms. Sophia, and we have a new family for Rosetta; we will not send her back to his home," Francesca replied.

"Okay, let me talk to her alone for a few minutes. Stay here," Angela instructed.

Angela went back into the living room and sat in the chair next to Rosetta. She faced the child and gently took her hand into her own. Staring directly into Rosetta's eyes, Angela asked, "Rosetta, did your boss do this to you?"

"Si, Miss."

"Were you afraid?" she continued.

"Si, Miss."

"Do you want this baby?"

"No."

"Do you want to have the baby and give it away?"

"No. I need to work. I don't want to be sick. I don't want to have a baby. Please, please, help me. I want to stay in America," Rosetta pleaded.

Angela called Francesca back into the room and returned to her seat on the couch.

"I am very sorry this happened to you, Rosetta. I promise we will help you. I just need to make sure that you really want to do this. Once it is done, it cannot be changed. Do you understand?"

"Si, Miss," Rosetta answered.

"The doctor will come in, and he will spend a few minutes with you. He will tell you about the procedure and make sure you are ready. He will give you a shot so you don't feel anything. You will stay here two days, until Sunday morning, so we can examine you and make sure you are well. Francesca is welcome to stay with you. I will be here during the day, and another nurse will stay with you through the night. You can come with me now, and I will show you to your room," Angela explained.

A narrow staircase took them from the corner of the living room up to the second floor in the colonial-style row house. It looked as if there were once three bedrooms, but now there were only two: one large room with two twin beds and one small room with an adjustable hospital-type bed. The room with the hospital bed was the operating room. It was immaculate, with a slate-gray linoleum floor, white Formica cabinets lining one wall, a stainless steel sink, and a variety of instruments. Built into the cabinets was a unit that looked like a toaster oven but was really a sterilizer for the surgical instruments.

The room with the two beds was where Rosetta would stay. Adorned in varying shades of pink with fluffy pillows on a chenille-blanketed bed, the room immediately welcomed the women—a haven from the rest of the world. There was a television, a computer, books and magazines. A small end table separated the beds, while two cheerful chairs hand-painted in pale yellow with flowers flanked the windows. The room was cozy and comfortable, inviting her to crawl into bed and pull the covers around herself. Rosetta liked the room and sat on the bed closest to the window.

Francesca helped her unpack her bag and change into the hospital gown Angela had provided. They watched television while they waited. Angela was busy preparing the other room.

Rosetta felt much better and managed to stop crying. Francesca kept talking to her about other things and tried to make her laugh. It was working; she felt much calmer.

The doorbell rang, and Angela peeked into the room. "That's the doctor now. We'll be up in a few minutes. Just relax."

Angela answered the door and sat with him in the dining room. "How was the city?" she asked.

"Very good. The clinic was busy, but I still managed to have lunch with a friend and head out before rush hour. So what do we have here?" he asked.

"It's Sophia's housekeeper's niece, Rosetta Gonzales. She is only sixteen and very distraught. She can barely stop crying long enough for me to explain things to her."

"How did it happen? Did she say?" he asked.

"Oh, that's the best part! Her boss raped her while she was cleaning his bathroom. Better still is the fact that her boss is none other than our conservative big shot, Senator Joseph Flanagan! So what do you think?" Angela asked.

"I think it's despicable," he replied, his face screwing up with disgust.

"No, I mean about doing the procedure," she clarified.

"She is a child herself. Of course, I am going to do the procedure. She is only sixteen. What would you want me to do, Angela?"

"In that case, everything is ready. Your scrubs are in the kitchen. Don't forget to put on your surgical mask," she instructed.

"I won't forget. I wish we could dispense with that formality. It's really so cold."

"Doctor, please. We have been over this before. This is a crime. We cannot take any chances. They will never identify someone they have never seen," Angela said.

"I know. It's just that I feel so bad for them, and I want them to know I will take good care of them. I want them to trust me, and it's a little difficult to do that with a mask on my face."

"I understand, but they will just have to look into your eyes and find the trust there. We are not taking any chances, and that's final. We need to be available to others. We can't risk it," Angela stated in a firm tone so that he knew she meant every word.

He changed quickly and scrubbed his hands in the kitchen. He would scrub again once he was upstairs: he liked to follow his hospital surgical regimen even though he was in the house. He had selected the house personally. It was located just five blocks from Riverview Medical, so he could have them transported immediately if anything went wrong. He took every precaution and purchased every item he deemed necessary for a state-of-the-art operating room. The sterilization unit, monitors, sonogram equipment, and surgical light were topnotch, a better quality than what he used in the hospital operating room. Private donations funded the entire operation. Each woman sent to them would never pay a dime for their help. They kept the patients for forty-eight hours, strictly adhering to recovery procedures until they were sure they were well enough for release. They never lost a patient, and all patients were required to attend a six-week follow-up exam in the doctor's office. Of course, he was not the follow-up doctor. A different doctor handled the follow-up exam so they could ensure confidentiality.

It was a very sophisticated program, with some of the best doctors in the tri-state area participating. The patients would come from a variety of sources, including friends of participants or from the doctors themselves. Every volunteer believed in helping and supporting each of the women through their situation. If they were caught, they would face conviction and imprisonment. They chose to support the program anyway. Doctors are funny that way. They would rather keep their patients alive than find them dead from an abortion opportunist. The local network, while secret, functioned as part of a large network with affiliates throughout the country. It was necessary. Most still couldn't believe *Roe v. Wade* had been overturned. All these years later, and still the majority found the situation unbelievable. They had organized to protect both women and children.

He finished scrubbing, put on his surgical mask, and ascended the stairs. He knocked gently on the bedroom door and stood in the threshold.

"Can I come in?"

"Yes, doctor. Thank you, please," Francesca responded.

"Call me Dr. Dee," he said as he extended his hand to Francesca and then to Rosetta.

He sat next to Rosetta on the bed and gently turned her face to his.

"Hello, Rosetta. I want you to know I am going to take very good care of you. Are you sure that you are ready?" he asked.

"Si, doctor," Rosetta answered, staring back at him.

She immediately felt at ease with this man. He appeared sincere and seemed to care about her.

"We will perform the operation in the next room, which Angela showed you. You will be awake, but I will give you a shot so you won't feel anything but a minor pinch. Do you understand?" he asked.

"Si, doctor."

"If Francesca would like, I can have her scrub in, and she can sit next to you and hold your hand. Would you like that?"

Rosetta beamed, nodding her head yes.

"That would be great. Thank you," Francesca replied.

The doctor continued. "It will take only a few minutes, and then you will be able to rest. I will give you Tylenol for the next day or so, since you may feel some cramping. It shouldn't be too uncomfortable for you. Are you afraid?"

Rosetta looked at him and realized that she was not nearly as afraid as before.

"Just a little."

"That's to be expected. Don't worry. You will be fine. Come with me so I can get you situated, and Angela will help Francesca scrub in."

He talked to them throughout the entire procedure. He tried to keep Rosetta calm and even managed to make her laugh a few times. Francesca was so relieved, and Rosetta sensed it. Rosetta knew Francesca was very nervous but was being strong for her sake. She thanked God for Francesca, who was like her own mother. Now that Francesca was happy, Rosetta could relax because she knew everything would be fine. She trusted Francesca with her life.

Just as he had promised, the procedure took less than twenty minutes. Francesca and Angela helped Rosetta into bed. Angela left to clean up and returned with two trays of food. The doctor insisted

Rosetta eat something. Angela quickly brought a tray with orange juice, tea sandwiches, and shortbread cookies. Rosetta nibbled at everything, sipped the orange juice, and lay back in bed. She was so tired. She had not slept in days, and it all caught up with her at that very moment.

The doctor came in to check on her and was pleased to see she had eaten and was resting comfortably.

"Rosetta, you did well. You are very brave. Everything went well, and you will be fine. Just rest and try to get some sleep."

He had such a soothing bedside manner. Rosetta wanted to hug him. She didn't know how to express her gratitude to this man. Tears filled her eyes as she tried to thank him. He shook his head as if to say, "Don't worry. I understand." He bowed his head to Francesca and left.

She would never forget the twinkle in his eyes.

June 16, 2021

Lehman **nominates Al Benazir to U.S. Supreme Court**

President Lehman nominated Al Benazir to the U.S. Supreme Court in an effort to fill the vacant seat created by the recent passing of Associate Justice Thomas Chesterfield. Judge Benazir is currently a justice on the New York State Supreme Court and has been serving the U.S. legal system since 1997. Al Benazir is forty-eight years old.

Chapter 16

IT was Saturday morning, and Gina had the entire day to spend with Nick. She had butterflies in her stomach and panicked over silly things like what to wear, how to style her hair, and how much makeup to put on. She was not vain, so these things usually didn't matter much to her. Now that she wanted to make an impression, she discovered she just didn't have the experience. She almost called Lisa but thought better of it at the last minute. How pathetic she would seem! Imagine not knowing how to dress for a date at thirty years of age!

She used minimal makeup, going for a "natural" look, while carefully selecting her Ann Taylor black crop pants with a summer knit cardigan, providing her a sophisticated but carefree appearance. She scolded herself for acting so ridiculous and checked the time. She still had nearly two hours before she would meet him at his house in Rumson, New Jersey.

She ate a banana to help ease the flutters in her stomach and checked her messages one last time. She realized she had nothing to do. She was ready with time to spare—how she hated that! She consciously pushed thoughts of work out of her mind because she did not want to let her obsession ruin her day.

The address was on Rumson Road, which meant the house could be an absolute mansion or a reasonable-sized home located in an outstanding area. She was not sure which she would prefer, but she would find out soon enough. Traffic was nonexistent leaving the city on a weekend. You had to wonder where everyone went once the workweek was over. She was off the turnpike and onto the

Garden State Parkway within a half-hour and would be in Rumson in less than twenty minutes. She was starting to get nervous again as she wasn't sure what to expect, and her apprehension was getting the best of her. It started to rain a little, and she hoped the sun would break through because she would prefer going to the racetrack in good weather.

She checked her directions once again and was now winding through Red Bank going toward Rumson. Once she was on Rumson Road, she nearly crashed while staring at the view. These were not houses—they were small hotels! Each one was larger than the last, with expansive grounds, mature trees, and massive gated entryways overlooking the Shrewsbury River. She reached the address but pulled off to the side of the road so she could check her notes carefully. The address could not be right. She stared at her notes and then at the entrance gate. The numbers matched, but the house was not what she had expected at all. She fought the urge to turn around and hightail it back to the city.

As her car stood at the black aluminum entry gates dwarfed by huge brick pillars, she realized she might be out of her league. She couldn't see a full view of the house from the street because it looked as if the setback was at least a quarter mile, and the landscaping created a privacy wall from the road. She hoped she had written down the correct address; it would be unbearably embarrassing to knock on the wrong door in this neighborhood.

Rumson had been a favorite location for many famous personalities over the last century and up to the present day. As she drove through the entrance, the road wound slightly down and to the right, with the house coming into view on her left. It was not a house; it was an estate, complete with two separate carriage houses, one garage building with at least six bays, and the main house. The main house was breathtaking. It had a covered portico entrance flanked by two wraparound porches and a round turret on the left. It appeared to be an updated Victorian farmhouse design in which the depth rivaled the width of the home. The entranceway and walking paths were constructed of tumbled pavers that ran throughout the immediate grounds of the house and attached the left porch to a gazebo that overlooked the river. It appeared as if it also overlooked the backyard, but she couldn't tell from where she was in front of the house. She hadn't known he was this wealthy. If she had known, she definitely would have avoided him. She would have assumed he was just another spoiled little rich boy. She was relieved he never let on. He was so down-to-earth.

Before she could open the car door, he came bounding out the front door in khakis, a golf shirt, and loafers. He looked like he could have been the valet, certainly not the owner. Gina laughed at the thought and immediately felt a little better. He had a casual air about him that she just couldn't ignore.

"Gina, I'm so glad you made it. I was starting to think I should have picked you up. I should have thought of it first—I'm sorry. Was the ride unbearable?" he rattled as he kissed her on the cheek and helped her out of the car.

"The ride was fine, no traffic, and I found the place in no time. You didn't mention I should be looking for a hotel!" she joked, figuring it was better to get her insecurity out in the open instead of trying to hide it.

"Oh, this. I know, a little embarrassing, so excessive. My grandmother had me build it. Actually, I let her build it. It was the last project she managed before she died, and it was very important to her. It's cozier than you'd think inside. Come on in."

He was right. Although immense from the outside, the house was welcoming as she walked through the door. The entrance hall did not have a two-story ceiling, but the whole floor seemed to have ten-foot ceilings with granite flooring and a view of the library and rear deck. The house slowly introduced you to its rooms without a grandiose display of excess. Each room was exquisite, with the kitchen overlooking the river through a wall of windows. Thick molding framed each window, creating a very traditional effect. From the kitchen, you could enter the deck, which overlooked a huge pool with rock waterfalls, a fieldstone patio, and the river as the scenic backdrop. Through the kitchen was the family room, decorated in dark woods and shades of celadon. It was difficult to explain how the house, although massive, could retain a comfortable and cozy atmosphere. She absolutely loved it, although she did start to wonder who this man really was.

A light breakfast was waiting for them in the kitchen, consisting of fresh coffee, juice, and scones with real cream. This was too good to be true—he just couldn't have prepared all this himself. She was about to ask him when an elderly gentleman entered the room.

"Gina," Nick explained before she could ask, "this is William. He will tell you he is the butler in an effort to gain sympathy, but don't believe him. He is like my father, and I don't know what I would do without him."

William introduced himself with a voice bearing dignity and a touch of an English accent. "Good afternoon, Gina. It's my pleasure to meet you. I have heard much about you in the last few days. I am glad you could make it out to the country today."

"I hope you heard good things. It is very nice to meet you too. I'm glad to be here," Gina stumbled.

"William, have coffee with us," Nick invited.

"No, thank you. I have a few errands to run, and I will catch up with you later at the gate," he answered.

Gina wasn't sure what to make of his statement, but she was still in awe of the house, so she didn't pay it any further attention. William left, and Gina sensed he truly was a father figure to Nick. They fell into easy conversation, and the world around them once again disappeared. Finally, Nick looked at his watch. "Gina, we have to get moving. We need to be there before the second race."

"Why? Do you have a hot tip in the second race, Dr. DePaolo?"

"As a matter of fact, Gina, I have a *horse* in the second race," he replied.

She was confused at first, and then it hit her like a punch to the gut. "You own a horse running in the second race?"

"I didn't tell you about my horse?" he asked.

"You know full well you didn't tell me about your horse!"

"Well, I am going to tell you everything about me today, Gina. I'll start with my baby. Her name is Lucky4Me, and today is her maiden race."

"Her maiden race! For God's sake, Nick, this is a big deal! You should have told me!"

"Why? You wouldn't have had to do anything different. I am just happy to be able to share the day with you."

"I would have dressed differently or been better prepared," she said, agonizing.

"Dress differently? What? Put on a huge brim hat, dark glasses, and a flowing dress? No, Gina, you look beautiful just the way you are. I don't want you or anyone to put on airs, especially not on my account. I would be honored if you would join me for my horse's maiden race today at Monmouth Park," he said as he bowed and kissed her hand.

She considered his request, saw his excited boyish expression, and threw caution to the wind.

"I would be delighted," she said.

They went outside, and he ran to the fourth door in the garage building. He must have hit a remote button in his pocket because the door opened automatically as he approached it. Seconds later, he drove out of the garage in a navy blue Jaguar convertible. Gina laughed out loud; she could no longer hide her shock.

"It's a car. What's the problem?" he asked, feigning confusion at her response.

"Yes, Nick. It's just a car," she answered as she got in the passenger side.

The sun burst through the overcast as they headed toward Monmouth Park. He pulled up to the valet and led Gina through the turnstiles into the front entrance. Gina loved Monmouth Park. When she was young, her grandfather had taken her every Saturday after Memorial Day until the Fourth of July. He said there was nothing like a horse race on a late spring day, especially at Monmouth. Built in 1870, the park was a "showcase at the shore." It was the premier venue for thoroughbred racing, complete with manicured gardens, an English walking ring, and a three-tier clubhouse.

Gina knew Nick could have entered the park through the private entrance for owners, but she took note of his desire to go to the race just like everyone else, through the front gates. Gina realized at that moment why she liked him so much: his wealth didn't matter to him one bit. As far as he was concerned, he was just like everyone else.

"Gina, I have a parterre if you would like to stay there," he asked.

"No offense, Nick, but I don't know what the hell a parterre is!"

"I'm sorry. It is the open-air box in the clubhouse. There is one reserved for me, and I thought you might be more comfortable there. They will serve you food and drinks. I really just want to stay here at the finish line and see the winner come in close up," he explained.

"Look, Nick, I *only* know the races from the gate at the finish line. I've been pressing my face up against that fence since I was three years old. If it's just the same to you, I would like to stay here," she answered.

He beamed. His expression could not hide how much he liked her.

Gina and Nick went through to the path where people could see the horses enter the track. Lucky4Me was number five and was wearing hot-pink colors. The horse was magnificent, a dark chestnut brown with a jet-black mane and one white-tipped leg. Gina excused herself and ran to place a bet. She couldn't help herself; her grandfather had taught her well, and a race was always more exciting with a little skin in the game. She bet the horse across the board (to win, place, or show) and combined it with the number two horse for an exacta box. She picked the number two horse based on careful technical analysis: she liked its name, Nick's Surprise.

Gina believed thoroughbred racing was one of the most thrilling activities in the world—just a few short minutes of sheer excitement! Gina pictured the horses rounding the last turn, the jockeys opening up for the last furlong, each horse pushing further and faster, nostrils flaring, people screaming, the announcer's voice rising as they broke through the finish, your heart beating so fast. Even if you hated racing, you were caught up in the moment, especially if you were by the finish line. Everyone would be jumping, hugging, yelling, and cursing. It didn't matter if you won or lost; the excitement in those few seconds could not be duplicated.

This would be the first time in Gina's life she had watched a race where she knew a horse owner. Truth be told, she *loved* the owner, and the familiar butterflies returned to her stomach. William was at the finish line, and Gina now realized what he meant when he said he would see them "at the gate." William and Nick were like expectant fathers, pacing back and forth, oblivious to everything around them. The horses walked to the starting gate, and Gina could see that Lucky4Me was walking gently, unlike Nick's Surprise, which seemed to be bucking every few feet. She didn't think that was a good sign for her exacta box, but you never know until it's over. Gina, William, and Nick positioned themselves just short of the finish line, leaning directly on the chain-link fence. They didn't say a word as the race, which was short—just five furlongs—started with a pulse-quickening "and they're off!"

It was hard for Gina to watch. Usually she would watch the digital screen, which showed the horses close up with the numbers of the horses that were in the lead printed on the bottom. She was so nervous she decided to focus directly on Lucky4Me and follow the horse around the track, ignoring the commentator and the visuals. She came around the bend and was behind at least four horses until they hit the straightaway. She shot out at top speed and pushed passed the pack, gaining speed and moving a nose out in front. Gina screamed when Lucky4Me crossed the line a full length ahead of the rest of the pack. She had no idea which horse came in second, but they were all yelling and screaming when Nick picked her up and swung her into the air. It would be impossible to forget the moment for as long as she lived.

Nick dragged both Gina and William with him into the winner's circle, ignoring their protests. They posed for what seemed like a dozen pictures, and then the jockey wanted to walk the horse. Nick hugged Lucky4Me's neck and planted a huge kiss on her face. The horse whinnied as if to answer his display of affection and then trotted off with her rider.

They all went to dinner together to celebrate. William tried to wiggle his way out of it, but Nick wouldn't hear of it. It was their first big win, and he wanted them all to celebrate. Gina was pleased he made William go to dinner with them. The excitement of the day had not worn off, and it would have been terrible if William had left them. The three of them had shared something wonderful, and it was only right that they should celebrate together. Gina won one hundred dollars on the race even though she didn't win the exacta, as the number two horse, Nick's Surprise, finished fourth. Lucky4Me had gone off as a little bit of a long shot, offering a very good payout and adding to the excitement of the day.

They decided on Italian and went to Buena Sera in Red Bank, which had become something of a landmark. It was a two-story restaurant with an open ceiling from the first floor to a loft-style second floor. The restaurant had been considered very kitschy at the turn of the century, with antiquities covering its brick walls, and diners would wait well over two hours on weekends to secure a table. The food was excellent, and the atmosphere was very casual. The restaurant was open with a high ceiling and tended to be noisy. The sheer volume allowed for a level of privacy during a dinner discussion without making you feel like you had to whisper. The three of them relived the events of the day and enjoyed a very pleasant meal. Between them, they enjoyed two full bottles of wine.

Their effects were beginning to show, as they all seemed a little giddy.

When they returned to the house, William excused himself to go to bed.

"It was lovely to meet you, my dear. Please visit us again soon," he said as he kissed her hand before retiring.

"It was great to meet you, too. Thanks so much, William, for allowing me to share such a special day with you two."

"Don't be ridiculous; the pleasure was truly all mine."

Gina and Nick decided to have another glass of wine on the patio. The river was beautiful, especially at night, and Gina could feel the quiet. It was more than just the absence of noise; it was as if the thick quiet of the night wrapped itself around her like a protective blanket.

They were looking out at the water when Gina finally asked, "Tell me, Dr. DePaolo. How does an extremely handsome, very wealthy, incredibly nice guy manage to stay single until forty in this day and age?"

He stared at her intently and figured he might as well get it over with. "I wasn't always single."

Once again Gina realized she had been shocked into silence. "I'm sorry. I didn't know. What happened?"

There was another brief silence, and then he continued. "She died."

That was it. The night was starting to twirl around her, out of control. She didn't know how to proceed, and the wine had erased any grace she might have possessed to handle the discussion. "Nick, I … I don't know what to say. When? What happened?"

"It was a long time ago, and I usually don't discuss it. In fact, I haven't talked about it in a really long time. I want to tell you … no, I *need* to tell you about it. I love being with you, Gina, and I want you to know all about me. I don't want there to be any surprises."

Gina wasn't sure where he was going with all this. Why would his past represent a problem for her? Before she could ask any questions, he continued.

"We were in college. She was in acting and I was pre-med. Her name was Stephanie, and we were wildly in love. She was a total free spirit and made me laugh all the time. We married while we were still in school and lived in a small studio in Gramercy Park. We were poor, but we were working on our careers and were totally in love. I thought I would be with her for the rest of my life. To this day, I am not completely sure what happened. Well, I know what happened; I just don't know why. You see, she died at home with me. I didn't know there was anything wrong until it was too late. I had come home from school, and she was lying down. She had not been feeling well, and I just figured she was resting. I went in to see her, and she looked very pale. As I sat next to her on the bed and held her hand, I realized she was very cold—too cold."

Nick's eyes were focused on a scene from the past, his face paled and his tone was one of genuine heartbreak.

"She looked at me and squeezed my hand so she had my full attention. I asked her what was wrong, and she didn't answer. I started to panic, but she squeezed my hand harder and pulled my ear to her lips. She asked me in a whisper to forgive her. I didn't know what she was talking about until I pulled back the covers. She was lying in a pool of blood. I knew I had to move quickly. I called 911, packed her with towels, and begged her to hold on. I pleaded with her, kissed her, held her, and ultimately, when I knew it was too late and she was slipping away, I forgave her. It was her dying wish, and I granted it. The ambulance arrived a minute later."

Gina was crying. She could not help herself. He was talking to the night, as if he was there alone. Gina was hypnotized by his words and devastated by his story. She could not speak. She simply held his hand.

"I'm not finished. Gina, she was pregnant, and she had an illegal abortion. She never told me she was pregnant. She knew I would have been happy and would have wanted the baby. That's why she didn't tell me. She didn't want the baby. I don't know if it was because we were young, or because we didn't have money, or if she thought it would have ruined her career. I don't know what her reasons were. I don't even know if it was my child. I had so many unanswered questions. I was devastated. I didn't want to get close to anyone ever again. I had strong emotions that needed closure, that needed to be resolved, and I knew they never would be. I plunged myself into my studies, and then my work. My grandmother made me come and live with her on weekends and helped me through the whole thing. She told me I would meet someone I loved as much as Stephanie one day. She made me focus on being a doctor, on building a career, and on creating a new life. That's why I have all *this*!"

Nick gestured with his free hand, waving toward the vast expanse that was his home. "I built and collected these things as a means of escape from my past. Gina, I love you. You are the first woman I have fallen in love with since my Stephanie. It's because of this that I need you to know everything. Gina, I wish Stephanie had told me she was pregnant, I wish I could have talked her into having a baby, I wish I had been more careful, but what I wish more than anything else in this world is that abortion were legal. If it were, she would not have died. I know she viewed her death as punishment for her actions. Otherwise, she would have sought help as soon as she knew something had gone wrong. I will never forgive myself, and I will never change my mind. You need to know how I feel, especially because of your career. If I am afforded the chance, I will work to legalize abortion."

He finally finished, but he didn't look at Gina. He stared out at the water as if it—their young romance—was over. He thought she would run now that she knew the whole story. Moreover, he thought she would leave because of his convictions. Knowing it might ruin his chances with her, he still had laid his soul at her feet.

Gina wished she was not feeling so tipsy. She wished she could form a coherent sentence reflecting her feelings, but she couldn't. She knew he was taking her silence as the worst possible scenario. She finally found some words.

"Nick, I love my grandmother, and she feels like you feel. I respect your position; I really do. I cannot imagine the pain you must have experienced. I see it firsthand all the time, and I know the devastation. I wish I could erase it for you, but I can't. I will tell you that it does not affect our relationship or us. Stephanie will always be a great love of your life, but I would be grateful to share a piece of your heart. As far as who I am ...I do a job that I believe in, but I do not condemn others for their beliefs."

Gina couldn't take it anymore. She stood up, pulled him to his feet, and held him with all her might. She pulled slightly back, searched his eyes, and gently kissed his face. He overwhelmed her. She wished she could stay in his arms in that place forever. Finally, Gina understood what all the fuss was about: being in love *is* awesome.

That is, until your cell phone rings.

Chapter 17

PATTI Darby was out of her coma, and Gina needed to get to the hospital. Patti was coherent and asking to speak with the cops. Gina couldn't wait until morning, so Nick made her a strong pot of coffee. She wished she had not drunk the second bottle of wine, but it was too late for that now. She was already sobering up but realized she was tired more than anything else. He asked her about the case, but she skirted his questions. She didn't want to discuss her work with him. She needed to keep him separate from that world, even though it was an unrealistic desire. She promised she would call him on Sunday and headed out. Rumson Road was harder to navigate in the dark, so she had to drive slowly until she hit the main roads. Once she was on the parkway, she was home free. There was not a lot of volume at 2:00 a.m. on a Saturday night.

The coffee made her feel much better, and as she drew closer to the city, her anticipation grew. This was exactly what she was hoping for. Patti Darby could tie everything together. Now Patti was awake and *wanted* to cooperate; she wanted to talk to the cops. As Gina drove away from New Jersey, the day started to become a distant, fuzzy memory, while the prospect of interviewing Patti Darby crystallized. Her senses sharpened as she mentally reviewed her line of questioning. This was what she needed, and she could barely contain herself until she arrived at the hospital.

The staff was expecting her, and before they allowed her to see Patti, they insisted on adhering to certain procedures. She would have to be gentle, she would have to wait for Patti to respond because her responses would be sluggish, she could not fire multiple questions, and she could question her for only fifteen minutes. They wanted to give her a chance to adapt to her new consciousness and did not want to risk any unnecessary stress. Gina knew the rules, which was why she needed to choose her questions carefully. She already knew the three questions she wanted to ask, but she didn't want to seem too aggressive. It had been two hours since Patti awoke from her coma, and although her speech was sluggish, she was capable of talking. They originally had wanted to wait until morning to contact the authorities, but Patti had requested to speak with the cops. Gina thanked them and entered the room as the nurse took her position just outside the entry.

Patti looked up at Gina and motioned for her to come close. Gina sat in the chair next to the bed about three feet from Patti's face. She leaned in so Patti could speak into her ear.

"Immunity …," she croaked.

"Yes, Patti, you have complete immunity if you tell me who did this," Gina confirmed for her.

Patti continued. "Horrible man. I will give you the address. Get paper."

Gina pulled out her notebook and handed it to Patti with her pen. Patti scribbled the address from memory without hesitation.

"Behind the green door. Go behind the green door. Many more in there. Please save them," she pleaded.

Gina was confused. She thought for sure Patti would tell her about two guys, not one doctor. Her mind started to race. What if they were not linked? What if the prior operation and arrest had nothing to do with Patti's case? Gina had thought for sure this would all go together.

Gina spoke slowly, "Patti, are you sure there was only one doctor?"

"Yes."

"Did he have an assistant?"

"Yes."

That was better; an assistant plus the doctor could equal to the two men they had arrested.

"A young girl," Patti whispered.

"I'm sorry. Did you say there was a young girl?" Gina questioned.

"Assistant is young girl," Patti answered.

"The assistant is a girl?" Gina asked.

"Yes."

This was starting to sound as if it was totally unrelated, and Gina was starting to panic.

Gina needed time to think and check out the address Patti had given her. If it was unrelated, she needed to get busy finding this guy. She had just two more questions, and she would be on her way.

"Patti, describe the doctor," Gina commanded more than asked.

"Heavy, white, black curly hair, dirty," she whispered.

This was definitely not Tony Arabia or Joe Primak. Gina was about to retrieve the photos when Patti asked, "My boys?"

Gina stopped dead and decided to slow things down and bring Patti up to date. "Patti, your boys are fine. Ginny Lui has been incredible. She is so worried about you and the boys. She is a wonderful friend. I will call her myself tonight. I am sure she will bring you the boys in the morning. Michael, your baby, he misses you the most."

Patti smiled and started to cry. Gina took Patti's hand. "I know what happened to you. You cannot take a chance like this again. Your boys need you. When this is over, you are going to promise me you will let me take care of your ex-husband."

Patti just nodded and cried. Gina opened her phone and dialed Ginny Lui.

"Ginny, it's Agent Vincent. No, no, nothing's wrong. I am sorry to call so late, but I have someone who needs to speak to you."

Gina held the phone up to Patti's ear so she could talk. "Ginny, it's me, Patti."

Gina took the phone back. "Ginny, it's Agent Vincent again. She is awake but very weak. She can't really talk on the phone. If you could take the boys up to see her in the morning, I think it will do them all a world of good."

Just as Gina was hanging up with Ginny, she asked Patti her last question.

"Patti, how did you find the doctor?"

"Clinic. Two guys. Blue Buick."

That was it. She had it. Patti linked them all together, and Gina was ecstatic. She retrieved the digital photos of Joe Primak and Tony Arabia from her phone. Patti positively identified them as the two men she had met at the clinic. It was all starting to fall into place. She still had some things that just didn't add up, but she was right there at the end. She had the feeling, the feeling you get when you know you are about to make solitaire or solve a puzzle: all the pieces are not quite in place, but you know you're going to solve it, and you just have to play it out. She needed to get to John Winthrop, but it was nearly 4:00 a.m. She weighed her options and decided to call. There was too much riding on this case for them to lose any time. If John wanted to, he could bring them back in for questioning, and he would have a better chance of finding them at home in the middle of the night.

She called his cell and waited. She got his voice mail, hung up, and dialed the cell again. She knew he would hear it. She just had to give him enough rings to respond. On the third call he answered, "Winthrop here."

"John, it's Gina. I need you. Patti Darby woke up, and she made our guys." Gina said.

Gina knew it was not registering for him yet. It would take a few minutes before he was awake and coherent. "John, wash your face, and call me back."

Within three minutes, her cell phone rang. "Hello."

"It's John. What's going on?"

"Patti Darby is out of her coma. She gave me the address of the so-called doctor who performed her termination. She also identified our guys as the men who gave her the doctor's address. She met them outside the clinic."

"So a different guy performed her procedure?" he asked.

"Looks that way. I was confused at first also. I thought we were completely off track until I asked her how she found the doctor. If this doctor has a large operation, it could be his money backing the defense of those two. It makes more sense as I think about it. What do you want to do?" she asked.

"I think I'm going to bring Mr. Primak and Mr. Arabia in tonight. This information should allow me a better interrogation than the last one. In the meantime, I will put Ben and Sally at the address of the doctor to see what they find. Gina, this is good. It's what we needed."

"I know. I will call you in the morning, John. I really need to get a few hours' sleep."

June 28, 2021

Al Benazir Elected to the Highest Court

The U.S. Senate has elected Al Benazir to the Supreme Court of
the United States of America. The Senate Judiciary Committee
approved his nomination by President Lehman last week and sent
it to the floor for a final vote today. The Senate approved the
nomination with a two-thirds majority. Associate Justice Benazir
will fill the seat vacated by the passing of Associate Justice Thomas
Chesterfield. Al Benazir is currently a justice on the Supreme
Court of the State of New York.

Chapter 18

IT was finally happening. After many false starts, this had to be it: the change. She was only fifty years old, but she was ready for it, actually looking forward to getting it over with. It was still a little early, but the way she was feeling, this was definitely *it*. She was hot all the time with bouts of nausea that came on suddenly without warning. Now here she was at her scheduled appointment, patiently waiting for the receptionist to call her name. She studied the expectant mothers in the waiting room. She daydreamed about the time when she had been one of them. When she was pregnant, the closer she came to her due date, the more often she found herself in the waiting room, wondering why she needed to come every week. They only weighed her and announced, "Any day now, Marina," which wasn't exactly news to her. Nonetheless, she smiled, remembering each of her four pregnancies, which had begun nearly thirty years earlier. When she had the fourth, her baby Vincent, she didn't think it was necessary to visit at all—she was updating *them* on her progress. She went to each visit anyway, anticipating the birth and the joy that accompanied each arrival. She wasn't sad it was over for her; she had a new baby granddaughter and another grandchild on the way. It was so true: the only thing better than being a parent was being a grandparent—all the fun and minimal work!

They called her name, and she proceeded to follow the nurse to the examination room. She was given the customary drill: remove your garments, urinate in the cup, wrap the lavender paper robe around you, and sit on the table. The procedure had changed very

167

little over the thirty-five years she had been visiting the office. Her original doctor had retired, but she was perfectly content with any partner who took his place. She went only once a year and didn't see the need for "interviewing" the new doctor; her baby-bearing days were over, and she believed anybody could do a Pap smear.

A young male doctor in his thirties entered the room and quickly paged through her file, which was loaded on the wall screen. Marina thought back to the paper file days and tried to figure out the last time she had seen one. It had to be over twenty years.

"So what brings you to us today? You're not ready for your annual checkup," he said, breaking her out of her file-folder reverie.

Marina stared at him blankly. This would be the third time she was answering the question—once for the receptionist, once for the nurse, and now for him.

"It's quite simple, doctor. I am going through menopause. I am constantly hot. I have dizzy spells. I go through fits of perspiring. I am nauseous a lot during the day. I just want to know what I should do to minimize the symptoms, and I will be on my way."

He reviewed her file, read the notes, tested her urine (for what, she did not know), and was noticeably quiet. Marina was accustomed to the usual banal chitchat that was associated with these visits and was mildly disturbed at his silence. He asked her a few questions about the lack of her period, the first date of her last period (she never understood the women who knew the answer to this question—she hadn't a clue), her last sexual intercourse, and another review of her symptoms. He took a quick blood sample with a penlike device that drew a few drops of blood into a chamber. He said he needed to run a few quick screens and would return in a few minutes.

She found the whole scene very odd indeed. She started to think he might have found something wrong, something he did not like, and she began to worry. Cancer, while more manageable than it once was, remained a serious threat and a leading cause of death. Just as her mind really started to run away, he entered the room.

"I have some news for you," he announced.

She was starting to wonder about him. His communication skills surely left something to be desired.

"Yes, doctor?" she asked as she leaned forward to get a closer look at his face.

"You are not entering menopause. You are pregnant," he announced with the same tone you would use for a hangnail.

"I beg your pardon—"

"Yes, you are pregnant. The urine test was positive, and the blood test confirmed it. From the information you have given me, I estimate you to be seven weeks," he reaffirmed.

"Doctor, that's absurd! I couldn't possibly be. Surely you must run the test again."

"I will run the test again, but I assure you, the blood test is very accurate."

"Please, run the test again," she pleaded.

Marina started to panic. She couldn't be pregnant. It was completely absurd! She was a grandmother, and her husband was nearing sixty! They were approaching their retirement years and senior citizen status. Surely this was a mistake. She could not have a baby, not at this age! She would be mortified. How would she explain it to any of them? How would she tell her husband?

He dutifully ran the test a second time and left her once again. He returned to the room and nodded a confirmation. "It's positive."

She was in a fog as she left the office. Her life seemed to be on mute, where she didn't hear any sounds around her, only the pounding of her heart. Her mind raced. Was it possible? She realized it *was* possible from a timing standpoint. They did make love. It wasn't a frequent occurrence, but they did have a nice interlude a few weeks prior. Her cheeks blushed hotly as the scene played in her mind. No, this was not possible. Just not possible!

Her hair appointment was at one o'clock, and she didn't know if she should cancel or not. She had absolutely no idea what she was going to do. Stephan had been doing her hair for twenty years; he knew her inside and out. If ever there was a person she could tell, Stephan was that person. She decided to keep her appointment. Leo, her driver, was waiting patiently outside for her. The one luxury she thoroughly enjoyed as a result of their success was her driver. He would escort her through all her errands, wait on crowded streets, and drive in circles until she returned. She loved Leo, and she hoped he wouldn't sense there was anything wrong.

Leo dropped her at the salon and dutifully waited in the lot. Marina wasn't in the chair thirty seconds before Stephan insisted she tell him what was wrong.

"Marina, my love, what is the matter? You look dreadful."

"Oh, Stephan, I don't even know how to say it."

"What? You know there is nothing you can't tell Stephan!" he exclaimed.

Marina looked up at him as the tears spilled down her cheeks. Stephan, shocked by Marina's emotion, immediately whisked her off to the coffee room and shut the door.

"Marina, please, all kidding aside, what is the matter?"

"Stephan, I'm pregnant." She choked on her words as sobs shook her small frame. "Stephan, I am a grandmother, with another on the way. This can't be possible!"

"Oh, there, there … Marina, please don't cry," he pleaded.

"No, Stephan. There is no way I can have this baby! I don't even want to tell him. I don't want anyone to know. It's not natural. I am old. I should not be pregnant!"

"Marina, please. We can take care of this. I know where you can go," he said.

She stopped crying and looked at him. "What do you mean?" she asked.

"I mean I know where you can go to terminate. I can call right now. I am sure they will take you."

"That's illegal. You know it's illegal," she warned, her red-rimmed eyes widening as she suddenly sobered.

"Marina, there, there. These things are taken care of more than you think," he explained.

"No, Stephan. I can't."

"Marina, it's completely up to you. If you want, I can call right now. Lisa can drive you over without your driver even knowing. It should only take a few hours."

"You mean go right now?"

"I don't see why not. You would need to pay, but I can give you the cash. It will be expensive, but I know they will take you quickly without a word. No names, no history, no records."

She stopped crying as the thoughts raced through her mind, calculating the possibility, dismissing the notion, reentering the option, weighing the pros and cons, and finally reaching a conclusion. "Stephan, make the arrangements."

Stephan made a few telephone calls, spoke with his assistant, Lisa, and instructed Marina to call Leo to tell him she would be longer than planned. They would take her immediately and have her back within two hours. It would cost five thousand dollars, but it would be over before she returned home for dinner. Stephan counted the cash from his safe and gave it to her in an envelope. Marina was one of his wealthiest clients. He didn't hesitate to lend her the money.

Marina was too stunned to be afraid. She never thought she would ever have to do this! She never had understood the women who did. Now she was one of them, and she felt guilty for the silent judgments she had dispensed so easily when the practice was legal. She remained focused on eliminating her problem. Now was not the time for a moral debate. She was at high risk for a miscarriage due to her age, which would provide her a convenient explanation for her misfortune should she need one. Lisa led Marina out the back door and drove ten minutes to the downtown section. It was a nondescript building, and Marina entered alone. Lisa would wait in the car until Marina was finished.

As she entered, the building seemed vacant, a warehouse of some sort. She tentatively walked through the long, narrow hall to a single green door. She knocked, and the door opened by itself. A young woman briskly walked toward her asking if the hairdresser had sent her. Marina nodded affirmatively but did not speak. She was too shocked to speak—the building was horrendous, and the girl looked more like a call girl than a doctor's assistant. The girl insisted on payment and grabbed the envelope from Marina's hand. The girl took Marina to the changing room where Marina could undress. There were plastic laundry baskets lining a wall. Marina neatly folded her Armani suit and silk shirt as she placed her garments in the basket. She pulled on a cloth gown, the old-style hospital garb used before "paper wear" became the rage. From the thinness of the cotton and the holes worn into the fabric, she assumed the garment must have been from the last century.

Marina consciously chose to ignore her surroundings. She knew she risked running screaming from the building the moment she let her mind accept what she was doing. She pushed all thought from her mind except one: *it will be over soon*. She would grin and bear it, as they say. No need to be a baby. Buck up, and take it like a man. Right, like a man would be able to take any of this! A part of Marina's brain actually laughed at the thought.

The nasty girl returned and asked Marina to follow her to what Marina would loosely describe as the "operating room." As she sat on the table, she realized it was the same style doctor's table with stirrups that she had been on earlier that day. She sat on the table, tightly wringing her hands in her lap, hoping it would be over soon. She wasn't really paying attention to the girl, who was rattling on about procedures, Tylenol, heavy flow, and so on. The girl's voice was background noise, nothing important or necessary, just noise. Marina just stared at her, as one would look at a bug in a jar.

He entered the room, and she refused to look at his face. She knew if she made eye contact, she would crack. *Pull into yourself tighter*, she commanded, as if the inner voice was in control, willing her to follow directions, to detach, and to let the situation proceed on its own.

She never lost consciousness. Yet when it was over, she couldn't completely remember being there. She successfully removed her mind from the physical activity. She vaguely remembered the girl announcing she could go. The girl asked if she needed help, but Marina ignored the question. She changed slowly, on autopilot, without any active thought. As she exited the building, the normal sounds of life roared back into her head. She could hear cars beeping, children playing, and radios blaring. She saw Lisa parked across the street and walked quickly to the car. She slid into the backseat and said, "Let's go."

Lisa helped Marina into the salon through the back door. Stephan had been anxiously waiting for her return and immediately began to fawn about her. She pushed him aside and sat in the chair.

"I just feel a little weak. Could you be a dear and fix my hair, and add a little color to this face?" she asked.

"I will have you good as new! See, all your problems are gone. Home to rest, and tomorrow it will be as if it never happened" he exclaimed as he began to work on her hair while Lisa worked on her makeup.

Less than three hours had passed when she returned to Leo and the car. She felt horrible and couldn't wait to get home.

"Leo, I'm not feeling well. Would you be a dear and just take me home?"

"Sure, we'll be there in no time," he replied.

As she sat in the back of the car and stared out the window, she began to think about her life, how fortunate she was—a great husband, beautiful children, grandchildren, success and prosperity. The American Dream. She remembered her own humble beginnings—apartment living with her parents and grandparents to make ends meet. She remembered her First Holy Communion. *What an odd thought to have.* Her grandmother was so proud of her, crying as she walked up the aisle to the altar. Her mother had made her dress, and while it was not as fancy as the store-bought, it was beautiful just the same. She thought of her wedding, how she loved her husband and was so grateful she had him. She was always afraid she would wake up and discover her perfect life was just a dream. But it never happened; her life was real! She had met and married the love of her life. She remembered the first house they bought. They were the first generation to "own" a home.

As her thoughts floated, she was comforted. What a wonderful life she led. God was truly good to her.

"Leo, I am just going to rest my eyes."

She would never open them again.

Chapter 19

JOHN Winthrop could not believe his luck. As soon as he mentioned the address, the blood drained out of their faces. He had them. He knew the feeling well. Their arrogance gone, he saw them squirm. Just like in poker, they blinked, and he would take them down. They were carrying on about their lawyer, justice, and rights, and he let them rant. He wanted their lawyer to come in. He would confirm for them what they already surmised: he had them, and they would have to deal.

He left them in the interrogation room as he grabbed a coffee and stood in the observation room. He could see them through the glass as he watched them argue. Primak, the weaker one, was carrying on like a schoolchild, pacing and looking expectantly at the other. Arabia was dark and silent, choosing to stew as he churned his options in his mind. Winthrop considered separating them but decided against it. Primak would crack at the sight of him; Arabia would be unaffected. Arabia had been running the show; that is, until now, when Winthrop was sitting squarely in the driver's seat—the only place he liked to be.

He was enjoying his coffee when Sally radioed in.

"Ben and I are at the site. Vacant one-story warehouse. No sign of external activity."

"Take your time. Sit outside and watch. Don't go in. Try to be inconspicuous. I'll have something soon. They're waiting for their lawyer," John instructed.

"You got it. We'll call in if we see anything interesting," Sally replied.

Robyn Dendrite bounded in, and John had to fight back the smile threatening to break his stone façade.

"What is it now, Winthrop? We've been through this. Unless you have something, I want them released immediately. This is harassment, and you know it!" she sniped.

"Patti Darby positively identified them. She is out of her coma and is quite able to testify," he drawled, slowly enough to let the impact hit her, enjoying the range of emotions he would see cross her face: shock, outrage, practiced indifference.

"Patti Darby is hardly reliable. She is just out of a coma, and I am sure she was more than a willing participant. Let me guess: you granted immunity."

"We did, but we didn't have to. She actually called us to the hospital. Not that it makes much difference. She gave us the address."

"What address?"

"The address of the illegal clinic they bring young pregnant women to, the clinic that terminates the pregnancies of those young women. Last I checked, that's a federal offense in this country."

"Let's just slow down a second. Did Patti Darby tell you my clients performed her abortion?"

"No. Patti Darby told us that your clients lured her to the doctor who actually performed the abortion."

"Well, now, that is very different than the original charges. How big do you think the operation is?" she asked, feigning indifference, as if he didn't know what she was getting at.

"We think it is a very large operation that your clients are very familiar with. If they are willing to share what they know, *and* I think it is worthwhile information, the original charges could be modified."

"Modified, my ass, John. I'll talk to them, and if it's as significant as you are suggesting, I think we'll need a dismissal."

"Go talk to them. See what they have to say. We'll talk about it then."

"How about you give us a little privacy?" she asked.

"I don't think so. You talk to them. I may watch, but I won't listen," he baited.

She didn't bite. She stepped into the interrogation room, faced them away from the mirror, and began to gather her ammunition.

John loved it when he didn't have to do a thing. Like for a maestro, it was just orchestration, and he was the master.

Twenty minutes later, she joined Winthrop in the kitchen of the precinct. He was pouring coffee from a freshly brewed pot, waiting for her to speak.

"Can I get a cup of that?" she asked.

"Sure thing. How'd it go?"

"I think you will want to work something out. I have some things that should be of interest."

He wouldn't rush it, wouldn't press her. He could take his time and play all day. He was a very patient man. "Really? How about you tell me what you have, and let me be the judge?"

"John, you are not the judge, but I've had enough of the games. He is a doctor, and he pays them for each girl they bring to him. They rotate clinics and just stand outside. The girls seek them out more often than not. They just give out a card with the address on it—that's all."

"Why did they move to perform Gina's procedure? There was no third party in sight."

"They siphoned Gina because they knew what she was willing to pay. They were tired of being paid nothing while he made big cash. When Gina agreed to pay twenty-five hundred, they decided they wanted the money for themselves. It was the first time they tried it," she explained.

"Yeah. Okay, spare me the bullshit! They decided on *that* day to perform a medical procedure they knew nothing about because they wanted the money?"

"John, whether they did it before or not doesn't matter. Think of the bigger picture here. They can give you this guy, and they are willing to do it. They estimate that as many as twenty procedures are performed on busy days."

"How would they know that?"

"They give out the cards and stop at the clinic to see the activity. They definitely don't trust the guy. He is an ex-doctor but makes more money than he ever did when he was legit."

"What does he pay them?" Winthrop asked.

"He pays Arabia a couple hundred dollars. Apparently Arabia keeps Primak working for peanuts."

"Great guys! Sounds like a real team," he quipped.

"What about Ashley Rydell? She didn't go to the address. She was at an abandoned tenement a few blocks away. Did they siphon her? Are they responsible?"

"They know absolutely nothing about Rydell. They say they never saw her, never gave her a card, and that the doctor only performed procedures at the warehouse. He never went anywhere else to their knowledge."

"Smells like bullshit to me. This whole operation has something to do with the Rydell girl. I'm sure of it."

"John, be reasonable. They don't know anything about Ashley Rydell. Even if they did, her own family doesn't want to solve the case. I am not sure the country wants us to solve the case. Leave well enough alone. Let's convict this guy, shut the operation down, and leave the Rydell case as a miscarriage."

He knew she was right. The family didn't want the case solved, so why should he? It wouldn't bring her back. Nothing could bring Ashley back. This would only add to their pain and embarrassment. It still infuriated him. She was so young and beautiful, with a promising life ahead of her. Ended, for what? He wanted to punish someone. He wanted someone to pay.

"Talk to Gina. I know she will agree. Go for the big fish, John."

"Fine, but I'm keeping these two until I bring the other one in. Any problem with that?"

"No, John. Just bring him in quick so I can get them out of here."

"By the way, exactly who is paying your bill?"

"Arabia is paying me. Why do you ask?"

"No reason."

She was good. He had to give her that. Truth was he liked working with Robyn Dendrite. He knew if he did his job correctly, she would recognize it and proceed accordingly. He also knew that if she smelled even a whiff of bullshit, she would fight to the death for her client. He had to appreciate excellence, even if it was on the opposing team.

He radioed Sally. "Come on back, and get the team. We need to set up surveillance. It's official: one ex-doctor and a fairly large abortion establishment."

"Do we have a name?"

"Yep. By the time you get here, we'll have the briefs prepared. I'm calling Gina now."

"Good going, boss. We'll see ya soon."

He would take this surveillance operation very slowly. This wasn't a hunch; this was the real thing. There was no room for mistakes of any kind. He would be bringing this guy in and putting him away. Just twenty-four hours before, it had looked like the whole case was dead. Now, one lucky break and the whole show came crumbling down. That's what it always came down to: a lucky break.

"Gina, it's John," he yelled into the cell phone.

"How did we make out?"

"I'd say we did pretty well. They turned on the guy to save their skin. Apparently they just give out business cards, and the evil doctor does all the murdering."

"Is that right? What was their explanation for me?" she asked.

"Oh, you're gonna love this—you were a test for them. They were tired of getting paid peanuts by the doctor, so they were taking your cash for themselves. They claim they'd never even tried it before."

"That's such bullshit!" Gina hissed.

"I know it, but we need to keep our focus."

"What about Ashley Rydell?"

"They don't know anything about her. Sentiment around here is to leave well enough alone."

"What do you mean, 'well enough'?"

"Gina, the Rydell family doesn't want it solved. Dendrite says we should look at the big picture and figure out what good we would be doing if we pushed the Rydell issue. She said you would understand."

"I do understand her point, John, but I can't stand just letting it go."

"I hear you," he agreed.

"Still, Robyn does make a strong point. Pushing the issue would just punish Cynthia and George Rydell. Last I checked, they didn't need any more punishment."

"Well, what do you think?" John asked.

"Let's just go get the bastard."

"You got it."

Chapter 20

S HE wore taupe slacks with a light mauve sleeveless silk
sweater—understated yet striking against her tanned skin. She
stared at herself in the full-length mirror. Her body still looked
acceptable. Her skin, although weathered, added dimension to her
face. Sometimes she felt as if she were looking at a stranger. Who
is that old woman in the mirror? In her mind, she looked the
same as she did thirty years earlier. She looked at herself again.
Still tall, stately, and slender, although large-boned. Not completely
horrible, especially when compared to some of her friends, who
seemed to shrivel and shrink daily.

Green eyes. She loved her eyes. She knew they were expressive.
As a young girl, she would talk on the phone and look in the
mirror as she watched her eyes light with laughter, burn with anger,
melt with sadness, and dance with clarity. The world could see her
emotions simply by looking at her eyes. She hoped they would look
at her today and sense her passion, her commitment. She prayed
for strength, but the fear was present. When the stakes were high,
the fear was always present. She had learned to welcome it. The fear
was a good sign; it always meant she was on the right path.

She twisted her pearls as her mind performed the calculation
for the millionth time. Summer was coming, which always made
her run through the exercise more often. Late June. The child
would be sixty at the end of June. That is, had the child been
born. Seventeen and frightened for her life, she had aborted within
eight weeks. Those were the days when your own doctor could help
you, the days before a complacent society too busy watching reality

TV had allowed a conservative administration to eliminate their choice. A country founded on the premise of freedom had allowed a political party to levy *their* ideals, *their* religious beliefs, and *their* practices on the entire population.

She didn't regret her decision to abort. No, her great regret was getting pregnant in the first place. Never would she forgive herself. She had made a deal with God that she would atone for her sin. She would help others avoid the mistake. She would educate and support but never judge. It was the least she could do. So stupid! She was just so stupid! If only she could do it all over again.

She had thought she was in love. He was ten years older, and they had an easy relationship. They were companions. He tried to leave her once, and she panicked. He was her best option for marriage, and she just didn't want to lose him. After all, they didn't give you a "love" handbook. Was there really was such a thing as breathtaking, heart-stopping, true love? He wanted to have sex and promised her that he would take care of everything. She thought it was her duty. How else would she keep him? Such a fool she was! She believed him. How naive! He promised her safety, all so he could have sex. Never would she forgive her stupidity.

She had discovered her problem shortly after Thanksgiving while putting up the Christmas tree. She went to place a ball near the top and nearly threw up on the tree. Losing her balance, she fell off the step stool and needed to sit on the couch to regain her balance. Something was definitely wrong. She didn't have a gynecologist, mostly because nobody had told her she needed one. Hell, she never knew how a woman got pregnant in the first place! Sure, she knew you had sex, but she had no idea how human reproduction took place. The discussion in health class lasted all of thirty minutes and left her with more questions than answers. People did not talk about sex or sexuality in school and never, *ever* did they talk about it at home.

A friend sent her to an OB/GYN not far from her neighborhood. She loved him immediately. Even though she was crying in the office, he understood, and he did not judge her. He counseled her, reviewed her options, and explained the procedure. He made her think about it for three days to make sure she really wanted to go through with it. The laws at the time did not allow him to perform the procedure in the hospital. Although legal, it was not widely accepted, and they had to go to a special clinic.

Having been given three days to change her mind, she still moved forward. How could she have a baby when she was still her mother's baby? No, she could not take care of a child. It just was not possible.

The procedure turned out to be simple enough, and with the exception of some slight cramping, she felt like herself after only two days. Her doctor saw her one week after the procedure to perform a physical follow-up as well as a training session. He taught her about reproduction using medical models. He told her how her period and ovulation affected her timing and her ability to conceive. He explained to her every contraceptive device that was available and made her select one. If she followed the directions, this would never happen to her again.

Given the same circumstances, she would make the same decision today. Her true regret, her true burden, was the pregnancy. The guilt, like a birthmark, was always there, sometimes not noticed but always present. Why hadn't she known any of the things the doctor taught her? Why didn't her mother tell her? She knew the answer: nobody ever told her mother. It was ignorance passed from generation to generation.

She would remember her unborn child until the day she died. If she helped just one person avoid an unwanted pregnancy, then her entire effort was worthwhile. Avoid the pregnancy. It was the only answer. It was so simple yet was never considered. It made her furious when she thought about it. It was totally absurd—a society that allowed medical coverage for Viagra but not birth control! A government that would protect and care for fertilized eggs in a dish while real children starved on the streets. Ridiculous! Yet an entire nation allowed it to happen.

No more. Today she would make a difference. It was time to stop the calculation. The child would be sixty had there been a birth. There had been no birth, so there was nothing to count. Nothing at all. No child. No birthday. No point to the whole damned exercise. It was time to move on. She glanced in the mirror one last time. Sophia was finally ready.

Chapter 21

EVERYTHING was falling into place. The masses were once again complacent. They were just as clueless as when *Roe v. Wade* was overturned in the first place. It was a society more interested in reality television than in their own social issues. The majority didn't even register to vote. Imagine that! It was a right paid for with the lives of their ancestors, and they didn't even bother to register. Of those that bothered, less than half actually showed up to cast a ballot.

Had the masses paid attention, if the media were responsible in their reporting, they would have seen the overturn coming. A depressed economy, continued war in the Middle East, third-world nuclear issues, and the constant struggle for fuel had shifted the general political focus from the progress of the pro-life platform to world issues. When *Roe v. Wade* was overturned, the majority was shocked, but it was too late. They had no one to blame but themselves. Ignorance. Most Americans didn't even know the role the Supreme Court would play in the decision, let alone who was on the Supreme Court!

Today that same complacency would bring their plan to fruition. Now that Al sat on the Supreme Court, they could plan the next phase. The event was in Red Bank at the Molly Pitcher Inn, a historic hotel and restaurant that overlooked the Navesink River. The inn was a grand hotel fashioned in the 1800s, with generous hand-crafted "window walls" overlooking the river. It was impeccably maintained yet traditional, and guests could still enjoy afternoon tea on the veranda.

Today the event would be a Chinese auction to raise money for the Scleroderma Research Foundation. Sophia was very deliberate in her selections, always trying to maximize her effort. She had actively supported scleroderma research ever since her best friend was diagnosed with it nearly fifty years earlier. Sophia hated the disease. She believed it to be a truly painful existence. First, the skin begins to harden. Once the skin feels like rock, the disease progresses to the organs and slowly turns them to stone. During this slow progression, the human mind must accept the excruciating pain until death represents the only merciful alternative. Major strides in research over the last decade offered the ability to curtail the progression, but a cure remained elusive. Sophia was looking forward to a successful fundraiser, followed by the more important after-event meeting.

The sun burned brightly in the sky, painting the scene in vivid color. Although it was hot, a smooth breeze flowed off the river, fanning those on the veranda. It was a remarkable day, the type of day when the sky is so blue you know there is a God and a heaven.

Once the auction ended, the team would be meeting in a hospitality suite Sophia had booked especially for the occasion. The auction lasted two hours and raised two million dollars. Not bad for an afternoon tea. Sophia was thrilled but nervous about the meeting. She excused herself and hurried to the suite. It would take at least a half-hour for everyone to assemble. The members of the team had mastered the art of simply trickling away, completely unnoticed, in a staggered fashion until they reassembled as a group.

Nicole arrived first, lacking the patience for a day at the Jersey shore.

"Sophia, let's get this show on the road!"

"Mayor Huerta, you are the epitome of a New York minute."

"Very funny, Sophia. Let's get going."

Within minutes, Al Benazir, the newly elected U.S. Supreme Court Justice, David Chabin of the Florida Supreme Court, and Senators Domenic Dispenza of New York, Gerard Schuman of

Pennsylvania, and Anita Hyde of New Jersey were all talking excitedly as they waited for U.S. Associate Justice Jane Letterer.

Jane swept into the room. "Sorry, I couldn't get away. Joe Sorino talked my ear off while staring at himself in the mirror over my shoulder."

"You have to stay away from the mirrors! If he gets a good view of himself, you will never get away. It's an addiction. I feel bad for the poor bastard," joked Anita.

Sophia called them to order as Dr. Nick DePaolo entered the suite. "Nick, we're so glad to see you. Everyone, let's give Nick a warm welcome," Sophia announced as she started the applause.

"Thank you. Please. It is very good to see you all. In light of your recent successes, I thought this meeting would be critical," Nick explained.

"We couldn't agree more. We are very pleased you could join us."

Sophia continued, "I would like to congratulate Al on his new position as a U.S. Supreme Court justice."

Once again, the room erupted in applause. David whistled, and the crowd laughed with enthusiasm.

"It is through the efforts of everyone in this room that we are moving forward. Al's placement was critical, but it remains only a step in the journey. Today we need to decide how we plan to proceed."

Domenic responded in an effort to contain Nicole Huerta, who was visibly anxious. "We need to decide which cases in the lower courts are positioned to move up quickly. It would be best if we found a case in either New York, Florida, or Rhode Island. I know Rita couldn't be here today, but she thinks she has at least one case that would fit the profile."

"I would prefer it not be a New York case. I have had too much visibility on the issue lately," Nicole said.

Sophia interrupted. "Let's not get too far ahead of ourselves. In addition to selecting the case, or cases, we need to think beyond the overturn. It's important for us to plan for the aftereffects. We must not make the same mistake again. The real work begins once we reach the goal. Education, daycare, counseling, birth control, and medical coverage will be major issues."

"I need to know how long the process will take. Are we talking weeks, months, what?" pressed Nicole.

David responded, "If we select one or two cases today and determine we have majority control, we can push the case through. Once the case is sent to the Supreme Court, it's Al and Jane's show."

"In order to minimize public attention, we need a diversion. A juicy headline redirecting attention could accomplish what we need," Al offered.

"I have Charlie Randazzo of the *Post*. Give me something he can sink his teeth into, and he will lead the pack," Nicole promised.

"I can move gun control to the front. We have a case now where a child shot and killed his 7 year old neighbor and best friend. The parents of the dead boy are suing Florida since they still do not require a permit or registration for any firearm. The case has gained a huge following. If we can focus the nation on that ruling, it will be easier for us to proceed," David explained.

"Is there anything juicy we can give him?" Nicole pressed.

"I think Charlie will be fine with that story. He never misses an opportunity to jump on the redneck south and their inalienable right to bear arms. Charlie's a player; he will run with whatever we give him," Sophia said.

A high-pitched, cackling ring broke their attention. Sophia, startled, hesitated before rushing to pick up the receiver.

"Yes? Oh. Yes. Um, who did he say he was?" Sophia asked the caller.

"Yes, yes, send him up. Thank you." Sophia gently replaced the receiver on its cradle. She slowly turned to face the group.

"That was the front desk. Senator George Rydell is on his way up."

They all began to speak at once, and Sophia held up her hand. "Let's not panic. How would he know we were meeting?"

Jane spoke for the first time. "I told him."

Silence. "Why?" Sophia simply asked.

"He called me. He said he knew we had a plan. He truly is devastated, and I think he is a changed man. I've known him a long time, and I believe he really wants to help the cause. He sees it as atonement for Ashley. I honestly don't think he could live with himself if he didn't do something," Jane explained in a cool, calculated tone.

"This better not be a Trojan horse! We are too close," Nicole spat.

Jane made a habit of never responding to Nicole's outbursts. Sophia quickly added, "Let's just ask the senator his intention when he arrives. We don't have to share any information, but we should at least hear what he has to say."

A second later, there was a faint knock at the door. Sophia glanced at the team one last time before opening the door.

"Good afternoon, George. What brings you here?" Sophia asked.

"Thank you for receiving me, Sophia."

"Don't be silly, George. I trust you know most of the people here," Sophia drawled.

"Yes, yes. Domenic, Al, Dave, Jane," he muttered as he nodded to each of them.

He continued slowly, "I want to help you. I know what you are doing, and I believe I can help."

"Why don't you just tell us what you're proposing, Senator," Nicole hissed.

"I have a case that could be elevated to the court," he said.

Domenic immediately asked, "George, what are the details?"

"We have a case in the Illinois Supreme Court—*Planned Parenthood v. Martin*. Just prior to Ashley's death, the court ruled in favor of Martin. Planned Parenthood has appealed to the higher court. It is the perfect venue for an overturn."

"Sounds too perfect to me. What's the catch?" Nicole asked.

"No catch. Let's just say the conservative right in my state has suffered a major blow since Ashley's death. It seems Ashley was the true love of my constituents," he explained.

"Have they filed the motion to appeal?" David asked.

"Yes. They are awaiting the response. This would give you a case that is already on its way. There would be no need for manipulation. The case is being brought to the top regardless of your efforts."

"I wouldn't mind a case coming from Illinois. I am sure Chicago could benefit from the decision as much as New York," Nicole said.

"George, there is concern that you are here to misguide our efforts, that your true loyalty lies with your party and your platform," Jane said more for the group than for George. "I can appreciate that. Jake Woodward has left me. He believes I am committing political suicide and has decided not to go down with the ship. I am not running for reelection; I am trying to live with myself. I lost my child to my platform, and I cannot accept it," he explained as he stood stoically before them.

"George, we are not simply moving for an overturn. We are planning a new and better program. We don't welcome abortion any more than you do, but we strongly believe it can be eliminated through other measures," Sophia explained.

"I don't know about that, Sophia. I just know Ashley would be here with me now if it were legal," George answered as he seemed to shrink before their eyes. He was once the ever-loud and boisterous voice of the right, and it was hard to recognize the man who stood humbly before them.

It was the first time he openly admitted his daughter's cause of death, and it was hard to ignore his grief; even Nicole relented. This man was on a mission he would not abandon. Anita moved it forward. "George, welcome. We were just about to review the court's position. Jane, can you give us a rundown?"

"Al has prepared the details for you," she responded.

Al brightened at this, as he was thoroughly enjoying his new position.

"Here is the rundown of where the Supreme Court stands today. Jane, Elizabeth Gentry, Tyler Morgan, and Richard Georgalas are pro-choice. With the exception of Richard, they each voted *against* the *Roe* overturn. I spoke with Richard directly to confirm his position, and he is an avid supporter. With my inclusion, we have the five we need."

"That leaves Offin, Marollo, Steel, and Winston. What is the climate? Do they have any idea this is coming?" questioned Domenic.

"Al has done a pretty good job networking within the group. They have been wrapped up in Chesterfield's death and Al's arrival more than anything else," Jane informed the group.

Jane was very pleased with Al Benazir. Regardless of their agenda, the rest of the justices knew Al was a great addition to the U.S. Supreme Court. "Is there any chance Elizabeth or Tyler will rule against us?" Sophia asked.

"No. They are patiently waiting for a case to arrive," Al replied.

Nick didn't usually participate in the political discussion, partly because he didn't completely understand how it all worked and partly because it was boring. He understood the general intent, but the finer points were truly lost on him. He spoke for the first time since his arrival. "What is the likelihood of our success?"

Nobody answered. Silence. It looked as if many were wondering just the same thing.

"Barring the death of another justice, we will see a ruling in our favor within four months," Jane said.

"Absolutely," agreed Al.

They enjoyed a toast and a lively discussion for the next half-hour. The group found it hard to contain their excitement. This was the only setting where they could talk of their plans openly, and once they left, they would have to keep their feelings private. They were careful to minimize their public reactions to events, to avoid media coverage, and to generally keep a low profile. Amongst themselves, they could finally open up and revel in their success.

The political machine was a huge monster, and although it was difficult to push in a direction, once it started moving, it was a thrilling ride.

Nick approached Sophia. "Can I have a moment with you?"

"Sure, Nick. Let's have a drink on the veranda. It's still light out, and the vista is gorgeous."

Nick laughed. Sophia was so dramatic and full of life. They sat at a table close to the railing, enjoying an unobstructed view.

"It's good to see you, Nick. How are things?" she asked coyly.

"Ah, Sophia, I think you know how things are. I am grateful you introduced me to Gina, which is what I need to talk to you about."

"Oh. Is anything wrong?"

"No, to the contrary. I am pretty sure I love your granddaughter."

"Nick, that's wonderful!" Sophia gushed.

"No, Sophia. It's not wonderful. I can't be with her if I don't tell her—*everything*. She needs to know *all* about me." He spilled the words rapidly before he lost his nerve.

Sophia considered her response carefully. "Nick, let's not be rash. What is it that you feel Gina needs to know?"

"Look, Sophia, let's cut the crap. I need to tell her about my role, the procedures I perform. She has to know. I can't build our relationship on lies."

"Stop it! She does not need to know. She prosecutes people like you! What are you thinking?" Sophia hissed.

"Sophia, I can make her understand. I want to marry her, but I can't even consider asking her while I keep this secret from her," he pleaded.

His statement visibly shocked Sophia. She had known they were getting along well, but she hadn't expected this. She quickly recovered her position. "Fine. If you feel strongly, then you can tell her—with one condition: you do not tell her until after the ruling."

"I don't know if I can wait—"

Sophia cut him off immediately. "Bullshit, Nick! After the ruling. No exceptions. We are too close to success, and Gina is too powerful. I am pleased you two hit it off, but nothing is going to get in our way, least of all your love life."

Her response was curt, not at all what she had intended, but she was serious. There could be no compromise.

More softly, she continued, "Why do you think she needs to know? What good can come from it?"

"It is not about her; it's about me. I want her to know who I am. If she chooses to love me after she knows everything, I will be ecstatic. If not, I certainly would understand. I think she deserves to know the man she may marry."

"Gina is very strong-willed. Her job and her beliefs go hand in hand. Abortion is murder, and she makes no compromise. Are you prepared for her response?"

"No, but I don't think I have a choice."

"We always have a choice, Nick. Just wait a little while longer. In the meantime, I think you should reconsider your position. It's not necessary to share every element of your past with her," Sophia warned.

"It's more than that, Sophia. This is too big of a deal for me to keep it from her. If she stays with me after she knows, then I know she loves me as much as I love her."

Sophia was thrilled by his words, but she didn't show it. She needed to be indifferent, at least for the time being.

"Remember, Nick, we need you. You are the only safe choice for these women. Until things change, you must keep it together. Are you worried about the integrity of the operation?"

"No, Gina has no idea, which is one of the reasons I feel so guilty. In any event, the operation is safe. Angela has everything under control."

"By the way, thank you for taking care of Francesca's cousin. She is very grateful."

"Don't mention it."

Chapter 22

JOHN was pleased with their progress. Sally and Ben were watching the clinic for patterns while he pulled together additional resources. He knew how he wanted to proceed, but he still had some unanswered questions for the two suspects. John did not trust Arabia. Tony Arabia gave the impression he would lie just for sport. Joe Primak, on the other hand, was a simple man who didn't appear to be capable of lying, at least not very well. John decided Primak would be his best bet. It was just a few questions, but they would be critical to the execution of the plan. He didn't want to make Primak nervous, so he held an impromptu interrogation with Arabia just so Primak would be comfortable when it was his turn. John made sure Arabia and Primak passed one another in the hall so he could note their eye contact. Arabia, thinking Primak would be answering more of the same questions, gave him a wink, which immediately calmed Primak. John smiled. The criminal mind could be so predictable.

John sat across from Primak and began by reviewing the basic details of the case one more time. He wanted Joe Primak to feel at ease, completely comfortable. Finally, when Primak stopped fidgeting in his seat and his hands were still, John asked, "What time does the doctor arrive at the clinic?"

"Around eleven o'clock in the morning. The girls arrive throughout the day, but we tell many to come at nine. The assistant collects the money and gets the girls ready for his arrival."

"Who is the assistant?"

"I don't know her last name. We only know her first name, Tatiana. She's mean. She never tells us anything. I think she's Russian because she has an accent."

"What does she look like?"

"Tall, thin, white skin, long black hair. I know she smokes because I have had a cigarette with her outside the building."

John nearly laughed aloud. They smoked outside! They treated women like cattle in a meatpacking plant, but they smoked outside! Classic.

"What day of the week is the busiest?" John continued.

"It is different all the time. Thursday is busy. He won't work on Friday, so Thursday is busy because nobody wants to wait until Monday. Yes, I would say definitely Thursday is the busiest."

"The doctor, David Schimmel—is he a real doctor?"

"I think so. Tony says he is. He just makes more money this way, I think."

"Joe, how much do you get paid?"

Joe began to rock back and forth while sitting on his hands. "I told you, Tony takes care of the money, and he takes care of me. I sometimes get two hundred, sometimes fifty. Once I got five hundred."

John felt bad for Joe Primak. He was like a child, and even under the circumstances, he didn't completely understand the trouble he was in.

"Do girls go to the clinic that you do not know about?"

"No, they must have a card. If they don't have a card from me or Tony, then they must come from a girl who went there before. Like, what's the word—a referral."

"Do you always give out the same card?"

"No, I have a stack."

John rephrased. "No, I mean do the cards change at all, or do they always say the same thing?"

"Oh. No, the cards are always the same."

"Can I have a card?"

"Yes, but I gave you one," Joe said, confused.

"I know. I would just like another," John clarified.

"Sure, here you go." Joe Primak handed John the card, which looked just like a common business card. It was a standard-size white heavy card stock with black letters in straight type that just had an address and the words "Monday through Thursday 9–5." *Nice hours*, John thought to himself.

"What does a girl do when she gets there?" John asked.

"She brings the money we tell her to bring. All the prices are different. I get confused, so Tony usually tells me what price to use. Sometimes it's a lot; sometimes it's a little. I don't know why. We write the price on the back of the card."

"Show me, Joe. What would you write on the back of this card if a girl were to pay, let's say, twelve hundred dollars?"

"Oh, that's easy. Give me it." John gave Joe the card and a pen. Joe neatly penned the numerals "1200" and proudly handed the card back to John.

"Then what happens," John pressed.

"The girl takes the card, gets her money, only cash—no checks—and goes to the building. She gives Tatiana the money, and then Tatiana takes her inside for the procedure."

"Is that what you call it—a procedure?" John asked.

"Yeah, the doc said it's not really an operation. Not anywhere near as dangerous."

"Have any of the girls died?"

Joe was nervous again. His hands fluttered from his face to his sides, and he started to rock again. John didn't really need the answer; Joe's actions told him all he needed to know.

"That's okay, Joe. I think we're done for now." John paused and then added, "Who gave Ashley Rydell the card?"

"Nobody, Tony said—" He stopped and then quickly continued, "We don't know anything about that."

The hesitation was all John needed—these two knew what had happened to Ashley! Unfortunately, John would never be able to prove it. It didn't matter. John was satisfied; Primak had given him everything he needed for the time being. Now all they had to do was plan the takedown.

The meeting was set for that afternoon at Gina's office. John didn't want Gina going in again. It was too soon after the last undercover operation, and he didn't think she could handle it emotionally. She would never admit it, but John had his reservations. Sally would be the better choice, except she didn't have Gina's finesse. Still, he would rather school Sally than risk Gina. It would definitely have to be Sally. The hard part was making Gina think that it was her idea. He had two hours to figure out just how to do that.

When John arrived at Gina's office, the team was seated and waiting for him in the conference room. Spirits were high since the pendulum swung in their direction. They knew they were going in for the kill, and it felt good. John called the meeting to order while Gina asked Robert to join them in the conference room. Sally, Ben, Curt Conroy, and Robert took their seats. Gina sat at the far end of the table, while John stood in the front of the room next to the full wall monitor. He painstakingly reviewed every detail of the case up until the current day using a variety of video, archive documents, photo stills, and surveillance media. John was meticulous in every phase of an investigation from planning through execution. Finally, he put up a slide reviewing the information and profile for Dr. David Schimmel.

John began, "David Schimmel *was* a certified doctor, but he has not practiced medicine for the last ten years. He ran a successful OB/GYN practice before he abruptly quit, referring his clients to other doctors. He claimed the rising cost of malpractice insurance combined with the reduced fees of managed medicine made it impossible for him to make a living. To the best of their knowledge, Primak and Arabia say he performs the "procedures" Monday through Thursday in the warehouse in downtown Brooklyn. Tony Arabia and Joe Primak are his "front men," responsible for securing clients. They hang out at the free clinics to draw out women who want to terminate. The majority of the clients come from the clinics or 'word of mouth' referrals. They are paid roughly 10 percent for their work, but it seems manipulation of the funds is possible and likely."

John took a breath and let all of the information sink in. All eyes on him, he continued. "Security in the building is light, and just about anybody with a card can gain entrance to the warehouse. They believe there is one camera trained on the front door, but neither Primak nor Arabia knows if it is in operation. Tatiana, the only other "employee," runs the operation, collecting the money, assisting the doctor, and preparing the women. I was unable to uncover any information on Tatiana. I'm afraid without a last name, she is a complete unknown. We need to infiltrate the building and secure evidence that will incriminate both Tatiana and Dr. David Schimmel."

He ended his presentation and let the silence hang in the room. He knew they were thinking, preparing, strategizing.

"Each of you take a moment to collect your thoughts. We will start our brainstorming session in a few minutes," John instructed the group.

He left the room to grab a cup of coffee and to listen to their chatter. He overheard Gina saying she wanted to go in as soon as the morning. He knew she would just assume she was going in. He took his time, poured the coffee, added the cream, stirred three times, and walked slowly back to the room.

"Okay, let's get started. Ben, you first. What are your thoughts?"

"We need to do exactly what we did last time. We need a female to go in and secure enough evidence to take the operation down."

"Sally, what do you think?"

"I agree with Ben. We need to get inside. We've watched for a few days now, and while we see females coming and going, we do not know if they're pregnant. They could be getting a damn pedicure for all we know."

John nudged the group. "What are our risks?"

"The risks are huge," Sally answered as if they were all a little daft. "All our information comes from two questionable subjects. We do not know for sure how many people are inside, if they have security, if they are armed, and what they are capable of if something goes wrong."

John was pleased. As always, Sally was the one in the group who could find everything wrong with a situation. The others would get pissed at her for cutting down their ideas without giving them any thought. John knew better. It was Sally's nature; her brain worked to find what was wrong with a proposition. On the surface she appeared to be a complainer, but in practice she was indispensable. Sally would identify every problem the team would have to consider before they took action. There was no better way to prepare, and Sally was the best at telling the others what she felt. The problem was, Sally wasn't much for troubleshooting once she identified the problems. He needed Ben for that. Ben felt that with enough thought you could overcome any obstacle; he had the consummate "can do" attitude.

"Ben, how do we minimize the risk?"

"We take another run at Arabia and Primak, making sure their information is consistent. We need one more week of outside surveillance to check for patterns and light-activity days. Curt can figure out the best camera options under the circumstances, with no visible wires. We select a topflight agent to go in, one who can take care of herself while we surround the building with enough firepower to blow it all to kingdom come."

Gina was conspicuously quiet, and John was waiting for her reaction. He was quiet, hoping she would jump in. He didn't want to push or manipulate the meeting.

"Who is going in?" Gina asked.

Silence. Finally John asked, "Who do *you* propose, Gina?"

"I think I should do it. I was kept out of the media the first time around, I know what I need to get out of them, and it's simply a repeat performance. I want to go in."

John nodded his head without saying a word when Robert spoke up.

"I think Sally should go in. Gina is a risk."

Gina's jaw dropped; she couldn't believe what Robert had just said.

Robert continued, "Before you get all crazy on me, hear me out. We don't know how many other women will be inside. We will need field agent skills to help protect those women in the event something goes wrong. Moreover, there hasn't been enough time since you went undercover last. This is too important for us to overlook the basic rules we need to follow. You don't even know the emotional impact the last surveillance has had on you. You have to be outside. Sally should go in."

Somewhat timidly, Ben spoke up. "I agree with Robert."

Gina sighed. She knew they had made a good point. Although she felt fine, once she was inside the building, her mind could bend under the pressure. They couldn't take the chance.

"How do you feel about going in?" Gina asked Sally.

"It would be my pleasure."

"It's agreed. Sally goes in." John turned to Curt, "What camera methods?"

"I think we use the nails, earrings, and baseball cap," Curt answered. "That would give me three video and audio feeds."

Robert disagreed. "Not possible. Nails with the baseball cap don't go—it would give her a questionable appearance. Pick a different third."

"Fine, I can add a bracelet and a hair clip. The hair clips are still a little flaky, but they get great panoramic shots. The bracelet could be a safety net."

The options were endless—modern-day surveillance made James Bond movies look like the Stone Age. Wireless video and sound in microscopic sizes gave them an amazing array of field accessories.

"I kinda liked the baseball cap idea," Sally quipped.

They all laughed. Sally was not one for jewelry—or any other accessories, for that matter.

"I think Sally makes a good point," Robert interjected. "She needs to feel and look completely comfortable. Let's give her the baseball cap and stud earrings. Nix the bracelet, hair clip, and nails."

"I need a third selection for backup. I have a bracelet that is a simple silver twist with a snake-head clasp that would fit with the cap and earrings," Curt said.

Robert, the authority, answered, "Perfect."

The rest of the planning went much the same way, with each of them building on the others' ideas until they were all satisfied. They would go in after a week of surveillance. Sally would dye her hair purple/black and dress "street" for the occasion. In addition to the surveillance van, they would arrange for fifty agents to surround the building.

As the meeting wrapped up, John could see that Gina was disappointed with the outcome. He had known she would be, and he had prepared the antidote. "Gina, I almost forgot. I took care of Joe Darby."

She immediately brightened. "What do you mean?"

"We ran down Joe Darby. Needless to say, he won't be seeing Patti or the kids anytime soon. I think he's on his way to Horsham—something about working on his cousin's farm," John explained.

Gina was thrilled, her earlier disappointment forgotten. "Can I tell Patti?"

"By all means."

Chapter 23

GINA waited until the team had left and Robert was back at his desk. She loved Robert, but at times he was too overprotective. She was still pissed at him for not supporting her in the meeting.

"So, why, may I ask, did you do that?" she asked him straight out.

"Gina, every point I made is valid. You ask me to participate, to give my opinion, and then you get mad. Is it that I should give an opinion *only* when it agrees with yours?"

Gina crossed her arms and gave Robert the flattest of looks. "No, that's not it at all. You know this is my case. You know how hard I've worked on it. If I don't go in, I lose control, and I don't want anything to go wrong."

"Gina, calm down. Join the rest of us. You can't always run the show. Sometimes you have to give others a chance. You never know—you may even be surprised to find they can do a good job!"

"I know all that. It's just that sometimes I think you do it to protect me, not because it's the right thing," she explained.

"Yes, Gina, I did it to protect you, but I would do it to protect any of us. That's the point: we minimize the risk. Your going in is a risk. Period."

"Okay, you're right. I don't know what's wrong with me today. I'm going to return a few calls, and then I'm heading out to see how Patti Darby's doing."

Robert leaned back in his chair and touched his chest. "I'm sorry. Did I hear you say I was right?" he asked, feigning surprise.

"Very funny. Yes, Robert, I said you were right. On a different note, did Nick call today?"

"No, I didn't take any messages. If he calls in before I leave, I'll route him to your cell."

"Thanks, Robert."

Gina was looking forward to seeing Patti Darby. In spite of her general rule to keep some distance between her cases and her own emotions, she really liked Patti and Patti's friend Ginny. They were good women, and Gina saw in them why someone might consider an abortion as the only answer. It didn't sway her opinion, but at least she understood why. Patti needed to survive, to protect her four boys, and she would do anything to accomplish that. Gina arrived at the hospital to find that Patti had been moved to a regular room and was no longer in intensive care.

"Well, someone is looking much better!" Gina exclaimed.

Patti looked up from the book she was reading. "Agent Vincent, how are you?"

"I am very good, Patti. I have some updates for you, and I wanted to see how you were feeling."

"Things are much better. They say I might be able to go home in the next few days. I really can't wait. I miss the boys so much, and poor Ginny—she has really had her hands full!"

"Somehow I think Ginny manages just fine. She is a great friend," Gina replied.

"I know. I couldn't survive without her. If it weren't for her, I don't know how I would make it."

"I have some good news. The information you gave us checks out. Turns out, it is very important to our current investigation. I will need you testify at some point in the future. As long as you are willing to do that, no charges will be brought against you."

Tears streamed down Patti's cheeks.

"Agent Vincent, I can't tell you how grateful ... I mean ... uh ... I didn't want to ... I just couldn't—"

Gina broke in. "Patti, please. None of that. What you did was wrong, but I would be a liar if I didn't tell you I understand. I at least understand what drove you to it. I must stress the danger in the decision you made. You carried a life, and while I know the situation seemed impossible, time would have presented alternatives. Please reach out for help in the future. We can help you. You do not have to live your life in fear. This was not the only way out."

Patti didn't respond; she couldn't control her tears and only managed to nod her head.

"As a matter of fact, I have even better news for you. Your ex-husband will not be around anytime soon. We were able to track him down, and certain associates of mine assure me he will not be bothering you. They tell me he went to Pennsylvania to work on a farm."

Patti laughed through her tears. "That would be his cousin Clement. Clement always needs help around his farm. Joe hates the police; he probably ran to Horsham."

"I guess he's the kind who can dish it out but can't take it," Gina said.

Bounding into the room came what sounded like a small army: Ginny and the boys.

"Mommy! When are you coming home?"

"Look, I made you a picture!"

"We are going to have a party for you!"

"Do you miss us, Mom? Mom, I love you!"

They jumped on the bed and spoke to her all at once while showering her with hugs, kisses, and pictures they had colored. Ginny stood at the doorway and smiled.

"Hello, Agent Vincent."

"Hi, Ginny. It's good to see you. I hear our favorite patient will be going home soon."

"Yes, and her fan club can't wait!"

"I was just telling Patti that we were able to track Joe down. We are reissuing the restraining order, and my office is flagging your address in the system. Any calls to Patti's address will be broadcast as urgent. For the time being we don't think you'll see him. After some consideration, he decided to go away for a while—a farm in Pennsylvania."

Ginny smiled. "I can't say I will miss him."

"I hear you. Anyway, I will leave you to your visit. I will let you know how things progress. Patti, remember, I am going to need you in court."

"You can count on me. Thanks so much," she replied.

Gina left the hospital feeling buoyant. It was as close to a happy ending as she could get. In her line of work, there were never any winners—dead mothers, dead babies, cruel, inhumane doctors, and criminal opportunists. She wished she could say she made a difference, but on most days, she didn't feel like she was part of a solution at all. Sadness, death, and tragedy were the trademarks of her profession, making it difficult for her to remember why she had wanted the job in the first place. Preservation of life was her mission, a goal she never seemed able to reach.

She immediately stopped her train of thought. She was feeling good, and she didn't want to ruin her day. Gina knew her propensity for depression and consciously worked to avoid it.

As she arrived at her car, the cell buzzed. "Vincent here."

"Gina, it's Robert. Prince Charming is on the phone; can I send him through?"

"Sure, thanks. Go ahead."

"Hello, Gina. Can you hear me? It's me, Nick."

"Yes, I can hear you. How are you?"

"Good. How about you?"

"I've been busy. Things are starting to heat up again."

"I figured that. I completely understand if it's not possible, but I was wondering if maybe we could have dinner tonight."

"I can't go to New Jersey. I need an early start tomorrow. If you want to eat in the city, then I can meet you."

"Excellent! I am already here; I had office hours today.

Where do you want to eat?"

"How do you feel about Little Italy? We can eat and walk the streets. I love the street vendors in the summer, but I never get a chance to go," she said.

"I'll make a reservation at Angelo's. Meet me around six o'clock. How's that?"

"Perfect. I'm looking forward to seeing you, Nick."

"Me, too."

She was thrilled! Her heart pounded in her ears while she was talking to him. She felt like a child, but she didn't care. He made her feel wonderful, alive, forcing the rest of the world and her cares to melt into the background. When she was with him, nothing else seemed important. She was heading home to shower and dress. Gina wanted to look good for dinner—she was really looking forward to her evening.

She decided to shed the slacks, tank, and suit jacket that were her standard summer garb and picked a pastel floral wrap dress. Tan strappy sandals, minimal makeup, and her hair pulled back with a single rhinestone clip made her look like a real "girly girl." She would cab it over and leave her car at home so she could enjoy a few drinks. It was better in the city without a car, giving her a complete sense of freedom. She could get a ride or walk no matter what time of day.

He was already at the bar when she arrived. Angelo's was a small restaurant with tables crammed into the front, a bar that ran along the left wall of the front room, and a full dining room in the back with more tables shoved in. The place was packed, and Nick was leaning over the bar talking to the bartender. God, Nick was so handsome! He was wearing a simple tan polo with olive pants. Her heart started that silly fluttering once again as he saw her from across the room and smiled.

"Gina, over here."

As if she hadn't seen him. He was the only one she saw in the crowd. She weaved her way through the tables to the bar, and he gave her a quick kiss on the cheek.

"What would you like to drink, Gina?"

"I think I'm in the mood for a chilled chardonnay tonight."

Within seconds, she had a large glass of white wine and a seat that he seemed to produce from nowhere. "Gina, sit here. Our table won't be ready for a while."

They talked, laughed, and drank for the better part of an hour, and Gina was starting to feel a little tipsy. Gina always remained in control and very rarely drank alcohol, but when she was with Nick, she broke all her usual rules.

Their table was finally ready, and they weaved their way to the back of the restaurant. Gina preferred the back room of Angelo's because the front was too active and loud. The rear gave diners a sense of privacy even though the tables were as close to one another as they were in the front room. Nick let Gina order for both of them because she knew the menu intimately. Spiedini and roasted peppers to start, a half order of angel hair with marinara each, followed by the veal chop for her and the osso bucco for him. They were the best dishes in what was arguably the best restaurant in the district.

"Gina, how's the case going?"

"I can't talk about it. Anyway, I'm having a good time, and I don't want to think about work."

"Sorry, I just wanted to see how you were doing."

"I'm fine. Really. My life is not just my work, although until I met you I can't remember the last time I did anything fun." Gina smiled over her glass.

"I know. I feel the same way. It's like I've known you all my life. I am more comfortable with you than I was with my wife. I hope you don't mind my saying it."

"Nick, obviously I'm not one to beat around the bush. I love that you say these things, and I feel the same way. My grandmother was right—she said you were perfect, and I have to agree. Nick DePaolo, you are too good to be true."

His heart dropped. He felt like saying, "I'm not that good. I have secrets, secrets that would make you hate me."

Instead he glanced down at the table and just changed the subject. "Do you want to go to Atlantic City with me this weekend?"

"I wish I could. Actually, after tonight, I may not be able to see you for a week or so. My work is at a critical point, and I probably won't be able to get away."

His expression fell. "Oh, for how long? Could I even meet you for lunch?"

"Just a week or so, but no, I won't even be able to meet you for lunch. I'm sorry, Nick, but things are going to be a little crazy for me. I promise I will call you as soon as there is a break in the action."

She didn't want to ruin the evening because they were both having a wonderful time. After dinner, they casually walked the streets of Little Italy and decided on Ferrarro's for dessert. Once the cappuccinos and cannoli arrived, Nick grew serious.

"Gina, do you ever think that it was better when abortion was legal?"

She was speechless—not so much because of the question but because he had asked it out of the blue.

"I believe a life is a life. There is no difference for me. A first-trimester fetus is a baby just as sure as you and I are sitting here. We must protect that life. If a woman doesn't want a baby, then she should take precautions."

"Gina, what if it were out of her control? Do you still think a woman should be forced to bear a child?"

"Nick, I really don't want to have this discussion tonight. It's how I feel; I'm not going to change. It doesn't have to impact how you feel. I can appreciate your position, and I've met women who have helped me see the other side of things. Still, I always arrive at the same conclusion: the baby needs to be protected."

"What would you do if it were legal again?"

"Nick, what is this all about? Why are you asking me these things? It's not going to be legal. I'm not going to change my mind. What are you driving at?"

"I just … well, I just wanted to know how you feel. I also want you to know where I stand. No surprises. Gina, if given the opportunity to make it legal, I would. Would you still want to be with me then?"

"Of course I would still want to be with you—our relationship is not defined by this issue. The only way this would be a problem for us is if you ever asked me to get an abortion: I wouldn't. Not under any circumstances, not for any reason, not for anyone. Barring that, this should not be a problem for us."

"Gina, I would never ask you to get an abortion. On the contrary, I want to spend the rest of my life with you, having children, building a family."

She nearly fell off her chair.

"Well, you certainly know how to take a girl for wild ride."

"I know. I'm sorry. I must sound crazy to you. It's just that I have really strong feelings that I haven't had in a very long time. I don't want anything to ruin it."

"Nick, what would ruin it? I love being with you. I respect your opinions, and I love how you respect mine. Now stop being ridiculous, and let's go to the Italian *chachka* store."

"What store?"

"*Chachkas.* You know, the Italian variety store. It's like an old five and dime but with Italian imports. Trust me, you're gonna love it!"

They roamed the store for over an hour, laughing and exploring every little gadget in the place: Italian flags, T-shirts, fans, string puppets, loaded dice, and a huge variety of Italian CDs. Nick bought an Italian opera CD and a "Kiss Me, I'm Italian" nightshirt that Gina eyed up. They had a great night, and neither of them wanted it to end.

"It's getting late, and I have to get an early start tomorrow," Gina said.

"Let me take you to your car. Where did you park?"

"I took a taxi over. I didn't feel like driving."

"In that case come with me to my car, and I will drop you home."

"No way, Nick. You can just go through the Holland right here. My place is clear across town. I'm just going to catch a cab."

"Don't be ridiculous. It will only take a few minutes to drive across town at this hour. Come on."

Nick gently led her by the arm to the corner lot where he had parked his car. His was the only car left in the deserted lot. It was the type of lot where you paid up front and kept your keys. This way the night attendant could leave whenever he wanted. Nick started the car and turned the air conditioning up—it was a hot, humid night, and the heat was unbearable. He popped in his new CD, and Italian opera was playing in a matter of seconds.

Gina laughed. "You don't waste any time, that's for sure."

"Signorina, may I kiss you?"

Gina caught her breath and nodded. He gently took her face in his hands and kissed her full on the lips. It was perfect. She didn't want him to stop, so she did what any New York girl would do. She kissed him back. It was a hungry kiss—she wanted more of him, and she didn't care about anything else.

"Nick, stay with me tonight," she breathed.

"Gina, nothing would give me more pleasure, but I can't. No, let me explain. I won't. We have the rest of our lives. Let's take our time."

Gina had never thought she would be on the receiving end of those words. She was more than a little disappointed, but she knew he was right. She wouldn't even be able to stay with him in the morning.

They necked like teenagers in front of her building. Gina saw Norm, her doorman, staring, so she waved. He timidly waved back.

"Nick, if I get any free time, I promise I will call. In the meantime, I'll be thinking about you every minute."

"Me, too, Gina. Thanks for a great night."

"Don't mention it, sweetheart."

She skipped into her building and hugged Norm. New love— was there anything more ridiculous?

Chapter 24

I T was Friday night. They had completed a full week of surveillance, and Gina hadn't seen Nick since their dinner in Little Italy. She missed him so much but didn't even have a chance to call. The team would meet every night to review the day's surveillance tapes. After a full week, they were able to collect a considerable amount of information and were ready to plan the takedown.

They spotted the doctor, David Schimmel, only once coming out the front door of the warehouse. They discovered he could enter the building from a connecting building with a garage. Tatiana came and went through the front door, opening by 8:45 a.m. every morning and leaving promptly by 6:00 p.m. every night. They watched four girls enter in pairs of two on Monday, two girls on Tuesday, only Tatiana on Wednesday, and three girls on Thursday. It wasn't nearly the booming business they had expected to find, but the team figured with Arabia and Primak behind bars, "sales" had taken a hit.

Because volume was not an issue, they decided Monday would be the day. There was little reason to wait, especially when each girl represented a terminated pregnancy. They would plan throughout the weekend and have everyone in place by the time Tatiana opened Monday morning. Sally was already in character with spiked dark black/purple hair, white powder makeup, blackish lipstick, a baseball cap, and a loose-fitting gray sweat suit. Curt tested Sally's video and audio feeds. Sally had to practice delicate movements to ensure quality transmission because Curt was afraid she might be too rough on the equipment.

They hadn't seen the doctor arrive or leave throughout the week. They had one video segment when he briefly stepped out the front door. Even with cars situated around the attached building, they were not able to mark his arrival or departure. In this respect, they would remain blind until Sally could provide them the information when she was inside. John didn't like loose ends, and he would have preferred knowing what type of vehicle they would be looking for if the guy managed to get away.

"I want the team to consider two more days of surveillance to ascertain arrival/departure times and vehicle type," John said.

"I don't think we have two more days, not unless we let Primak and Arabia out to get the doctor new clients. Without those two, volume is very low. Sally showing up with a card will raise more questions and put the whole plan in danger," Ben warned.

"Gina, what do you think?" John asked.

"We have to go in Monday. Girls are still filtering in with the cards they put out on the street, but Ben's right—soon that will dry up, and Sally will enter a questionable environment. We'll have to rely on tight placement around the perimeter in the event he runs. Has he been spotted at the home address at all?"

"Not once. We've had round-the-clock coverage at his last known address, and we have not seen him once. Tenants claim they don't know who lives in the apartment. It's a tight building, requiring card access, and there's no doorman," Ben informed the group.

"So we only saw him once all week, and we don't have a current address. Is that correct?" Gina asked.

"That's it," Ben answered.

"We go in Monday. Time will only muddy this up, and it will take us further away. We need to catch him at the warehouse," Gina announced.

"It's not perfect, but I agree," John said.

It was 5:00 a.m. on Monday morning, and fifty armed agents surrounded the single-story warehouse for a complete three-block perimeter. Each agent had orders to subdue but not kill the subject.

Gina had the option to stay in the van with Curt or pick another surveillance point. Gina decided to take her position on the second story of an abandoned brownstone, where she had a clear view of the side fire door that connected the warehouse and the neighboring building. Gina felt that if someone in the warehouse were to run, the door leading them to the side street would offer more privacy and a variety of buildings to hide in. Gina always put herself in the place of the pursued. She situated herself outside the exit she would use if she were in their place.

Many of the women brought friends with them to the warehouse. Not Sally. The team decided Sally should go unescorted. If Sally was alone, they wouldn't give their security a second thought. Sally's card had twelve hundred dollars written on the back. John handed her the envelope containing twelve one-hundred–dollar bills. "Be careful. Be alert. Be cautious. Just say the word, and I will come and get you," John instructed.

"I'm ready. Don't worry. We're prepared. Curt has me all wired up," Sally replied.

"Remember what we practiced. Enter the building, find Tatiana, and give her the card. Try to collect as much video as possible. If you are afraid for any reason, do not hesitate. Call us in. No heroes," John warned.

"Yes, boss." Sally gave John a hug and assumed her position.

At 8:48 a.m. Tatiana arrived as usual. She opened the front door of the warehouse with her key after parking her brown Chevy Cavalier on the side street. At 9:35 Sally walked three blocks to the building and entered the front door carrying a knapsack. Once inside she saw a vacant reception area behind a window with a long corridor off the left side of the reception area. At the end of the corridor was a green door. She approached the door and knocked loudly twice. Tatiana opened the door while Curt and

Ben got a full, clear audio *and* video feed in the van. There were four monitors, three of which were picking up the feed from Sally's camera accessories, while the fourth came from a camera mounted outside the van in the bicycle rack.

Sally handed Tatiana the card, announcing, "I was told I could get help here."

Tatiana took the card, turned it over, looked Sally over, and asked, "Do you have the money?"

Without a word, Sally handed her the envelope.

Tatiana took the envelope, counted the bills, and put it into her pocket.

"Follow me."

Tatiana led Sally down the stairs into the basement. On the lower level there was a corridor with rooms off each side. Two rooms had beds lined up in neat, orderly rows. It resembled a very old army ward. It looked as if each room was empty, but Sally couldn't see every bed from the hall. The last room on the left appeared to be the "operating room," but Sally couldn't be sure. Tatiana was moving briskly, and Sally nearly had to run to keep up. At the end of the corridor was a large musty room with laundry baskets lining one wall.

"Take your clothes off, and put them in one of the baskets. Put this on." She handed Sally a cotton hospital gown.

Tatiana continued. "You will wait here until I come for you. The doctor will be here shortly. I will take you to the room next door, and it will take only a few minutes. You may rest in one of our beds for a few hours. You must leave by six o'clock tonight. Take Tylenol for the next few days. Bleeding should be expected but not too heavy. If you get sick, don't come back. Go to a hospital."

Before Sally could ask a question, Tatiana abruptly left the room. She changed into the gown quickly so she could look around and get as much video of the interior as possible. She put her clothes in her knapsack and the sack in the laundry basket. She went to look for a bathroom so she could wander the hall for the sake of the boys in the van. She looked through each of the "ward" rooms, which held the beds. There were a dozen beds in each room, and both rooms were empty. Sally was the only patient of the day. Just as Sally was entering what she thought was the operating room, Tatiana came down the stairs and yelled, "Hey, what are you doing?"

"I was just looking for a bathroom," Sally replied.

"In the back of the waiting room. Here, let me show you."

Tatiana brought her back to the room with the laundry baskets and opened the only other door in the room, showing her the bathroom.

"Sorry, I thought it was a closet."

"Just stay here and wait until I come for you. No walking around," Tatiana warned.

Sally filmed the bathroom and panned the waiting room one more time. Just then, Tatiana returned with another patient. A young girl, late teens, entered the room and Sally listened to Tatiana run through the instructions again. This was just what the team had been hoping to avoid. The girl was scared. She stared at Tatiana wide-eyed and asked only one question, "Can my boyfriend come in?"

"No, he must wait outside. Don't worry, it will be over before you know it," Tatiana replied.

Tatiana left the two of them alone, and Sally had to squelch the urge to talk to the girl. She had to appear aloof and disinterested. The girl asked Sally if she knew where the bathroom was. Sally pointed to the door but said nothing.

The girl changed in the bathroom and dropped her things in the basket next to Sally's. She sat on a bench; they were locker room–type benches painted a dark gray and placed in the center of the room.

"How long have you been waiting?" the girl asked.

"Just a few minutes," Sally answered.

"Do you know how long it takes?"

"No, this is my first time here," Sally said.

"Me, too. I wish I didn't have to be here."

Sally wanted to scream at the girl, "You don't have to be here! You could go home! Have your baby and put it up for adoption or keep it! You don't have to do this!" Instead Sally said, "Yeah, me, too."

They waited nearly two hours. It was almost lunchtime and they barely talked the entire time they waited. Sally was afraid to say anything, and the girl looked as if she was ready to bolt with each passing minute. Sally hoped the girl would become so afraid that she would leave on her own. Just when they thought they couldn't take it another minute, Tatiana came down the steps.

"The doctor is here. Just give me a few minutes to set up. You … you're going first," she said to Sally.

She then turned to the young girl. "Your boyfriend is getting a little nasty. I've had to ask him to leave five times already. I need you to get dressed and go tell him to stay outside. He cannot come in again. Do you understand?"

"Yes, yes, I'm sorry. I'll be just a minute."

Sally hoped they could find a way to keep the girl out there. This was a huge break. They just had to get to the boyfriend first. The team heard everything Sally did, and she hoped they would move on it.

The young girl quickly dressed and ran up the steps and out the front door. She saw her boyfriend sitting in the car and leaned in the window.

"Carm, what the hell are you doing? Why are you harassing her? The doctor just came, and they are getting mad at me! You can't go back in. You have to wait for me to come out." she hissed.

"Get in. Now!" he growled.

"Why? What's wrong?"

"Lena, just get in the car."

The girl was confused, especially because Carm never spoke to her that way. She knew something was wrong, so she got in the front seat. Crouched in the backseat on the floor was Ben.

Ben whispered, "Lena, you are not going back inside. The doctor is very dangerous, and you cannot go back in. Do you understand?"

"Yes ... but ... I ... I need to ... I gave them our money ... I can't—"

"Enough!" Carm yelled.

"I didn't like this idea from the beginning! We are not going to do this, Lena. Let's not make a bad situation worse. We *are* going to get married, we *are* going to have a baby but we *are not* going to do this!"

"The nurse will come out looking for me."

"No, she won't. Even if she does, who cares? We'll sit here and argue in the car. She won't want to cause a scene," he said.

"Why don't we just leave?" Lena asked.

"I'm sorry, Miss, but that would compromise our position, and we can't have that," Ben explained. "Just stay here in the car talking back and forth. The assistant can see that you two are talking things over."

The team figured it was better to have the girl outside than risk her well-being in the building.

Inside, Tatiana escorted Sally to the operating room and instructed her to lie on the table.

He entered the building as he always did, through the building next door. He would park a block away, walk to Second Avenue, and enter what was once the Key Food. He walked the length of the block, passing through three abandoned buildings before he entered the warehouse from an interior door he had installed. He never entered the front or the sides of the building, protecting his identity at all costs. Not that it mattered—not once had he come close to being caught. If it weren't for the two idiots, he would still be safely making a fortune. This was the closest the law had ever come to his operation, and he could kill the both of them for it. Arabia was smart; he'd lined up that Dendrite lawyer. She would get them off, and he didn't have to get involved. At first, he thought he would have to hire them a good lawyer, but they managed just fine on their own. Sometimes things did work out for the best. He needed them out soon, or he would have to find new front men. His clientele diminished more each day. Maybe it was a good time to take a vacation—close the shop down until the boys were out again. That is, unless they were convicted—but convicted of what? He knew they had double-crossed him and were busted for attempting a "procedure," but he didn't think they would implicate him. Still, he couldn't take the chance. Today would be the last day. Definitely a better plan. He would shut down for a few months. No big deal.

He entered the interior door, which put him in the back of his warehouse on the ground floor behind the old reception area. He quickly went through the green door to the basement to find Tatiana. He had two patients. One was already on the table, and other one was … where was the other one? Never mind. That was Tatiana's job, not his. He entered the operating room and saw a gothic punk rocker–type lying on the table. Jeez, they came in all shapes, colors, and sizes. She looked afraid, but then again, they all looked the same. Like frightened animals. They would always stare at him. He didn't feel like talking today. No small talk bullshit today. Just do the job and shut it down. He checked the instrument table and selected two off the counter. He checked the straps on the stirrups and made sure they were tight around her ankles. She really looked afraid, like a caged animal. This one might freak. He'd better get Tatiana. Just then, Tatiana entered the room and settled the girl down. Good. He wouldn't have to make chitchat with anyone. He approached the subject and began to separate her legs when she totally lost it. The girl was nuts! Screaming and yelling for help. What the hell was wrong with this one? He didn't like it.

Didn't like any of it! He grabbed the emergency syringe and put the girl out.

"Tatiana, abandon now! Get the safe!"

Tatiana ran to the back room while he ascended the steps two at a time. He heard yelling outside and saw men entering the front door. What the hell was going on? Oh, my God! It was a raid! A four-number sequence on the keypad above the light by the rear door—a brilliant plan, his idea of course. If the situation was too hot, he had the building wired. Tatiana, unfortunately, would be missed, but it was unavoidable. By the time she grabbed the safe it would be too late for her and the one on the table. He knew Tatiana would never leave the safe, greedy little bitch! Five seconds, and the building wouldn't exist. He would have to exit the side door, but the explosion would cause so much confusion he could be halfway to Guam before they knew what happened. He hit the keypad, entered the sequence, and flew out the side door.

When Sally started screaming, the team went into action. Twenty agents ran toward the front door, but only two made it in before the whole place blew up. John was screaming orders into the radio, agents were strewn about Third Avenue, and Ben left the girl and her boyfriend and ran toward the burning building.

Sally was in there. He had to try to get her! Sally was in the building! John saw Ben running toward the front door and ran after him.

Gina was on autopilot in the brownstone. It was the closest thing to hell she had ever seen! As soon as the explosion hit, she saw *him* come out the side door. She raced down the steps, taking them four at a time, out the front door, and down the block.

He'd blown up the building! He'd blown up the goddamn building! She ran as fast as she could. Was she the only one who saw him? She was gaining on him.

"Stop! FBLI! Police! Stop or I'll shoot!" Gina yelled.

He made it out the side door and down the steps before the blast hurled him into the street. Beautiful. He made it. Just had to get down the block, and he was home free! He'd be in Barbados by nightfall. He'd planned every detail of this day. Foreign bank accounts, property, and a full set of identification were all prearranged. He'd thought of everything. He was halfway down the block before he heard her. Stop. FBLI. Was she nuts? He wasn't going to stop. Not for her. Not for anyone. He was out of here! His hut on the beach was the only thing on his mind.

He was still running! She had to stop him! The reality of the moment hit her harder than the blast. He'd killed Sally, blown the whole damn place up! Oh, God, she would have to shoot. She had no other choice.

"Please! Stop! I am going to shoot! Stop!" she screamed.

She bent down on one knee, braced for the shock, and pulled the trigger three times in succession. All three caught him right in the back!

He fell to his knees and then fell face forward to the ground.

She shot me? The bitch shot ...

He was dead by the time Gina reached him. No pulse. She had killed a man. Oh, God! Orders were to subdue! What had she done? Why was she so cold? She was shaking, uncontrollably shaking.

The agents radioed John that the suspect was down. John ran down the street and saw her. She was in shock. He knew the signs immediately. He took his jacket and wrapped it around her as he led her away.

"Gina, it's okay. You had to do it. Gina, you did the right thing. Good job, Gina. You did a good job."

She was unresponsive, staring off into space. He would have both Gina and Ben treated for shock. His two strongest team members were down for the count, and the third was dead. It was the worst possible scenario.

John had Robert escort Gina and Ben to the hospital in an ambulance. John would be on-site for hours trying to clean the mess up. The only luck they had all day was the civilians, both the girl and her boyfriend, were unharmed. It would remain the only thing John could be grateful for. The rest was a complete disaster.

Chapter 25

ROBERT realized he wasn't cut out for the field, especially because he found himself desperately missing the safety of the office and his desk. He was a complete wreck, and they were relying on him to escort Gina and Ben to the hospital. *Escort Gina and Ben!* He thought he needed an escort, for Chrissakes! Robert traveled in the ambulance with Gina, while Ben was in a second ambulance that followed close behind. It was bad. Very bad. Sally was dead. He didn't know what to do, feeling completely helpless. The whole affair was a runaway train, and he couldn't stand it.

Gina grabbed his hand as the ambulance careened toward Maimonedes Hospital.

"Robert, I killed him."

"I know, Gina. Don't worry, you had to. You are very brave, Gina," he muttered.

"I never killed anyone before. I don't know how—"

"Gina, not now. Rest."

They gave her a shot, a mild sedative, nothing that would put her out completely, just a little something to take the edge off.

"Robert, what about Sally?" she asked as the sedative took effect.

"Not now, Gina," he replied just as she dozed off.

They arrived at the hospital and were admitted immediately. No emergency room gymnastics for them. Robert couldn't believe the way they were whisked through administration and situated in a matter of minutes. The efficiency was unbelievable—he never saw anything like it in the civilian world.

They placed Gina and Ben in private rooms next to one another in a private wing of the hospital. Three field agents were already in surgery. Five others were already in their rooms in the same wing. A trauma team was waiting to examine Gina and Ben, leaving Robert in the hall to pace and wonder what he should do next.

He knew one thing: no fieldwork for him. He was sorry he had ever brought it up to her. Stupid, wanting to move into other areas. He liked being in the office, making schedules, taking calls. He was not cut out for pulling bodies off the street! No promotion for him. They could keep the fieldwork—he would be an inside assistant for good. His heart just couldn't take this shit!

Robert was a complete wreck, not knowing what to do with himself. If he was at the office, he would be making calls, notifying family members, and acting as a central information center. That was exactly what he needed to do now—make calls. Ben's wife, Jody, would be first because she would need to get someone to watch the kids before she could get down to the hospital. Should he call Gina's mother? No, definitely not. She would have to decide when to notify her parents. He could call Nick. Yes, that was a much better plan. Even if she got mad, he could always say Nick called him. I mean, Dr. Nick DePaolo did call her practically every day anyway.

Robert set up a makeshift office in the waiting room of the hospital wing, commandeering the one phone for his sole use. This was his forte, and he was feeling much better already, like a fish back in water.

He quickly dialed Jody first. "Hi, Jody. It's Robert with the agency."

"No! Not Ben! Please!"

"Jody, he is going to be fine. Please listen. There was an explosion, and Ben has some minor injuries and severe shock. How quickly can you get here?"

"My mom can be here in a few minutes. I'll be there within the hour," she said.

"Great, I will be waiting here for you," Robert said.

"Oh, Robert, one question—why is he in shock? What happened?" Jody asked.

"Sally's gone. He was trying to save her."

Jody simply hung up the phone.

Robert knew Jody was a strong woman. She had to be, being the mother of five children, four of them boys, and having a federal agent for a husband.

Robert called Nick's office in New Jersey and then his office in New York. He was not at either location. He called Nick's home number, and a man answered the phone.

"Hi, this is Robert, Gina Vincent's assistant. I was hoping to speak with Dr. DePaolo."

"Hello, this is William. I am afraid Dr. DePaolo is unavailable," William replied in his subtle English manner.

"William, normally I would not leave such a message, but I'm afraid it is urgent that I speak with the doctor," Robert explained.

"I do hope nothing unfortunate has happened. Please give me a number, and I will try my best to raise him for you," William said.

Unfortunate? Raise him? Who is this guy, so proper and all?

"Thank you, William. That would be splendid indeed," Robert added in an effort to match William's eloquence of speech. It didn't work—he just managed to sound like an idiot.

He gave William his cell number and then quickly checked on Gina and Ben, who were both resting comfortably with a little help from Dr. Xanax. Once the sedatives wore off, the trauma psychologists would begin working with them immediately. Robert radioed John and gave him an update on the health status of the team. It still sounded like massive pandemonium in the background, and Robert couldn't wait to hang up. John promised he would be on his way shortly.

Robert had nothing to do but wait. His cell rang, and he took the call in the waiting room.

"Robert, it's Nick. What's wrong?!"

"There was an accident, but Gina is fine. They were working a case, and there was an explosion. Many of our agents were injured, but Gina was not. She is being treated for shock. We are at Maimonedes in Brooklyn. I am here now, and I decided to call you instead of her mother. I hope you don't—"

"Don't be ridiculous! I'll be there within the hour. Robert, thank you! I appreciate your contacting me."

Robert hoped Gina would be as enthusiastic about his decision. He would wait to speak with her directly for further instructions on what to tell her parents.

Nick flew into the hospital flashing his medical ID to anyone who would look at it. He pushed his way into the hospital wing until the two armed guards at the front door restrained him. They paged Robert to the door, where he checked Nick's identification and cleared him for entry.

"It's nice to finally meet you in person, Dr. DePaolo."

"Please, Robert, just call me Nick. I really appreciate your calling me."

"She is mildly sedated and is sleeping right now. Nick, she killed a man today. The suspect was fleeing the scene, and Gina shot him. She didn't have a choice, but she did let off three shots. All three made the mark."

"Damn! She's never killed anyone, has she?"

"No, never. She was pretty shaken up. We also lost an agent, a member of our team. It's a devastating loss for all of us. Gina was supposed to go in, but the group decided this other agent would be a better choice. If Gina had her way, she would be dead right now."

The words didn't penetrate at first, but slowly the realization hit him: She would be dead. She would be dead right now.

"Nick? Dr. DePaolo, are you okay? Can you hear me?" Robert asked.

"She would be gone? I would have lost her? I can't believe it," he repeated as the color completely drained from his face.

This was the first time Robert met Nick in person, and it was evident that this was more than just a casual relationship. Dr. Nick DePaolo had very strong feelings for Gina, and it was clearly apparent. Under different circumstances, Robert would have been thrilled to see how much Nick cared for Gina; however, right now, it looked like Robert would just have another basket case on his hands—not exactly what he needed.

"Nick, I called you hoping you could help me help her. I thought if she saw you, she might come around. But, please, don't tell her I called you. Tell her you called in, and I told you what happened. She would be furious if she knew I contacted you."

Nick knew he was right. She would be furious, no doubt about it. He really didn't want to lie to her. *No lies.* He figured he would just avoid the subject.

"Robert, can I see her?"

"Sure, right this way. Physically she is fine, no injuries. It's just the shooting combined with the explosion—"

"This is about the explosion! Of course, they were in a Brooklyn hospital. Gina was supposed to go undercover and be in that building today, wasn't she?"

Robert raised his eyes from the floor. "Yes."

"She told me this was her case. Why didn't she go in?"

"Partly my fault combined with the team director, John Winthrop. John thought it was too soon after the last undercover operation. I can't say that I disagreed with him, especially since she nearly fainted a few days after that one. Sally was definitely the better choice, and I said so at our planning meeting. The team agreed, and Gina didn't argue. I know she will blame herself for Sally's death. I know Gina."

"Well, let's just take it one step at a time. Can I see her?" Nick asked.

"Sure, I'll wait right here."

Nick brushed past the guard and entered the private room. There was one hospital bed, a bathroom, a closet, and a small seating area. It was larger than a standard hospital room and looked like they were trying to mimic a hotel room. It was a weak effort.

He knelt beside the bed so his face would be level with hers. He didn't want to sit on the bed for fear of waking her. Her face was beautiful, so determined, driven, yet soft and expressive. He'd almost lost her! In that moment he knew, beyond a doubt, that he loved this woman more than he had ever loved any other.

He studied every little nuance of her face, her hair, the shape of her lips, the single freckle she had to the left of her nose. He'd almost lost her!

"Nick, what are you doing here?" she whispered so low he wasn't sure if she had spoken at all. "It's so bad."

That he heard. No question, she was talking.

"Gina, I know. I'm so sorry. I came as soon as I heard. Gina, I love you. I need you to know how *much* I love you!"

In her head, she thought maybe she was going crazy. She wasn't hurt, so why was he so concerned about her? He was beside himself, and she couldn't understand why.

"I love you, too, Nick. I killed someone today. I was supposed to just 'shoot to subdue,' but I killed him. I never killed anyone before," she continued to explain.

"I know, Gina. Robert told me everything. I know how bad it all seems, but it will get better. You will be able to get through this, and I am going to help you. Please, Gina, I need you."

"Nick, what's the matter? I will be okay. There is nothing wrong with me. I wasn't in the building. I should have been, but I wasn't."

Just then Gina remembered Sally was in the building; she remembered that Sally was gone, truly gone.

"I'm sorry, Gina. I was just so worried. I don't want to lose you like I lost …"

She knew he was thinking about his first wife, and she understood why he was so rattled.

"Nick, it's all right. I understand, but really, I am fine. I wasn't hurt. I just never thought we would lose somebody. I can't even believe Sally's gone. I think of the explosion, and I know she was inside, but I just can't think of her as dead. It's like my mind just won't accept it."

"It's the first stage, Gina—the first stage of grief, and there will be more. I know you feel fine, but you are going to experience a range of emotions that are foreign to you. I know firsthand; I've been through it."

Gina knew Nick was right, but she still didn't feel fragile or unstable; she simply felt sadness and shock. She had taken a life. An agent who was dedicated to preserving life had actually killed a man—now, that was truly a paradox. Another ... what was the word ... oh, yeah ... *irony*.

"Nick, is John here?"

"Um, no ... just Robert. Do you want me to get him?"

"Yes, I need to talk to him for a minute. Can you stay with me a while?"

"Gina, I am not leaving until you throw me out! Let me get him."

A second later Robert rushed into her room, sat on the bed, and grabbed her hands.

"I was worried sick! You were in a freakin' trance!" he exclaimed as only Robert could, while he kissed her forehead.

"Tell me, where is the team?"

"John is still onsite. Ben is in the next room, also being treated for shock. Three agents are in surgery because of the explosion, but we expect them to pull through. Five others have a variety of cuts and bruises. It looks like we are going to make it through with just the one fatality. Gina, it could have been much, much worse, you know. I still can't believe Ben wasn't hurt. He nearly dived into the fireball to get her, and John pulled him away."

"Can you get me John on the radio?"

Robert immediately radioed John and handed the set to Gina.

She heard a variety of activity, but it seemed much quieter to her than when she had left the scene.

"Gina, how are you doing?" he yelled, making sure she could hear him.

"John, I'm fine, and I can hear you well. Don't yell. I have a little headache."

"Oh, so now you're a comedian? I'm on my way to the hospital, and I will talk to you when I get there. Right now, everything is under control. Just try to keep it together for me. I need you, Gina."

"Sure thing. I'm going to visit Ben. Robert tells me the other agents will pull through. Have you called Sally's mom?"

"No. After the hospital, I am going to her house. I have to do it myself, and I have to do it in person."

"Do you want me to come with you? I think I can, you know ..."

"No, Gina. I don't want you to come with me. I can take care of this myself, and I need you to take care of things at the hospital for me. Can you do me that favor?" he asked as if he were talking to a child.

"Yes, John. I can do that," she replied.

Gina got out of bed and walked into the hall. She hated hospital garb. It was impossible to be taken seriously when wearing such a ridiculous outfit—made of paper, no less!

"Gina, you shouldn't get out of bed!" Robert yelled as he ran to her with Nick right behind him.

She turned and glared at him. If looks could kill, Robert would surely have been dead and buried right on the spot.

"I need to speak with Ben—alone. Just give me a few minutes—okay?"

Nick answered, "We'll be right here, Gina. Go ahead."

Nick knew there was no way Gina would put up with the coddling. He also knew she needed to take control of the situation, for her own welfare more than anything else.

When Gina saw Ben staring at the ceiling, a wave of grief washed over her, taking her completely by surprise. They hugged each other. Tightly. No words, just the deep painful sobs of sadness shared between two people who felt exactly the same way.

Jody ran into the room, breaking their embrace. "Ben! Ben, are you okay? Please, baby, are you okay?"

Gina thought to herself, *This is good. He can calm her down.* For the moment, she felt much better, although she couldn't help but feel the respite would be short-lived.

Nick was sitting in the guest chair in her hospital room patiently waiting for her to return. He stood up as soon as she entered and attempted to help her into the bed.

"Nick, would you please stop it? I'm not injured; I don't need help getting into bed."

"I'm sorry, Gina. I'm just worried about you. Really worried."

"Don't be. Now, tell me, how are things?"

"Gina, stop. I've missed you, and not a moment goes by that I don't think about something I want to tell you or some place I would like to take you. It has really killed my productivity. All I want to do is be with you. But, on a serious note, I have some things I need to work out with you."

"Oh. What things?"

"Not now. As soon as you get out of here and have a chance to sort things out, then we'll talk about it. It's only important that you know I want to spend some private time with you as soon as you get the chance."

"Sure. I would love that. Really. Are you sure it isn't something you want to talk about now?"

"No. Really, Gina, this is not the time or the place. But do promise me, you will never do this to me again!"

Gina laughed weakly. "I wish I didn't do it to you in the first place. Believe me, I don't ever want to go through another day like today."

"Is there anything I can get for you? Do you want me to call Sophia?"

"Oh, thanks, but no. Robert will call my mother, who will notify the free world within thirty minutes. I haven't given him the go-ahead just yet, but I suspect I'll let him call her within the next hour. I don't want them to find out in the news—my mother would give me pure hell. I just have to prepare myself for their arrival, which can be somewhat overwhelming."

"Do you want me to stay with you until they arrive?"

"That's great of you to ask, but it would only raise more questions that I am not prepared to answer for them, especially not today. John is on his way over, and I am going to need to go over a few things with him. I appreciate your coming. I'll call you in a few days. I promise."

Nick didn't want to leave her—not today, not ever. He knew she was going to have a rough time dealing with the events of the day, but he respected her need to work. She was "in gear" and not at all prepared to detach from the issues at hand—just another trait that made him love her even more.

He bent down, kissed her gently on her lips, and hugged her tightly for a brief moment—an embrace so strong he could almost feel the transfer of soul from one body to the other. He was afraid. He had almost lost her, and he realized he could not handle it again. He was in love.

She was sorry to see him go but truly had other things on her mind. Her bigger concern was John Winthrop. *Where in the hell is he?* Gina thought.

As if on cue, John walked into the room. He didn't say anything, just stood there, looking much larger than the hospital room, like a giant who was very tired.

Gina sat up in her bed. "John, where are we? How bad is it? Do we have a final count?"

He continued to stand as if the room itself made him uncomfortable, unsure what to do with himself. "Well, it's bad, but it definitely could have been worse. The only civilians were the girl who entered the clinic and her boyfriend, and Ben was able to keep them in the car. That left only the doctor, Tatiana, and Sally in the building. The doctor blew up the building just before he exited the side door where you saw him. Seems he had it set that way for an emergency, but we will know more once the building cools. The fire is out, but the building is hot, real hot. Apparently the doctor made no effort to save Tatiana."

"Not very surprising, at least not to me. I keep going back and forth in my mind. On the one hand, I am horrified I shot him, but then I think about what he did, and I feel guilty for being *pleased* that I killed him. I'm happy he's dead, relieved he didn't escape. Is it horrible for me to feel this way?" She begged for his insight.

"Gina, it's perfectly normal. It is the human condition, and in many instances it is very predictable. You *should* feel happy that a horrible murderer who had little regard for anyone, including his own assistant, is dead. It's also natural for you to regret being the executioner. Our call is to protect life, not take it away. I'm afraid one just doesn't come without the other."

John was exhausted. Although his eyes were still bright, filled with thought, compassion, and grief, fatigue was visibly setting in as he rubbed his neck and stretched his back. Looking at him, Gina felt silly for being in a hospital gown lying in bed. What the hell was wrong with her anyway? She got out of bed and sat in the visitor's chair, which afforded her a modicum of professional appearance. She motioned for John to take the seat next her, and he did.

"John, did you find her?"

"Yes."

Neither of them said anything for a long while. There really was nothing to say. He had found Sally—or more appropriately, her remains—after the explosion.

Finally, Gina broke the silence. "What about the assistant?"

"Yes, we found her also. She was by the safe. She must have been trying to take the contents of it. We think she was in flight; we don't believe she ever thought he would kill her."

"What set him off? Do we know? What did Curt say?"

"He only replayed once—he was too busy getting the cleanup and rescue video. It seems Sally reacted violently when he approached the operating table. Her reaction seemed too extreme, at least to the doctor, because instead of calming her, he fled immediately. He yelled some sort of command to his assistant and disappeared. The video showed him injecting something into Sally. She may have been dead before the explosion, or at least heavily sedated."

"I don't know, John. I don't know how it all went wrong so quickly."

"You know what is so ironic? From a mission standpoint, we are successful. We accomplished our objective. We reached our goal. The clinic is gone—completely. The doctor and his assistant are dead, so there is no need to investigate, prosecute, or jail. From the taxpayer's perspective, this alone is cause to celebrate. But I'm sick, completely sick to my stomach. In thirty years of service, I have only lost four agents, and this is by far the most difficult. I mean, hell, Gina, it's life investigation for Chrissakes. We consider this division 'safe'—perfect for those who have had enough 'action.' I just can't believe it."

He was talking, not crying, not yelling—just talking. It was an appeal to Gina to hear him—not respond, just to hear him. Gina sensed that John had very few people in this world he could talk to. Gina was grateful he counted her among the few.

"John, before you protest, please hear me out. I want to go with you to Sally's house. I want to help you tell her mother." "I know, Gina. I know you want to come with me. That is exactly why I already went there. I just left her house; that's what took me so long."

"Oh, John. How bad ... what did she ... what did you say?" Gina stammered.

"She knew, Gina. As soon as she opened the door and saw me standing there, she knew. They always know. Why else would a federal agent be knocking at her door? She saw the explosion on the news and realized within a few seconds of seeing me. I watched her accept the most devastating news of her life. She didn't speak, and she didn't cry. You know what she did? She asked me if *I was okay.*

She asked me if she could help me. Can you believe it? I told her how Sally saved many lives, how she was very brave, and all along she looked at me to see if she could help *me*! Then, do you know what *I* did? I cried, Gina. I sat down in her living and bawled my eyes out while Sally's mother comforted me."

Gina didn't know what to say to him; she didn't know what to do at all.

"John ... oh, John. I'm so sorry. Your tears are important to her, much more important than your composure. She knows, in spite of her unmentionable loss, that Sally Lister, her beautiful baby girl, died a hero."

Her words fell flat in the sterile gray hospital room.

September 6, 2021

Planned Parenthood v. Martin goes to U.S. Supreme Court

The U.S. Supreme Court will begin deliberation of the Illinois case *Planned Parenthood v. Martin*. The case once again brings the issue of abortion and reproductive rights before the highest court in the land. A ruling in favor of Planned Parenthood could once again legalize abortion in this country. The court ruled in 2006 (*Mather v. Tutola*) that abortion infringed upon the constitutional rights of the fetus, rendering a complete overturn of the 1972 *Roe v. Wade* ruling where abortion was first made legal.

Chapter 26

.

NICK sat in his kitchen staring out the double doors to the river over a fresh, hot mug of morning coffee. He was lost in deep thought, altogether oblivious to the view or his surroundings. William was in the kitchen preparing breakfast, and Nick was completely unaware of his presence, indicating to William just how preoccupied Nick was.

"Nick, what is causing such concern? Gina is still meeting you today, is she not?"

"Oh, good morning, William. No ... I mean, yes, she is still meeting me today. Unfortunately, that's the problem. Today I tell her."

"Nick, you look ill. Surely if the lady loves you, she will respect, if nothing else, your honesty."

"No, William, this is completely different. She has spent her career prosecuting abortionists, and I am going to tell her today."

"I do understand. I am not daft, you know. I simply think you are making much too much of this. I know you love her and are compelled by forces, which I am sure I do not understand, to tell her everything. Well, fine, then go ahead and get on with it. If she takes issue with you, it is best you discover this now as opposed to later."

"I am afraid I will lose her. I am afraid she won't love me enough to overlook what I tell her."

"Nick, I love you like a son—you know this. I think the world of you. I am so proud of your achievements. However, you are now a man, not a boy. Your character is solid, and I think you need to tell Gina whatever you must and deal with the outcome in the graceful fashion that I have grown accustomed to."

"Direct hit. You've sunk my battleship."

"I do not find your response to my guidance humorous in the least."

"Oh, cut it out. I know you are right, as always. I am just going to 'get on with it,' as you say."

"Very good. I will see you this evening."

Nick still had an hour before he would be meeting Gina. She was visiting her grandmother, and they had agreed to meet for lunch in Freehold. He had suggested Federicis, which he loved. They had the best thin crust pizza and house salad complete with thick, creamy Italian dressing, salami, and provolone.

He felt like a schoolboy, but he knew telling her was necessary. If she didn't want to see him again, then so be it. At least he will have been honest. The bigger problem would be Sophia. Sophia would be furious if she knew he was going to tell Gina, especially because she wanted him to wait until after the ruling. Nick didn't care. He didn't know how long the ruling was going to take, and he didn't want to wait anymore. Hopefully, Gina wouldn't go off, or worse yet, arrest him. She could if she wanted to, but he really didn't think it would come to that—at least, he hoped not. The café was located at the intersection of Main and South Streets, the heart of downtown Freehold. He arrived first and took a table in the back. Usually he sat at a table in the front room by the windows, where you couldn't help but look at the people walking down the street. The tables in the back were private. He might need privacy, especially if she flipped.

She breezed in, and he caught his breath—she was prettier every time he saw her. God, he had to get control of himself. It was so unlike him to be this way. Usually confident and slightly aloof, he was not used to having a woman really get under his skin.

"Hi, there, Doctor," she chimed as she gave him a kiss on the cheek.

"I'm so glad to see you. I've really missed you. How are things?"

"It's been tough, but I'm hanging in there. Sally's funeral was hard—on all of us. We have wrapped up most of the loose ends, and things have finally quieted down. It's good to be out in the country."

"Well, it's not exactly the country, Gina."

"It's not New York City, that's for sure."

"Gina, I'm really happy you could meet me today. I know how difficult things have been for you, but I really need to tell you some things I've been holding back. I meant what I said at the hospital. I love you, and before I go on and on, I want to know if you feel as strongly as I do."

"Well, nothing like getting right to the point!"

"I'm sorry. It's just that I have wanted to talk to you since before the … uh … accident."

"No, it's fine. Really. I was actually just trying to be funny. Anyway, I feel strongly about you too. I can't tell you how many times I've just wanted to call or drive out to see you. You are a bigger part of my thoughts than you could possibly imagine."

Gina couldn't understand where the conversation was going, but she sensed that it was serious, at least for Nick.

"Gina, I have told you how I feel about abortion. I told you I would prefer that it were legal, and I feel very strongly about my position."

"Yes, Nick, we've been through this. I understand."

"No, Gina, you don't know everything. I have performed procedures that are illegal."

"I'm sorry. I don't know what you're driving at. What procedures?"

"Gina, I perform abortions in a safe medical facility. I have done this in addition to maintaining my main practice. I do not charge. It is not for profit; it is simply out of necessity. I do it to keep them alive, to keep them from doing it themselves … or worse. I do not regret my decision, but I need you to know. I love you and want to marry you, but I could never keep this from you. I just hope we can move beyond this together."

Gina was stunned. She was always stunned when Nick had something important to tell her. Why was he telling her this? Didn't he know what she did for a living?

"Nick, I am not sure why you are telling me this, but I don't want you to say any more. I don't want to hear it, not another word! I can't imagine why you want to tell me this, especially knowing who I am. Don't you dare clear your conscience at my expense!"

He had been afraid this might happen—she was reacting exactly as he had hoped she wouldn't. "Gina, please, let me explain. I had to help these girls. I am a professional doctor. I knew when they were going to put their lives in danger, and I knew if they were completely incapable of going to term. I did it to help them."

Gina was furious. She could feel her teeth clenching and wanted to slap him. She couldn't believe what he was saying. She wanted him to stop; she wanted it to all go away.

"Just stop it! I don't want you to say a thing! Not a single word! This is what I do, Nick. I find people like you, *especially* people like you, and I arrest them! Do you want me to arrest you, Nick?"

Before he could answer, she grabbed her purse and ran from the restaurant.

Her mind was reeling. How could it be? Why did he tell her? He was an abortionist! She'd known he was too good to be true! Handsome, funny, single, wealthy—he was definitely too good to be true. But she had never expected this! Nothing could have prepared her for this. Did her grandmother know? It wouldn't surprise her. Not one damn bit. Sophia was Sophia, and she didn't let the incidentals get in the way of her plan.

What was she going to do? Fury, shock, sadness, and a variety of other emotions overwhelmed her. She couldn't settle down, couldn't focus, and without any warning or the ability to stop it, she had an all-out panic attack.

No use in fighting it. She rummaged through her purse, opened the vial, and popped a Xanax, which was already cut in half, ready and waiting for such a moment.

She drove back to the city, struggling to catch her breath and to stop her heart from beating out of her chest. By the time she reached the door to her place, the pill had kicked in and she was exhausted—completely, totally, physically and mentally exhausted.

It was Saturday, so when she dropped onto her bed, she knew there was only one way to deal with how she felt: lockdown.

October 11, 2021

U.S. Supreme Court to Rule on Reproduction

The U.S. Supreme Court is expected to render a decision on *Planned Parenthood v. Martin* as soon as next week. If the Court rules in favor of Planned Parenthood, *Mather v. Tutola* would be overturned for the first time since 2006. *Mather v. Tutola* rendered abortion illegal in the Unites States, providing all fetuses protection under the Constitution from time of conception.

Chapter 27

"GINA, I have four calls from him, and it's not even nine o'clock! Please call him, if just to get him off my back. I can't accomplish anything with him calling every damn minute!"

"Are there any other calls?" she asked, completely ignoring his remarks.

"Gina, pleeeeeease call him so I can get some work done. As far as other calls, your grandmother called again. She wants to meet you either in the city or at the house. It sounded urgent. You'd better at least call *her*!"

"Fine. I'll be on the cell."

She had successfully avoided everyone for weeks. After her thirty-six-hour lockdown (refusing to answer the phone, wash, dress, or leave the house), she had finally pulled herself together and gone to work the following Monday. Since then, she had dodged every call from Nick, and the calls had escalated to nearly a half dozen calls per day. It took longer for her grandmother to catch on that something was amiss because she had been calling only for the last week. Sophia was a force she would have to deal with—sooner rather than later. Gina planned on calling her today.

Gina didn't know if Sophia knew about Nick or not. The truth was, Gina didn't feel like dealing with any of it. If she called Sophia back, she would surely get some sort of sermon or third degree as to why she wasn't with Nick. Another possibility was that Sophia knew about Nick and had set them up anyway. In either case, Gina would be having a discussion she didn't want to have.

Gina tentatively dialed the house. "Hi, Grandma, it's me. Robert said you called."

"Hello, Gina. Why have you been avoiding my calls?"

"Grandma, I am not avoiding you. I've just been so busy. So much paperwork since the Brooklyn case."

"Yes, yes, dear, I'm sure it must be very hectic, the federal bureaucracy and all. Gina, it's very important that I speak with you, in person."

"I'm sorry, Grandma. I don't know if I'll be able to—"

"Gina, cut it out! I don't have time or patience for this.

I know what happened with Nick, and I need to speak with you in person. There are things you clearly do not understand. If, after we meet, you still feel the same way, then you are free to continue ignoring us all."

"I am not ignoring anyone."

"Gina, please. When can I see you?"

When Sophia set her sight on something, nothing would deter her, absolutely nothing. Gina figured it was best to give in early because it consumed a lot less energy.

"I'll come out to the house this afternoon," Gina replied.

"Fine. I will see you then."

Gina was tired. It seemed as if her world was slowly unraveling around her, and she didn't know what to do about it. It took an enormous effort to ignore Nick, and Gina just didn't have the stamina. She still wasn't completely sure of Sophia's role in the whole affair, but she was beginning to believe it was more extensive than she had thought. She loved them both, and they had lied to her. She wasn't furious; she was tired—very, very tired.

Just as she exited the tunnel, her cell rang. It was Robert—again.

"Yeah, what's up?"

"Listen, you are going to have to break down and call this guy. I have no idea what he did to go from Prince Charming to the frog, but you need to return his call. A 'William' just called to speak with you on his behalf. That very fine English-sounding gentleman. You are going to have to tell me more about him, my dear."

"*William* called? That's odd."

"Yep, that's what he said. 'It may seem odd that I'm calling, but … .' In any event, Missy, he sounds like a great guy, and you should at least call him back."

"All right, already! What number did he give you?"

"He says it is the house number, and he hopes you will ring him. What does this William look like?"

"Robert, would you please cut it out! He's like a father to Nick. He is just a very nice and proper Englishman. Although I must say, he is handsome."

"Description, please," Robert demanded.

"Sixtyish, about 5'10", medium weight, bald but in a good way, with those round wire-rimmed glasses. But I don't think he would be interested, Robert."

"You just let me worry about that."

"No, I mean, I don't think he is gay."

"Gina, puhleeeze—male, handsome, never married, housekeeper, in his sixties … I mean, do you live under a rock?"

"He is a butler! A butler. Robert, you had better not offend him. I like William; he is a very nice man."

"Don't worry. I don't plan on offending him. I was just inquiring, that's all," he sang.

"I'm on my way to my grandmother's. It's time to deal with them all."

"Finally! Just make sure you call William back. Are you ever going to let me in on what's going on here?"

"Nothing is going on, Robert. I'll talk to ya later."

With that, she clicked off the call.

She kept thinking about William. He was such a nice man, and he treated her wonderfully. She knew it had to be important for him to contact her, especially because he was not the meddling type. She had absolutely no reason to avoid him and decided to return his call. She dialed the number, hoping that William would answer and not Nick.

"Good afternoon."

"Hi, William. It's Gina. My assistant mentioned you called."

"Gina, so delighted to hear from you, my dear. I do apologize for disturbing you, and I hope you will forgive me for putting my nose where it definitely should not be."

"William, you are not bothering me in the least. What's up?"

"I know you had a falling out. I do not know all the details, nor do I want to. I just want you to know how devastated he is. I do not know what price one must pay for true love, but I fear he is paying it. Now that I am saying it aloud, I must admit I sound foolish. I only know that he is absolutely beside himself."

"Oh, William, I know he is. I am so sorry, and I do love him. I just don't know if I can speak with him yet. I'm very angry, and I don't want to fight. It's very complicated."

"Matters of the heart usually are."

"I'm not sure why my grandmother introduced me to Nick or why he agreed to meet me. I don't know how they considered us a perfect match."

"Weren't you the perfect match? I know I thought you were. I have never seen Nick so alive. I believe I saw the same light in your eyes. The road is never straight, but with work it can be navigated."

"Normally, yes, but in this case I just don't think it's possible."

"Gina, just think about it. Agree to meet him, just to give him a chance to talk. You each need closure. Just ending it like this is not fair to either of you."

"You're right. I can't make any promises now, but maybe in a few weeks …I just don't know."

"That is all I can ask for. Thank you, my dear. I do hope I get a chance to see you again."

With that he was gone, and Gina was depressed. She liked William, and she loved Nick. If only she could erase the whole damn thing like it never ever happened. Actually, she missed him.

She wished he had never told her. Secretly she didn't care about any of it. She just wanted to be with him. Enough! She was going to see Sophia, and she needed to be prepared. The severity of the issue was starting to fade. She missed Nick. What did she want?

She turned off the power to her phone. She would need the ride to collect her thoughts. She would hear her out but would not let Sophia steamroll her—not this time, anyway.

Sophia was in the office with the interior designer planning the annual Christmas decorations. Sophia always did it up "big" for Christmas; she had ever since she was a young girl. She spent a small fortune each year decking out the house and the grounds for the Christmas season.

"Hi, Grandma. Close to that time of year?"

"Gina, hellooo! Yes, I would like everything ready the week before Thanksgiving this year. I am planning a toy drive for the Thanksgiving weekend, and I thought it would get everyone in the holiday spirit."

Sophia finished up with the designer and led Gina to the kitchen. "I have lunch for us, dear. Your favorite: Waldorf salad."

"Thanks. I haven't had it in so long."

Sophia jumped right in. She was not in the mood for small talk and preferred getting right to the point.

"Nick loves you. I know he told you about his side activity, and I think we need to talk this over."

Gina couldn't believe Sophia was telling her this right up front, boldly admitting she knew all about it.

"Grandma, I don't believe you! How could you fix me up with him knowing what he did?"

"Gina, cut it out. Nick DePaolo is a great doctor who provides a great service to women in this country. Think about it. He didn't need to risk his career. He is a successful doctor with more than enough money. He didn't do this for personal gain. He did it for desperate women—women you meet every damn day of your career. Please, Gina, put aside this holier-than-thou bullshit for a second and think! You, yourself, told me you felt bad for the women you investigate. He felt bad also, only he decided he would do something about it. Why he ever told you is completely beyond me! He apparently loves you very much to risk telling you, of all people, his secret. Now, I do not want this to get out of hand, but I think it truly needs to be put into perspective."

Gina was speechless. Her grandmother was actually irritated with her. She could hardly believe it. Irritated with *her*!

"Grandma, I really don't want to fight. Surely you can understand the difficulty I have in dating an abortionist! Surely the irony does not escape you!"

"Gina, really! I know your job is important, but Nick DePaolo is not an abortionist as you say. He is not an opportunist. He helped women who otherwise would have truly hurt themselves. He helped girls who were raped, young girls who didn't even know what had happened to them. Gina, you see it every day. Have we eliminated abortion in this country? Come on! Think about it. Does the law work? Have the abortions stopped? *No*, they haven't! You know it, and I know it. I am not asking you to advocate it either. I am asking that you respect a difference in opinion. If it were the year 2000, you would consider Dr. Nick DePaolo a great doctor, top in his field!"

"It's not 2000; it's 2021, and it is illegal in this country to terminate a pregnancy. Period. As a matter of fact, it is my job to uphold that law, lest we all forget!"

"Fine. What do you plan on doing?"

"What do you mean?"

"I mean, what do you plan on doing now that he's told you this? Are you going to arrest him? Investigate him? What?"

"I wasn't planning on doing anything. I do know I can't see him anymore."

Gina didn't know where Sophia was going with all this, but she sensed Sophia had a plan. Sophia always had a plan.

"Well, if your beliefs are so strong, then I believe it is your obligation to investigate. If you do not, then you will be committing a crime. Isn't that true?" Sophia asked.

Gina faltered, and she paused a moment before replying. "Well, yes . . . but I stopped him before he revealed too much. I did not get any of the specifics, so I was just going to avoid him."

"Gina, listen to me. If you do not investigate and arrest him, then you will be committing a crime. Isn't that true?"

"Yes, but it is my judgment."

"Exactly my point."

"It's not the same!"

"It *is* the same, Gina. The world is not black and white. Ask yourself why you didn't even consider investigating him. It's because you did not consider him a criminal. On some level, you know he is not a threat, that there is some merit to his actions. Otherwise, you would have had him thrown in jail. I know it, and so do you."

Damn her! Damn her for always being right! Why didn't she prosecute Nick? Why did she drop it and just run away? If he were a threat to anyone, she would not hesitate to stop him. On some level, she did not think of him as a criminal. Was it because she loved him? No, that really wasn't it. Even if she loved him, she would arrest him if he put another person in danger. She just didn't consider him the same as the doctor she had killed. He didn't kill women and babies for money. He really believed he was helping, and Gina knew firsthand that he was. She knew how many died every year by their own hand or by that of a butcher. She didn't know what she believed anymore. She was lost. The more she tried to sort it out, the worse it became. The fear, uncertainty, and pain threatened her, played with her, tricked her. Confidence and conviction, her longtime companions, were absent. They had served her well her entire life. Where were they now? Would they ever return?

Gina drew a deep breath and firmly faced Sophia, "You've made your point. Now let me talk, and don't interrupt. I don't consider him a criminal—not for one second. I saw too much good in him to consider him a threat to anyone. Still, it doesn't change the fact that what he did is illegal, and I should have turned the information over to someone who *would* investigate. I personally, as well as professionally, believe abortion is a crime. You know this. Now factor in the recent cases I've worked on—the death and tragedy that I have seen firsthand—and then tell me you don't understand why I am beside myself over this!"

"Oh, Gina, I do understand. I do. I just know there is more to this, and you know it, too. You have your doubts about the system; you told me as much the last time you were here. Abortion is rampant, and women are dying. These are facts we cannot ignore anymore. Gina, think about it. If we took all the money we spent on prosecuting this law, we could work to eliminate the need for abortions. Do you really think we accomplished what we set out to do?"

In good conscience Gina could not argue. She knew it herself. The women were persecuted, prosecuted, imprisoned, or killed. Meanwhile, the rapists, the crooked doctors, the back-alley abortionists were not held responsible. Death was all around her, every day, because the law did not really stop the killing.

"Grandma, what do you want from me?" Gina surrendered.

"I want you to seriously consider the situation. I want you to evaluate your own thoughts over the last few months. Then, and only then, if you still feel there is no way you can come to terms with what Nick did, I want you to arrest me."

"What? What are you talking about?"

"When you're done arresting me, you will also have to arrest Francesca. Oh, and your cousin Lily, the girl next door, Joelle, and at least a dozen others."

"What do you mean?"

"Gina, I sent the girls to Nick. Each girl was desperate—their personal situations could not be ignored. He did it for them—for me. Go ask Francesca. She begged for help for her niece. Go ahead!"

"Stop it, Grandma. I have had enough for today. Really, I don't think I can take any more. You accomplished what you set out to do. I understand why you feel this way. But what you fail to realize is that this causes me to reevaluate my whole life—my career, my values, my position. It is not just about Nick. Who am I? What do I believe? I just don't know anymore. Grandma, I just … don't … know," Gina sobbed, her voice breaking.

"I know, Gina. I know, baby. It's not about Nick. It's about you. I know. I know."

Sophia held Gina. Each of them was exhausted—grandmother and granddaughter in a completely new place. Gina wiped her eyes with the back of her hand as her cell phone flashed, chimed, and jumped. She welcomed the intrusion.

"Agent Vincent here."

"It's Robert. You need to get to New York Hospital."

"Why? What's wrong?"

"Lisa is in labor, and she wants her coach. What was it she said? Oh, yeah, 'Tell her to get her freakin' ass to the hospital nooowwwww!'"

"I'm on my way! Robert, can you go there now? Tell her I am on my way. Stand in for me until I get there! Please!"

"I will go there so I can tell her in person, *but* I am *not* standing in for you. I will calm her and tell her you are on your way, but that's it. Now get going," Robert commanded.

Gina threw her arms around Sophia and screeched, "Lisa's in labor! I gotta go! We'll talk later, Grandma. I love you!"

Chapter 28

SHE made it to the hospital in just under forty-five minutes—a record, if she did say so herself! She flashed her badge to the security guard, who promptly let her leave her car just outside the front doors—still the *best* perk her job offered. Breathless, she ran to the information desk asking for maternity, delivery, or wherever the hell they put you when the baby was coming! A perky nurse with a kind face escorted her down the first corridor off the entrance hall and through double hospital doors into the maternity ward.

It wasn't exactly difficult to find, with large storks carrying babies painted nearly six feet high on the walls. Once they were in the ward, they turned right once again, heading down a smaller corridor with four doors on either side. The nurse led her to the last door on the left. It was the birthing or delivery room, decked out in designer fashion with coordinating bedding, wallpapered walls, and custom draperies. Gina was stunned; she had *never* seen a room like this before. Before Gina could recover from the room's designer fashion, she saw Lisa. But even more shocking than the sight of her friend was the sight of her assistant—Robert was holding Lisa's hand and wiping her face with a towel.

"I thought you weren't going to fill in for me," Gina taunted.

"Oh, and look who's here. What choice did I have? I tell her you are on your way, and she goes into a full-blown contraction. I nearly dropped myself! I couldn't exactly walk out."

Lisa was sweating profusely, and her face was extremely pale. She had just finished a contraction and was gulping air in an effort to recover.

"I'm glad you made it. I was getting worried. Robert took good care of me. Thanks for sending him." Lisa rattled off, breathless.

"How are you feeling? What's going on?"

"Gina, pleeease. No stupid questions—she may kill us both. She morphs into Lucifer during one of those contractions," Robert deadpanned.

"Lisa, how far apart are the contractions?" Gina asked, ignoring Robert's assessment.

"I don't know. I think four minutes. They said I was only five centimeters dilated and that it would be a while."

"How long ago was that?"

"Before Robert arrived. I have kind of lost all track of time."

Just then, another contraction contorted Lisa's face, and her whole body tightened, almost as if an invisible force was pushing her body into a ball.

"Breathe, Lisa. We practiced this, remember? You have to breathe through it. Focus. Breathe. Count," Gina instructed.

"Oh, boy! She is gonna whip your ass as soon as she gets the chance!" Robert warned.

"Stop. She has to do this. This is what we practiced. We are prepared for this," Gina explained as much to Lisa as to Robert.

Lisa pleaded, "Gina, *it is not like they told us!* I want to die."

"Come on, now. Settle down, take a breath, and find your focal point. We can do this, Lisa, you and I. Come on—breathe!"

"Gina Marie Vincent, you stop coaching me this very instant, or *I swear I will rip every hair out of your head!*" Lisa yelled.

"Told you so," Robert whispered.

Gina realized she was causing Lisa more stress and thought she should fetch the doctor, or even a nurse, for an update on exactly where Lisa was in the labor process.

"Lisa, I'm going to see if I can find someone who can update us. Okay?"

"How about you find an anesthesiologist? I have been waiting for one since I got here," Lisa demanded.

Gina quickly ran from the room after Robert gave her a nod indicating he would stay until she returned. This was not what Gina had pictured at all. She had known it would hurt, but *this*— Lisa was beside herself in pain. She hadn't expected this at all. Lisa wasn't the least bit reasonable, and it didn't seem like anything they had practiced would be useful to them now. Gina had seen babies delivered before, mostly accidentally in the field, the "it's too late to make it to the hospital" deliveries. She never really had witnessed the labor part, the part that led up to the baby's arrival. It was *wicked*, just wicked. There was no other way to describe it.

Gina grabbed the first nurse she saw, who instructed her to return to the room. She promised someone would be along shortly. Gina went back to the room, where Robert was once again patting Lisa's forehead with a towel. Lisa was between contractions and once again looked a little more like herself.

"Hey, lady. Good to see you. Robert is a keeper. He can stay with me anytime." Lisa said.

"Lisa, how bad are they?"

"Gina, let's just say, no amount of breathing, panting, or 'hee heeing' is going to help with these things. It feels like someone is taking a bat and whomping me full force across the stomach. Knocks the breath right out of you and then follows up with the most wretched tightening cramp you could ever imagine. Oh, no, here's another—"

Just then, as if on cue, Lisa clenched her teeth as another contraction contorted her face—body tightening, face reddening, knuckles whitening, vein bulging, and then, mercifully, releasing. It was twenty seconds long, all up, all in. Gina didn't know if she could stand another. This was no joke. Mother Nature could be a real bitch!

"Gina, I'm afraid. Really afraid! I knew it would hurt, but I never expected this! They are actually getting worse!"

Lisa looked relieved as she yelled out her fears. It was as if telling everyone was taking the burden off.

"G, I don't know if I can do this," Lisa confessed.

"I know, Lisa. I'm sure it's bad, but you'll make it," Gina offered as she held Lisa's hand. "Robert, go see where the hell the nurse is!"

Robert scurried from the room, leaving Gina a little more confident. With that one command, they both felt more like themselves—Gina taking charge while Robert saw to the details. It wasn't thirty seconds before Robert returned with the nurse, who entered clucking and soothing.

"Now, now, dear, where are we? Oh, yes, I see. Good girl. Very good. You are doing so well. Excellent. Coming along very nicely. Ms. Talbot, you are doing a great job for you and your baby. Very good."

Gina squelched the urge to beat the nurse. "Exactly where are we, Nurse … ah … Norton?" Gina found the nurse's badge and addressed her by her proper name; that always carried more authority.

"I'm sorry. Who are you?"

"I am Gina Vincent, the birthing coach."

"Oh, yes, I see. Well, Ms. Talbot is six centimeters dilated, and the contractions are still about four minutes apart, although the intensity is increasing."

"Ms. Talbot requested an anesthesiologist. Do you know when one will arrive?"

"Oh, dear, I'm sorry. Let me check on that right now. Yes, yes, it definitely should have been by now."

The nurse, clearly flustered after checking the chart, quickly left the room babbling on about her return with the doctor. Gina sighed with relief. Action always made her feel better. Lisa just braced herself for the worst. Fear etched five horizontal lines across her forehead.

"Lisa, have you finalized the names yet?" Gina asked in an effort to keep Lisa's mind occupied. The breathing exercises were clearly useless.

"If it's a girl, Chelsea. I love that name; it reminds me of the Chelsea section. G, remember the first time we went out downtown?

The art houses, lofts, cafés—it was so cosmopolitan. I will never forget that day. If it's a boy, I still have no idea."

Just then, another contraction hit. This time an involuntary screech escaped her lips. Lisa tried to brace herself against the tightness. Gina winced at the sight of her. The severity of her pain was visible in her twisted facial expression. Gina realized she was holding her own breath until it was over. Childbirth was definitely not for the faint of heart. When it finally ended, Gina once again changed the subject—diversion would be the only strategy that could help Lisa under the circumstances.

"This room is awesome. They decorated it beautifully. I never saw a hospital room like this before," Gina said.

"This is just the birthing room. After the baby is born, I go to a regular room. They figure you should be in beautiful surroundings when your baby arrives. It is supposed to be soothing and help me feel comfortable. The truth is, when I got here I noticed how pretty it was, but after the first heavy contraction it all disappeared. The room is just a blur. I really think they have the plan backward—they should give me the pretty room as a reward for this!"

Gina completely agreed with her friend. What use was the pretty room if you were in so much pain you didn't even notice it? Just then, a young Middle Eastern man in green scrubs entered the room. "I am Dr. Aboud, the anesthesiologist."

Dr. Aboud checked her chart, read the machine that was monitoring the contractions, and watched as another contraction arrived. Once it was over, he quickly announced, "I will give you an epidural where I can regulate the medication. As you draw closer to ten centimeters, I will have to shut the pain reliever off so you can deliver. Do you understand?"

Lisa looked at the man as if he had ten heads. "I don't care if you hit me over the head with a Coke bottle. Just help me!"

Dr. Aboud smiled; he was no stranger to labor. "I'll have you fixed up in just a moment. I'm afraid you will have to clear the room, even your husband."

"Oh, he's not my husband. They are my birth coaches. I couldn't decide on one," Lisa lied.

"In any event, they need to leave, but once the epidural is in, I promise they can return."

Gina and Robert left the room as the doctor instructed. Gina called out, "I'll be right outside the door, Lisa. Just yell if you need me. I'm right outside the door."

Barely five minutes had passed when the doctor announced they could come back in. Gina rushed in and was shocked to see Lisa sitting up, completely relaxed and smiling.

"G, I love that man, more than I have ever loved any man in my life."

Dr. Aboud chuckled. "All the women say that. I am glad you are feeling better. I will check back soon."

"You look like you feel a helluva lot better." Gina said.

"I feel great! Awesome! Now, what were we talking about?" Lisa asked.

"We were talking about this beautiful room. I can't believe you feel so much better. That epidural must really be something." Gina looked at the digital read on the monitor. "Lisa, you are having a contraction, a mother of a contraction! Don't you feel anything?"

"Not a thing," she answered.

Robert quipped, "Gotta get me an epidural. That is some strong shit!"

Lisa was able to relax enough that she actually took a short nap. Gina and Robert did not leave her for a minute, and as long as the hospital wasn't throwing Robert out, they were all very content to stay together. The nurse came to check on her and indicated it would be very soon. She returned with the obstetrician and Dr. Aboud, who checked the feed to Lisa's line. Lisa's obstetrician was Dr. Neidermeyer, a fortyish woman with cropped brown hair and a wide, square smile.

"Lisa, it's time," the doctor said, gently waking Lisa from her nap.

"Oh, Dr. Neidermeyer. Time? What time?" Lisa asked, rubbing her eyes.

"It's time for you to go to work, my dear. You are ten centimeters, and the contractions are very close. Dr. Aboud will turn down the epidural so you can feel them again. You need to feel the contractions so you know when to push—okay?"

"Sure, Doctor, I know. Time to push," Lisa said, still not fully comprehending the program.

Dr. Neidermeyer turned to Gina. "You must be Gina. Lisa has told me all about you. She is very fortunate to have you as a birthing partner."

"Nice to meet you, Doctor, although I am not sure I completely agree with your assessment of my birthing capabilities. I feel like a square wheel."

"Don't worry. The important part is coming. Stay close to her head, hold her hand, and take her lead. You'll do fine," Dr. Neidermeyer said as she turned to address Robert. "And you are ..."

Lisa answered before either of them could respond. "Doc, he's a dear friend. Please let him stay."

"No, Lisa, I'll be in the waiting room. Really, I do very well *away* from the action," Robert said, the double meaning not being lost on Gina.

"Lisa, it's better if it's just you and your coach. I will let your friend come back in once the baby is here, I promise," Dr. Neidermeyer explained.

Robert kissed Lisa's hand. "You will do mahvelous, simply mahvelous, dahling!"

Lisa smiled and waved as Robert left the birthing room. Dr. Aboud adjusted the flow of pain reliever to Lisa's feed. The worry lines returned to Lisa's forehead, indicating she once again felt the contractions. The nurse adjusted the bed, placed Lisa's feet in the stirrups, and in one quick motion pulled the center of the bed out. She looked like a magician—the bottom of the bed was gone. Vanished! One big surprise after another!

"It's a birthing bed. It is specially made to adjust to the delivery," the doctor explained.

Lisa was sweating once again. Her skin was white, and her hair was wet and pasted to her head. Her eyes were wild with fear as the contractions hit her faster and stronger. She squeezed Gina's hand tight. Her nails cut into Gina's skin. Gina didn't feel a thing. She was mesmerized. The delivery had a life of its own. Lisa didn't speak; her body just adjusted to the rhythm of the contractions.

"Okay, Lisa. Another one is coming. Make it work for you. Don't lose any of it. Get ready. Go," the doctor instructed as the next contraction hit.

Lisa tightened her grip on the rails. Her face was nearly purple, her veins bulging, while her eyes squeezed into tiny slits as she pushed from the depths of her soul. The veins snaked red around her eyes, and she actually burst a few vessels. She sucked in a deep gulp of air and wiggled her butt slightly back on the bed before she repeated the whole process again and again.

Gina felt the room fall away from her, unaware of everything except Lisa and the doctor's instructions. Everything around them was a blur, and the only clear images were those of Lisa, the bed, and the doctor. They were sharp, focused, and clear, surrounded by a fuzzy cloud. The world was reduced to this small moment in time and space.

"Good job, Lisa. One or two more pushes, and your baby is here. I see the head. Don't push until I say. Make the most of the contraction, wait for my lead, get ready … *push!*"

Lisa took a deep breath, squeezed Gina's hand, and summoned strength from God knows where! She let out a groan that came from the center of the earth, pushing with every muscle in her body, when the head popped out of her! Before Lisa could suck any air back in, the being shot out of her in a rush of fluid! Lisa's body deflated back onto the bed.

"Beautiful. Lisa, you have a beautiful baby girl!"

The doctor held the baby, cord still attached, so Lisa could see her. "Gina, would you like to do the honors?" the doctor asked.

Propelled by unseen hands, Gina stood next to the doctor, took the scissor-like instrument, and cut the cord. Never would words ever accurately describe the emotion she felt at that moment. Elation, awe, exultation, jubilation, triumph—those words came close, but it seemed to Gina that the moment called for a new word, one created just for the occasion. Truly, it was a miracle, a divine intervention that humbled the human condition. Tears streamed down their faces, tears they were completely unaware of as they hugged, cried, and hugged some more.

"G, I have a baby girl. A beautiful baby girl. Thank you, oh, thank you, God," Lisa cried as they placed her baby on her chest.

"You do, Lisa! She is gorgeous, just perfect!" Gina sobbed.

The pediatrician stepped in from the shadows of the room and retrieved the baby from Lisa. As the doctor assessed the infant's health, Gina followed them everywhere, never letting them out of her sight. Dr. Neidermeyer finished up with Lisa.

"Lisa, I'm going with Chelsea. I'll be right back," Gina said to her childhood friend.

"Don't leave her for a second, G!"

"I won't, I promise."

As soon as they finished weights, measures, finger and footprints, Chelsea and Gina returned to Lisa. They cleaned Chelsea up and put a little pink woolen hat on her head. She was the most perfect being Gina had ever seen in her life—heaven on earth, a true little angel. Lisa held Chelsea close to her chest while Gina went to tell Robert the good news.

"G, bring Robert in here. I want him to see his godchild!"

"You're kidding?" Gina asked.

"No, I can't think of two better godparents: my best friend and her faithful assistant.

Seconds later Robert was staring at Lisa and Chelsea, bawling like the grownup child he was.

Gina held Lisa's hand. "You did good today. Very good, my oldest and best friend. I have another surprise for you."

Lisa looked at Gina, confused. "What surprise?"

Gina walked to the door and brought Mr. and Mrs. Talbot into the birthing room. "I have two very proud grandparents dying to meet their very first granddaughter—Ms. Chelsea Talbot."

Lisa's parents rushed to her side. Her father stared at the baby while her mother cried hysterically. "I'm sorry, Lisa, but I had to call them. I didn't want them to miss out on one of the most important events in their life. I hope you're not mad," Gina quickly explained to Lisa.

Gina didn't expect Lisa to answer; she knew it was more than all right. They were a family, a complete family, and there was nothing like the arrival of a child to adjust everyone's perspective. Lisa's mother doted on her, while her father held her newborn baby girl. It was a perfect moment. Gina could not control herself—she excused herself to the waiting room and cried. A true breakdown, nothing held back, like the crumbling of a dam, she just cried and cried.

Robert found her in the waiting room curled up in a corner chair. Most bystanders left her alone, figuring some sort of medical tragedy had befallen her or a family member. He rushed to her side, not sure what could possibly be wrong.

"Gina, what's wrong? Why are you crying?"

"I'm sorry. I don't know what's wrong with me. I was so happy, thrilled actually, when the baby came. Then out of nowhere, I can't control myself. I can't stop crying."

"It's all right. Gina, really, you have been through so much. I've been expecting this. You need to grieve; you need to get it all out. I think you should give in to it. Cry louder," he soothed.

She smiled through a tear-stained face, "You always know how to make me laugh." Gina sniffled and wiped her eyes on the back of her hand. "Robert, I love him, and I miss him. I'm sad over Sally, but I'm devastated over losing him. I don't know what to feel or what to do. I want to be with him. I don't care what he did; I just want to be with him."

"That's the real problem, Gina, isn't it? You can't continue this charade. There is no shame in loving him. I don't care what he did; we are fortunate to find true love only a few times in our lives, if ever. Don't blow it, Gina. Go to him. Go to him now."

"I can't. You don't know what he did. Robert, he performs procedures—*illegal procedures*!"

"Gina, of course I know. I swear your naiveté can be sweet but also very irritating. Our job is not so much to catch them all, only the dangerous ones. This has been going on since the beginning of time, and it will go on long into the future. He is not asking you to change, only to understand him. Now stop being so righteous and go to him."

"I don't know what I would say."

"Just show up at his door. I venture a guess you won't have to *say* anything!"

"I can't just show up at his door."

"And why not? Now is the perfect time. You have great news about your godchild being born, so why not share it with someone you love? Go give Chelsea a hug and Lisa a kiss, and then get the hell out of here!"

"You really think I should?"

"Yes, dear, I really do."

She drove, blinded by the fear of losing him. She tried not to picture herself chickening out at the last moment. The thought of her car parked on a rural country road in central Jersey would be enough for her to turn around. She consciously had to fight the voice that threatened her actions. *Just go with it*, she commanded. *Don't think; just drive.*

It was early evening when she arrived at his house. The round, burning orange ball that was the sun was just setting over the river, leaving streaks of dark purple and burnt rust in the sky. The scene was straight out of a painting. Real life could never produce such a picture. She sat in the car, memorizing the scene while willing herself to go in. What was she doing? Had she lost her mind? It was crazy but liberating. She was happy. She felt alive. It was right. Never before had she experienced such conviction. With her heart racing, hands shaking, and palms sweating, she tapped the doorbell, hoping he was home.

He answered the door before the second ring, shocked to see her. There she was on his front porch, as if it were a dream. For a moment, there was nothing but silence, that awkward, elongated silence—when a day's worth of thought is compressed into a few seconds of mind-racing frenetic activity.

"Hi," was all she managed. It was a weak, nervous squeak of a greeting.

He broke into a huge smile as he lifted her off the ground and buried his head in her hair.

"I have missed you so much," he breathed into her ear.

"Me, too."

Chapter 29

SOPHIA had cleared her schedule so she could stay in the house. It could be anytime now. She wanted to be home where she could monitor the response. CNN, MSNBC, and a variety of other stations were playing on the six LCD displays installed in her library. It was a brilliant plan, and it had progressed without a kink, the most serious threat being Nick's confession to Gina. Sophia was not one bit concerned. By the time Nick had bared his soul, the execution of the plan was in its final stage, and nothing would prevent its success. The team had thought of everything.

Snippets in the news informed the public of the Supreme Court case, but, just as planned, the media unknowingly helped them redirect the public's attention. Scenes of hard working Floridian residents ranging from farmers to little old ladies were arguing their right to purchase and own firearms without restriction. This is their country, their freedom and the government had no business in this matter.

They did not meet as a group. They kept a safe distance from one another as the last stages of the plan unfolded. They devised a chain of communication to keep each other informed. Al Benazir would start the chain. He would call David Chabin, who would call Nicole Huerta, who would call Rita Conover, and on it would go until everyone received the news. Sophia knew the decision was imminent. Rita called her with an update, and she in turn called Anita Hyde. Although they knew the outcome, it was still a nerve-racking wait. They had the five votes they needed to overturn. Letterer and Benazir were on the team, and Gentry, Morgan, and

Georgalas were on the record as pro-choice. It was a mere waiting game.

Sophia knew the decision would not be the culmination of their effort but simply the beginning of a large-scale movement. The real work would begin after the decision. The team had prepared preliminary plans to ensure they worked toward a desired state. Agencies would need to be disbanded, funds redirected, family centers created—there was no end to the plans the team had devised to reach the new goal. It was not a matter of money. The money spent to enforce *Mather v. Tutola* would simply be redirected to the new initiatives.

Sophia was still worried about Gina. Gina's entire agency would disband, leaving Gina without a job. Sophia's hope was that Gina would be mainstreamed and transferred to the FBI once the FBLI was eliminated. Gina was a young, intelligent, capable agent— Sophia had no doubt Gina would be able to recover.

Sophia sat at her desk and opened the large, black leather journal with the red leather spine—it looked more like an old-fashioned accounting book than a journal. Sophia kept meticulous notes. She rubbed her fingers over the numbers neatly printed in the columns. She reviewed the information frequently; it kept her focused, driven. These were the figures that had fueled the flames of change—3.4 million, the number of deaths caused by illegal abortion in the United States; 1.2 million, the number of female convicts imprisoned due to illegal termination; 90,000, the number of men convicted for terminating a pregnancy. Imagine that. Ninety thousand men impregnated over a million women! That, or divine conception was a common occurrence. The figures were impossible to ignore. Women *and* children died at an incredible rate. Over a million women had been forced to leave their families and serve their sentence as convicted felons. Men, on the other hand, were elusive. The numbers did not lie. Men, neither tried nor convicted, allowed the burden to fall to the women. How could this have gone on so long? In an effort to take a huge moral step forward, the entire country had taken ten steps back. It was inconceivable, yet there it was, in black and white.

She turned the page and continued to review her notes. Forty-six, the number of women she personally helped secure a safe abortion; 110, the number of women she supported financially to bring their pregnancies to term; 405,000, the dollars she personally spent supporting the children brought to term. And so the pages continued, listing every fact, figure, and dollar amount spent on the issue. It was her justification, impeccably maintained and updated for accuracy. She knew the figures by heart, yet she reviewed them every day. One person *can* indeed make a difference.

And so it was on Monday, January 24, 2022, while Nicole Huerta, the New York City mayor visited a women's shelter; George Rydell, who along with his wife returned from Paris, where they survived the first Christmas without their daughter, Ashley; Jean and Rich Annapolis celebrated what would have been their daughter Jennifer's seventeenth birthday; Patti Darby started her first work shift of her fourteen-hour day; John Winthrop replayed the surveillance video of the bombing for nearly the thousandth time; Lisa Talbot, who, along with her parents, planned her daughter Chelsea's christening; Gina Vincent traveled from Rumson, New Jersey, to her office in Manhattan; and Dr. Nicholas DePaolo delivered a healthy set of twin boys that the news hit the air for the first time.

January 24, 2022

Mather v. Tutola Overturned 6–3!

The U.S. Supreme Court issued their ruling in *Planned Parenthood vs. Martin*, ruling six to three in favor of Planned Parenthood. The decision held that *Mather v. Tutola* did severely infringe on the constitutional right of the mother, rendering the 2006 ruling overturned. For the first time in fifteen years, abortion is legal in the United States of America.

Chapter 30

I was time for a celebration. Sophia wanted a party, and by mid-February, almost everyone was looking for an excuse to go out. The hustle of the holidays was over, the winter cold kept everyone indoors, and the promise of spring was not yet in the air. Yes, it definitely was time for a party!

As much as she wanted to have a victory gathering, she could not. Just as they discreetly planned their event, so they secretly toasted their triumph. So it was, when Nick asked Gina to marry him, he provided the perfect premise for Sophia to host the mother of all parties. Most of the team was included in Nick's guest list, while Gina's roster included most of her former coworkers at the FBLI. In all, nearly two hundred guests would attend, including such dignitaries as New York City Mayor Nicole Huerta and New Jersey Senator Anita Hyde.

Nick and Gina had been inseparable since the day she stood on his doorstep. The ruling only served to shift her focus farther away from her career and onto her personal life. In the days after the ruling, there was much commotion about what would come of the agency. How would they implement the change? Who would be responsible? As always, careful planning ruled the day, and the transition was much smoother than anyone expected. The FBLI's first task was the release of all convicted female citizens, who each received a pardon from Andrew Lehman himself, the president of the United States. Abortionists, on the other hand, would serve out their prison terms, as they had put the health of the mother and the fetus in jeopardy. Second, the employees of the FBLI could either return to service in the mainstream FBI or take a position in the newly formed BLS, the Bureau of Life Services, which would work to implement the new agenda.

For Gina, there was no decision: she would work with the new agency. Gina personally met female prisoners she had helped arrest on the day of their release. The joy as they reunited with their families was cathartic for Gina. She never felt completely comfortable putting women in prison. She had wrestled with her demons with each arrest. The only justifiable arrests were those of the abortionists. Nailing the abortionist saved two lives—the mother and the child. These arrests she would never regret. Still, in spite of the outcome, she would never advocate abortion—never. She did, however, come to terms with the fact that it was not a decision appropriate for the government.

Gina was looking forward to the engagement party also because it would be a sort of going-away party for her coworkers at the agency. John Winthrop, Ben Addison, and Curt Conroy were all returning to service in the FBI, while Robert was joining Gina in the new division. Robert was adamant about remaining Gina's assistant—no new boss for him.

The house looked spectacular. The conservatory, which one entered from the living room reception area, was decorated completely in ivory. Live roses, gardenias, and hydrangeas were arranged in varying shades of white and ivory in huge centerpieces on each table, along with thick garlands that framed each window. Ivory candles, along with ivory linens and china, gave the room an ethereal glow. The piano played in the center hall as guests arrived and enjoyed champagne, caviar, and sushi.

Lisa Talbot would be the maid of honor, William would be the best man, and the wedding would be at the Rumson house in early June. Gina and Nick had a gift for making their guests feel special, as if each one were an integral part of their affair. They spoke personally with each one, sharing a drink or brief conversation, always thanking them for being a part of their special event.

It was an elegant affair that passed much too quickly for the guests of honor. Gina reminisced with her coworkers, sharing funny stories and memories of botched cases. At one point, she toasted Sally, drawing cheers and tears from nearly everyone for her deceased friend. Nick and Sophia met briefly in the library with the team members, sharing a private toast at their success and hope for a brighter future. Robert met William in person, and true to form, they hit it off instantly. To Gina they seemed the mismatch of the century, where the extremely reserved and soft-spoken William sharply contrasted with the brash, colorful, and opinionated Robert. William appeared to enjoy Robert's antics, and the two seemed indelibly attached to one another.

As the evening wore on and the guests thinned out, more intimate groupings and discussions ensued. By 1:00 a.m., Robert was entertaining William and Gina with office stories, while Nick and Sophia were sharing a moment in the library.

"Thank you for a great party, Sophia. Really, it was outstanding."

"Nick, don't be silly. I loved every minute of it. Nothing gives a grandmother more pleasure, except maybe a *great*-grandchild."

"Let's not get ahead of ourselves," he chided, but he quickly sobered. "On a more serious note, I want to apologize for not listening to you. I'm sorry I didn't wait until after the ruling to tell Gina. I know it could have ruined everything. I just wasn't thinking clearly."

"Rubbish. I never expected you two to hit it off so quickly. If anyone is to blame, it is me for insisting the two of you meet. I, too, was playing with fire."

"I'm grateful you introduced us, in spite of the risk. I love her, more than I could ever imagine."

"Nick, you have no idea how much her happiness means to me."

"I can't believe how different everything is after only ten months. Not only my life, but the whole country. I mean, we did it. We really did it. From a late-night discussion to a constitutional change—it's truly amazing."

"I only wish we had planned it sooner. So many years of suffering, for what? To think the Rydells would still have Ashley. How many Ashleys? How many broken families? It's so sad. I only hope we can work to make it better. Our job is only beginning."

"When do we go to work?" Nick asked.

"I spoke with Jane Letterer, and she thinks we will need a meeting to outline the important elements of change. Once we concur, it will be a matter of dividing our efforts in each of our venues. We will need to form new alliances and align with many groups to implement the necessary plans. We don't want to repeat the mistakes of the past. Education, birth control, medical coverage, job protection, and daycare must all be overhauled. We need to create a better plan. I think we have seen what we are capable of; it's just a matter of implementation."

"I am still surprised at the lack of media coverage leading up to the decision. I mean, it's no surprise that I am not really clear on the workings of the political machine, but I would have thought there would have been more controversy while the court was deliberating."

"Nick, public attention is focused by the media. The media determines what the masses will discuss. However, I am surprised the decision itself did not cause a controversy. I thought for sure they would take to the streets protesting the overturn. I expected dead baby pictures, protests, maybe even violence."

"I have a theory on that. I think more people than we even know suffered the last fifteen years. Even the most conservative individual will waver when forced to face a loss. Look at the Rydells. George Rydell was one of the strongest pro-life advocates in the country. He ultimately became an integral part of the ruling. If he felt this way, I am sure there are many others."

"I'm sure you're right," Sophia responded, and then under her breath, she said, "so much loss, so much unnecessary pain."

"Sophia, I've been meaning to ask you, and I keep forgetting. At our last meeting we were set on a 5–4 ruling—at least that's what I thought I heard. I'm still unclear how the vote came in at 6–3. We did plan on 5–4, didn't we?"

"That was a real shock to all of us. You got it right: we were definite on five, but when the decision came in, we picked up another justice."

"Really? Who was it?"

"Justice Joseph Marollo voted our way."

"Does anyone know what caused his change of heart?"

"Ben said he had been very melancholy since the passing of his wife and was visibly less controversial on the subject." "What happened to his wife?"

"I'm not sure. I know she died suddenly. It was very sad. I didn't know her very well, but we did work on a few fundraisers together. She was a very generous woman—I can't believe I don't remember what she died from. I do know it was fairly recent," Sophia explained.

"What was her name?" he asked.

"Marina."

Epilogue

I T was a cool spring day when they installed the podium for the inaugural ceremony. They expected one thousand people, including family, press, and government dignitaries. She would be the youngest individual named to head the Bureau of Life Services in its twenty-year history. As they unloaded the chairs and rolled out the temporary green outdoor carpet, the sky looked gray and overcast. Rain could ruin the ceremony or cause its cancellation altogether. As the electronics were being tested and the satellite feeds were being completed, the sun peeked through the clouds, offering a glimmer of hope for the first time. The ceremony was scheduled to begin in one hour.

The press arrived first, as always, securing the best possible placement of their microphones and cameras. Family and friends arrived next and took their places in the designated section, ensuring front-row seats for the immediate family members. Government officials arrived last, as expected, taking their place within minutes of the opening remarks. John Winthrop, Secretary of Health and Human Services, would swear in the director of the Bureau of Life Services. John Winthrop had served as secretary of the department for the last three years since he was sworn in on Monday, January 19, 2043, at the age of seventy-three. He had personally recommended her. She deserved the position, and he couldn't think of a better candidate to head the Bureau of Life Services.

She would hold the position for four years, and she promised a new level of life support services. By 1:05 p.m., everyone was in their place, and John Winthrop was announced. As he stepped up to the podium, his gaze swept the audience and rested on her sitting demurely in the first row. Her father sat next to her, along with her brother and sisters, as it was a big day for all of them.

He thanked everyone for their attendance, and without the delay of a lengthy oratory, he announced the new director of the Bureau of Life Services, Ms. Nadia Harrison. The applause thundered, and they all stood and watched her slowly ascend the stage and approach the microphone. He gave her a hug and quickly took his seat. It was her show now.

"I am Nadia Harrison, and on behalf of the United States Government, I am honored and humbled to accept the position of director for the Bureau of Life Services. Many people are responsible for this day. I would like to begin by thanking them publicly.

"I lost my mother, Sarah Louise Harrison, when I was still an infant. My father, Nate Harrison, has been responsible for raising my four siblings and me. Dad, thank you for your hard work and for your unwavering support of my endeavors." Nate, sitting in the front row, could not hide the tears streaming down his face.

"I would like to thank Sophia Renato Cavanaugh, who has been a mother, a confidante, and a friend for as long as I can remember. Her financial support helped me complete my education, and for that I am eternally grateful." Sophia, sitting next to Nate, joined hands with him as Nadia paused to acknowledge each of them while the crowd offered extended applause.

"Finally, I would like to thank Mr. John Winthrop, who noticed my dedication to the department and worked with me personally, providing career counseling and guidance. His mentorship is responsible for my induction today, and I hope my efforts will be worthy of his attention.

"Today is a pivotal point in our country's history. Not only am I the youngest person in history to be named to this position, but, as you may have noticed, I am *female*." Her delivery was excellent, and the crowd laughed as if on cue.

"We have a rich history in this country, and over the last twenty years, we have much to be proud of in the area of human services—more specifically, life services, which has truly changed the quality of life for millions of Americans.

"Since 2022, we have implemented a responsible approach to reproductive services. We are the first country to implement mandatory physician visits for all teenagers as part of their immunization and health history, ensuring each child receives appropriate medical information with respect to sexuality and reproduction.

"The implementation of free birth control, offered not only by our free clinics, but also by our private organizations such as Planned Parenthood, the YMCA, and participating private physicians, is responsible for the reduction in teen pregnancies from 15 percent to fewer than 2 percent over the last 20 years.

"Our complete overhaul of our school curriculum, eliminating 'abstinence only' education and favoring responsible education on human sexuality, is largely responsible for our success.

"Sexual education and reproduction curriculum mandated and implemented in grade two and continued through grade twelve ensures responsible, educated, and healthy young Americans.

"The Single Parent Support Act of 2036 offers unprecedented services, including day care, job protection, medical coverage, and group support. By registering at the local family center, a single parent can gain access to affordable daycare programs, legal support if their job is in jeopardy due to their parental status, and access to medical care for both child *and* parent, as well as formalized support groups that allow single parents to meet and combine their efforts to raise their families.

"Our family centers are world-class facilities run by a combination of funding from private, government, and nonprofit organizations. They are the culmination of what Americans can accomplish when they put their minds to fixing a problem." The crowd rose to its feet as their applause thundered for over a minute.

"The Abortion Reform Act allowed us to institute responsible guidelines for abortion procedures within the mandatory twelve-week window. Our counseling, adoption, and financial support services are second to none. In this country, we offer support so a woman can deliver her child without fear of starvation, homelessness, or loss of income."

The crowd once again rose to its feet as their applause lasted a full sixty seconds.

"Our physicians are trained, ensuring safe medical procedures. Never again will we eliminate necessary medical training due to political pressure. We are a responsible nation that values all life, that of the child and the mother.

"We are a country that strives to improve and advance the well-being of all. We are a people capable of banding together, in spite of differences, to reach a common goal. We have reached unprecedented figures in the reduction of homelessness, improved child welfare, and improved adoption services. Yes, we have many reasons to be proud.

"However, just as the journey of a thousand miles begins with a single step, we must continue to move forward. We can improve and hope to eradicate our largest issues. As the director of the Bureau of Life Services, I commit to the following:

"The inclusion of adoptive services in all family planning centers, the release by the parent of fetal material for research and biotechnological advancement, increased employer support in the form of tax deductions for those who conform to work and family guidelines, and requested volunteer service of those couples seeking termination—a simple request to give back to the program that helped them.

"We have found that common sense combined with education can make an impact, and we have the numbers to prove it. The key to our success is open, honest discussion combined with courage. We must openly discuss our problems and work to identify creative solutions. Finally, as a people, we must have the courage to change.

Nothing can stay the same. We must continue to evolve in a forward-thinking direction for the benefit of all.

"I commit to you that I will actively address the issues our families face today. I will work to provide responsible programs that support families. Most important, I promise to change what does not work in an effort to improve the services we provide.

"We are a country founded on freedom, with an objective to establish justice and protect basic liberties. It was important over 250 years ago, and it is still important today. I am committed to this cause. My name is Nadia Harrison, and in memory of my mother, Sarah Louise Harrison, I humbly accept the position bestowed upon me today."

As she stepped away from the podium, one thousand people rose to their feet and produced overwhelming applause. She bowed her head to the audience and turned her attention to John Winthrop. She raised her right hand and took her oath in front of the world. Her family couldn't break through the mob of media that swarmed around her as she tried to descend the steps.

Nate stood and faced Sophia.

"How can I ever thank you for all that you have done for me and my family?"

"Your beautiful children and their success are my thanks. Nadia will help more people in her career than I have in my entire life. My only wish is that your wife could have been here to see her."

A Word from the Author

M ANY people ask me if I am pro-life or pro-choice and what position my novel takes on the subject. My answer is simple: I am pro-solution. What I mean is that our current efforts, energy, and arguments on both sides of the issue do not provide a real solution. My intent when writing *Overturned* was to simply explore the question, "What if?" Would we solve the problem or would we create more? In the end, I believe that regardless of faith, values, or belief systems, we must join forces to get to the root of the problem. Addressing the result will never allow us to reach our true goal: the prevention of unplanned pregnancies.

It is my hope that this story prompts the reader to explore the issue in depth, beyond the surface arguments, and reach an individual conclusion that sparks creative, innovative ideas for the benefit of all humanity. Many people do not realize that the gravity of the situation is very real. The possibility of an overturn exists today as strongly as it did when I originally wrote this story in 2002. In all this time, I continue to see enormous effort, funding, and energies spent on the law and the arguments of both sides. These efforts should be focused on the issue and potential solutions.

I am a faithful, practicing Catholic who struggles and prays that my opinions are not offensive to my God and my beliefs; unfortunately, I will not know this until my time in this world ends and I prepare to answer for my life and my deeds. Nevertheless, between now and then I choose to show compassion, forgiveness, and support to each individual who crosses my path. In the end, love does indeed conquer all, and once we understand this, all disagreement should dissolve into a common effort that improves our existence and that of one another.

In closing, I envision a world where the need for the outlaw of abortion is unnecessary because, as a society, we managed to eliminate the real issue: unplanned pregnancy.

www.ingramcontent.com/pod-product-compliance
Lightning Source LLC
Chambersburg PA
CBHW020434030726
47495CB00006B/1796